How Things Unravel

By

Robert T. Hunting

HOW THINGS UNRAVEL Copyright ©2019
Line By Lion Publications
www.linebylion.com

ISBN 978-1-948807-14-2
Cover Design by Thomas Lamkin Jr. www.tljonline.com
Editing by Jedlica Editing

LINE BY LION
PUBLICATIONS

All characters herein sprang from my fertile imagination. To those with an understanding of Lyme disease, please know I stayed close to the facts. Close, but as this is a work of fiction, I adjusted here-and-there in order to move the story forward.

To Carrie. *Tu es amor meus*

In three words I can sum up all that I have learned about life. It goes on.

Robert Frost

Chapter 1

Katie Maines placed her elbows on the small table of the coffee shop.

"I've got to do *something*, Bailey." She pushed a strand of her chestnut-brown hair behind her ear and scanned the interior. Only the usual assortment of guys checking out Bailey. Nothing new. She ignored them.

Her long-limbed sister, two years younger, and the sole inheritor of their father's red, pomegranate hair, set down her caffè latte. She studied Katie for a moment. "So what exactly will you do?"

Katie again gave the room another fast once-over. "There's the thing. Nothing yet's come to mind. All l know is Hawksley's got murder in his heart. If I don't protect him from himself, he'll take the law into his own hands." She slowly shook her head. "Time's running out on me."

Eleven months earlier.

Lunch pail under his arm, Hawksley Pardee shut the rear door of his clapboard cottage. He approached the detached garage in the back, bent, grasped the handle of the wooden sectional bay door and pulled upward. Inside, he slid behind the wheel of his green Accord, and backed the car out of the garage. Once clear, he slipped out from under the steering wheel, closed the garage door, and put himself behind the wheel again.

His thoughts returned to his wife, Darlene, nagging him to get an automatic garage door opener. "What, we're the only ones who don't have an automatic garage door opener? Are we in the Middle Ages?"

Hawksley remembered his reaction. "Don't know why you're making such a fuss over this. How much energy does it take to pull up on the door?"

Darlene had fended off the question with a skyward roll of her eyes. "I'm not making a fuss, and what about when it's raining or snowing, huh? Be nice to sit in the car and open it from there."

Hawksley had raised his hands in surrender. "All right, all right. Fine. I'll price it out and we'll fold it into the cost of the kitchen renovation."

"Good. We can afford it. Nancy has one. Not like she's rolling in money."

Hawksley found it tiring listening to Darlene constantly bringing up Nancy. Sometimes he swore Darlene made her vows to Nancy, not him. He steered his Accord down the tight, shared driveway, grateful he'd never scraped against either house. Out in the morning sunshine movement caught his eye—Nancy Picton, on her front porch, bending to pick up the morning paper. *The Indiana Report*. Four years older, she reminded him of a skinnier, but prettier Delta Burke.

Nancy looked his way and waved. He tossed an obligatory return and pulled out onto Delaney Street, past Brian Kimball's house. A fast glance at his unwanted neighbor, he shook his head and drove on. Bad news, Kimball.

On principle, Hawksley had developed an immediate antipathy toward the drug dealer. For an instant, two sets of eyes locked in on each other, Hawksley nodded and broke off contact first. Thirty-six, lean and slope-shouldered, Kimball kept his salt-and-pepper hair short. His skin reminded Hawksley of those anti-smoking commercials showing smokers' faces with sunken cheeks and deep vertical lines.

In no particular hurry, Hawksley drove along his street filled with old houses, clapboards like his, tract houses, and the new monster homes. Gentrification had nudged its way into the neighborhood. Several times a month Hawksley received junk mail from realtors eager to sell his house; prices were lower than in Louisville. "Neighborhood's changing," he'd told Darlene. "Wait a few years, and the land will be worth more than the houses on it. Another ten, and I bet none of the original owners will recognize the neighborhood."

The other day he laughed at a bumper sticker, *Mug a yuppie. Jesus would approve.* Gold, but not as funny as *Jesus is coming. Look busy.*

On the spur of the moment Hawksley took the Ohio River Greenway, and stared at the vast expanse of water. A car behind him honked and denied him a longer gaze across at

Louisville. He stepped on the gas and made for W. Main Street and his usual morning stop, *Has Beans Café*. Inside he ordered coffee and took a free newspaper from the rack. He'd see how the Reds were doing.

Coffee finished, Hawksley checked his watch. Time to go. Five minutes later he pulled into the parking lot of *Houghton Plywood and Veneer Manufacturing*.

Six years earlier, only a few days past his eighteenth birthday, Hawksley had turned his back on college. He and his guidance counselor did a cost analysis. In theory the long-term benefits of a degree outperformed a blue-collar job. In theory. But those three years would put him in a deep financial hole. In debt with no guarantee of a job. Not worth it.

In his senior year at high school he'd hoped he might land a football scholarship. Nothing, unless he counted tiny Makefield College, a Division III school. The Oregon school wrote and told him his marks were good enough for a tryout. *If* he made the team, he might be eligible for a financial aid package.

Tryout. Might be. He'd tossed the letter in the can and set aside immediate plans to further his education. Later, maybe, he'd check out night courses at the University of Louisville.

He next gave himself over to finding a job. He applied at Houghton, a closed shop, belonging to *The Brotherhood of Progressive Pulp and Paper Workers*. To his surprise and delight, they called him in for an interview. Jobs weren't going begging in New Albany, and Houghton had a reputation for good wages. The company started him as a trainee in the drying facility. He didn't like the long shifts, but liked the pay and the full benefits. A hard, diligent worker, Hawksley received favorable progress reports. In his sixth year, Houghton promoted him to shift foreman in the drying facility.

Now, card in hand, the former safety of the New Albany High Bulldogs punched in at quarter to the hour. He donned his coveralls. Industrial goggles on his forehead, noise-cancelling headset around his long neck, Hawksley yanked his hard hat over his disheveled hair and marched off to the veneer feeder.

If asked, those who knew Hawksley might describe him as average-looking. He and his two siblings, Madison and Logan, inherited their father's good, clear skin, and their mother's full, caramel-brown wavy hair.

The elder Pardee's own hair thinned by the time he stepped out of his teens. At 53, only a few wispy strands remained. Yet in spite of his drinking and smoking, his skin remained smooth, even held a touch of pink.

With a narrow forehead and pointed chin, the son of Daryl Pardee looked out at the world through close-set, chestnut brown eyes, separated by a long nose with a slight bump. His face bore the five o'clock stubble popular among males his age.

Hawksley's personality drew others to him. His high school yearbook read, "If you can't get on with the Hawk, you can't get on with anyone." People liked him for his sense of humor, thoughtfulness, and general interest in others. Yet his self-image never quite aligned itself with the wider world. Many a time he'd ask himself why didn't he did not see in himself what others saw?

He once recalled a conversation with his best high school friend, Katie Maines, who asked him why he played football. "I don't get it, Hawk. You don't fit the mold of the dumb jock type. Not like Gardiner. Surprised he doesn't use his knuckles to move himself forward."

Hawksley stifled a chuckle. "Careful. You don't want Gardiner to hear you."

"Like I care," she snorted. "No, really, you're not like the other jocks, walking around like you own the school. You're nice, not stupid, don't go gaga over the cheerleaders, and you don't sit at the jock table in the cafeteria. Well, mostly not."

"I want to fit in, to be liked."

"And you don't without being a jock?" She paused. "I like you. So do a lot of others."

"I like you too."

"And yet... Ah, never mind." She shook her head. "Men."

Chapter 2

Weary and achy, Hawksley rolled his shoulders and unlocked his car at the end of his shift. Day's done; weekend's ahead, he told himself. He'd have a nice hot shower, change, and see what Darlene's wanted to do.

The radio on mellow rock, Hawksley powered down the window. He left the parking lot of Houghton. *Desperado* came over the speakers when a sneezing fit overtook him. "Allergies," he said aloud. "Time of year. Guess it's the price you pay living close to the river."

Three additional sneezes encouraged him to leave the river. He powered up the window, turned on the air conditioner and headed for the historical district on E. Main. "Go see my favorite place," he muttered. Early in his marriage he'd often head straight home from work, eager to be with Darlene. Now he wasted time in the historical district. He never tired of admiring these well-preserved Civil War mansions on their manicured lawns. "I ever win it big, this is where I'm gonna live."

The last lingering rays fought a losing battle with the approaching darkness when he entered the back door of his house.

"Dar?" He raised his voice. "I'm home."

No one answered. He headed for the kitchen counter and found a note on the kitchen table. *Next door at Nancy's. Hope you don't mind. Your dinner's in the fridge.*

Hawksley's stomach muscles tightened. He crumpled the note. "Why does this not surprise me? Mind? Yeah, I mind. Starting to mind a lot." Not given to irrational jealousy, he still harbored resentment at the hours Darlene spent next door. They'd already had two major fights over it. "You live *here*," he'd told her during their last fight, "in *this* house, not over at Nancy's. I come home, and where are you—at Nancy's, tipsy, and smelling of perfume? Not *your* perfume."

Her eyes blazed at him. "What are you saying?"

Chin extended, eyes narrowed, Hawksley whispered. "Uh, guess, Dar. Guess what I'm saying."

Her mouth tight, Darlene kept her gaze on him, and at last spun around. He watched her tight jeans accentuating her sylph-like figure, and disappear from the room. "Here we go again," he muttered. It always ended the same way. He had to come to her and beg for forgiveness. Until then, no sex, no kisses, no conversation; only the deep freeze.

His singular triumph centered on a prenuptial agreement. Darlene hadn't yet moved in with him when he broached the subject. She'd insisted they didn't need a pre-nup. She vowed she'd never leave him, nor would betray his trust.

He held firm. "My name and only my name is on the mortgage agreement. Leave things as they are for now. Maybe later…"

He'd once made the mistake of blocking her way in the kitchen during a fight. She'd moved to go around him. "Get out of my way."

"Not until you talk to me, and stop being so childish."

Her eyes flashed. She grabbed a dish from the counter and threw it onto the floor. It shattered. He stared at the shards. "Nice. Mature. Pleased with yourself?"

She'd stormed past him. He found a broom and again puzzled over the beauty he'd married, and the emotional mess inside her.

He pushed the memory from his mind. Where had life, their life gone wrong, he asked himself? He remembered when he first met her in Loo-A-Vul, at the *Moonbow Pub.*

For young people, everything happened in Louisville; nothing much happened in New Albany. If you wanted fun, any kind of fun, you went to Louisville. Pubs, movie houses, meat markets, concerts, all there.

Some of his old teammates pestered him to come to a pub with them. He agreed, but said he'd drive in his own car. "I've seen you guys behind the wheel after you get extra happy. I want to come back over the bridge, not be in it."

By ten p.m. the pub had overflowed with revelers. The five friends took their place in the outside line. At last they made their way in. By good luck another group left and gave up their table. The friends hurried over, signaled for the server, and called for their first pitcher of beer.

Hawksley surveyed the dark cavernous room, and spotted the beauty. At once he suffered the same fate as all the other horn dogs vying for her attention. If anyone made eyes dilate, she did. His gaze followed her every movement, from her crowded table, to the small dance floor and back: a woman's woman, everything about her, from tight jeans, tube top, high heels, makeup, detailed red fingernails, long glossy tresses, oozed femininity.

Rick Mikita, the Bulldogs' former punter whacked his arm. "Dude, those jeans gotta be painted on."

Hawksley's hormonal impulses insured Makita's message never reached him. He kept his eyes locked on the goddess across the room.

Mikita waved a hand in front of him. "You *there*? She's hot, but ask me, lot better chicks in here."

The hand wave caused Hawksley to pull out of his fantasies. Had he been so obvious? His face reddened. He gave thanks for the low lights. "Let's get more beer," he said, eager to change the subject.

The band finished a number. The lead singer said, "Lotta fine ladies in here, gents. What say we get mellow and give them a chance to check out the men in this Ladies Choice?"

Hawksley's friends soon found themselves led to the floor. To his surprise, the tube top beauty made her way over to him. He squared his shoulders, sat upright and offered up his best smile.

She approached, and asked Hawksley if he wanted to dance. They stepped out onto the floor. She moved into him, but not too close. He inhaled her intoxicating perfume.

The number over, she remained with him. Thrilled, Hawksley took this as a good sign. He worked hard to engage her in light conversation, worried he'd run out of things to say. She stayed with him through the end of the set, and didn't resist when he held her hand.

He spent the rest of the evening with her, and ignored the jealous stares he received from other males. She told him she too lived in New Albany, not far from him. She told him she worked as a cosmetician.

"Sounds interesting," he lied, even if he knew or cared nothing of the world of cosmetics.

"And what do you do?" she asked.

"I work at *Houghton*."

"Oh, yes? Doing what?"   He told her. "I hear it's a good place to work."

He nodded. "It is. They pay well and treat their employees well too."

They sat out the remaining numbers and talked. She kept up long, lingering eye contact, laughed at his jokes, and asked personal questions. At closing time, she accepted his offer of a ride, and said goodbye to her girlfriend.

Hawksley's friends winked and made rude, suggestive gestures behind her back.

He had every intention to drop her off at her apartment, but they never made it. They spent the night in the bedroom of his new house. Three months later, against the advice of his family and friends, they married at city hall.

Early in the marriage Hawksley learned Darlene was prone to moodiness, especially in the mornings.

"What's the world done to you this early in the morning?" he once asked her. "It's a brand new day. New opportunities. New experiences."

"Lemme alone," she replied. "I don't wanna be bugged until I have my morning coffee, all right?"

Coffee, and spending an hour working on her makeup, alone and without conversation. He'd learned to eat breakfast by himself.

She also wanted things—lots of things, expensive things, including status. She oohed and aahed at Tony and Nancy's new home, what they had, and compared it to what she didn't. She dragged him to the open house, charity tours of the well-heeled. He came to discover the tours came with more than an admittance price. She'd sulk for the next day or so, lamenting their inferior status. "You never want anything better," she said.

He replied with a fast shrug. "Not true, and besides, if it bothers you, why'd you marry me? I'm a simple man with simple needs."

The microwave dinged and brought him out of his reverie. He poured himself a glass of milk. A bright light of truth entered into his consciousness. It made him face what he'd always known—they had little in common. When he peered into the future, it scared him. He set down his milk and mumbled, "I guess I've either had my head in the sand or up my ass. Can't say I wasn't warned about rushing into marriage."

Darlene bounced into the house an hour later, smiled sweetly, and kissed him. "Sorry I'm late. Girl talk, you know? I'll make it up to you. Wanna have some fun tonight?"

The prospect of having her in his arms wiped away his recent stored-up resentments. His eyebrows shot up. "Really? Yeah, sure."

Later, his lust slackened, he stared up at the ceiling. *If they ever put pussy-whipped in the dictionary, there'll be a picture of me beside it.*

Chapter 3

Two days before the Memorial Day weekend, Stan Gainey and Ellen Maythorpe, approached Hawksley at work. "Saturday's supposed to be a good day for fishing," the affable Maythorpe said. "Whattaya say about joining me 'n Stan? Go get some bass."

"Where?"

"Blue River."

Never married, the tomboyish, middle-aged Maythorpe, enjoyed a reputation for being a year-round sportswoman. Equally liked, she could talk point spreads with men, or the latest diets with women.

Hawksley considered the offer. "Yeah, okay. Pretty sure we haven't got anything on this weekend. I'll check with Darlene first."

'Great."

"And don't go showing us up, Ellen," Gainey teased her. "Leave some fish for us."

"Ah, you big cry baby," she shot back. "Can't stand the competition, huh? Don't worry. If you don't catch anything, mama will give you one of hers."

At five the following morning, an eager Hawksley stood in front of his house. With Darlene's blessings, he looked forward to the day. "Go," she said when he broached the subject. "Enjoy yourself. What time do you think you'll be back?"

"Knowing Ellen and Stan, it'll be a full day. They'll want to stop somewhere to eat after we're done, so I'm guessing around six, seven maybe."

Gainey pulled up in in his pickup, towing his boat trailer. Hawksley climbed in the back. "Mornin' all."

"Mornin,'" the other two still-sleepy fishers said in unison.

Less than fifteen minutes past the city limits they heard a loud, metallic snap. The pickup fishtailed. Gainey brought it under control and checked his rearview mirror. Trailer and aluminum boat leaned dangerously to the right side. He swore, slowed, and pulled the pickup onto the gravel.

"Damn, Gainey," Maythorpe shouted, "don't take us into the ditch."

"Yeah, yeah, yeah. Settle down."

All three climbed out of the truck. A quick inspection and Gainey diagnosed the problem. "Som-bitch. Trailer leaf's busted. I can't fix this, no fuckin' way."

A long profuse apology laced with expletives followed.

"I knew we should'a stopped for coffee first," Maythorpe said.

Gainey gave her a long-suffering look and let out a whoosh of air. "How the hell that help anything?" Cellphone in hand he called Triple-A and arranged for a cab to retrieve his guests. "No point in you staying," he said. "Take the cab. I'll pay you back next Tuesday."

Ellen and Hawksley declined the offer of repay and commiserated with his misfortune.

"Happens," Gainey said. "Sorry it did, but don't let it ruin your day. I'll drop your gear off when I get back in town."

Maythorpe and Hawksley took the cab. They stopped at a diner for breakfast. Close to seven-thirty they said goodbye.

Disappointed with the events of the morning, Hawksley walked the nine blocks back home. He'd talk to Darlene about maybe going over to Louisville for dinner and a movie.

He let himself in the back door. It surprised him to hear Roxy Music's *Avalon* on the stereo. His eyebrows furrowed in respons e. Darlene didn't much care for rock.

Another surprise awaited him—the pungent, unmistakable smell of marijuana. When did Darlene ever smoke pot? He followed his nose until soft feminine voices reached him. He moved closer to the sound, and heard a familiar, intimate sound. Doubt gave way to full suspicion. Anger knotted his stomach; instinct coiled his muscles. Self-preservation, his brain told him. His mouth turned to sandpaper.

A plan came. With little sound he stepped back and reached for his camera dangling from a coat hook. Battery on, he waited a few seconds and returned to the doorway. He spied a naked Nancy, head between the legs of his wife. Eyes closed, Darlene fondled her breasts while Nancy ministered to her.

His hands trembling, Hawksley held the camera at arm's length. He studied his subjects through the LCD and snapped the first picture. The camera clicked, the flash went off. Darlene's eyes flew open. Nancy's head shot up. Both screamed when the flash illuminated the scene a second time. In panic, Darlene kicked Nancy away and yanked at a blanket to cover her nakedness. Nancy scrambled for her clothes on the floor.

The flash went off a second time, and a third and fourth. The two lovers had managed to cover their nakedness. Nancy made a feeble attempt to wrest the camera from Hawksley. He held it out of reach. "Don't even," he snarled, his face contorted. "Get out!"

Something in his face and voice told her everything. She slunk past and out of the bedroom. He heard the back door shut, walked to the stereo and turned it off. When he returned to the bedroom, Darlene had slipped on a bathrobe. She would not meet his gaze.

Hawksley forced himself to speak in a measured tone. "You slut! Amazing. I never bothered to see beyond your looks." He slowly shook his head. "They write country songs about fools like me. I don't know if I'll ever get over this humiliation. But the worst is you did this in our home. Here. You had so little respect for me, you couldn't fuck her in her house?"

She wouldn't answer, gave him her back, and busied herself dressing. Dressed, she gathered makeup, jeans, t-shirts and undergarments. She shoved all into a large tote bag. Done, she grabbed her purse, moved past a stock-still Hawksley, and without a word left the house.

He'd later remember it as the longest day of his life. Shock, disbelief, anger, all competed for prominence. He snorted while he tore off the bed sheets and tossed them on the floor. A simple twist of fate: Gainey's trailer broke down, and Hawksley had returned home to find Darlene and Nancy in bed. How long had the affair been going on; how long had Darlene played him for a fool?   The answer came at once. *Forever, dummy. All those days and nights over at Nancy's. For sure they weren't trading recipes, or talking about makeup and shoes.*

The day at last wore out, yet a despondent, angry Hawksley couldn't quiet his mind. Fatigue at last claimed him, and he fell asleep on the couch, avoiding the bed.

He woke three hours later. His stomach growled. He should eat something, but he didn't feel like it. He ignored his stomach's protests and instead cleared out closet and drawers of anything related to Darlene. He chucked them in a careless heap on the dining room floor. He'd deal with them later. Eyes heavy, he at last grabbed a blanket and returned to the couch.

Early the next morning Hawksley called the plant. He left a message on the office voice mail to say he wouldn't be in on Tuesday.

He ate little throughout the day, drank too much coffee, and replayed what he'd walked in on. How, how could she have done this to him, in *his* house? When had her words of love become lies? Dark thoughts of Darlene's betrayal at last gave way to sadness, to feeling abandoned, isolated, certain he'd come undone in every way possible.

Hours later Hawksley's rational mind took over. Okay, enough, it said; you've been neck deep in your pity party. Life goes on. She's a shit, not coming back, and you're not taking her back. Now, time to get on with the rest of your life.

He headed for the bedroom and reached for new sheets. He'd be damned if he'd sleep on the old ones. Should he even bother keeping them? Anger in his quick, furtive steps, he picked up the old sheets and held them at arm's length. Not the sheet's faults, he told himself and dumped them in front of the washing machine. Tomorrow he'd give them a good wash.

Hawk readied for sleep, set his alarm, and climbed into his bed. He slept through much of the night, although he dreamt about Darlene and earlier times together. In the morning he showered, shaved, and reviewed his plan. Ten a.m. found him on the sidewalk in front of the bank with three others, waiting for the doors to open. He closed their joint account, surprised she hadn't cleaned it out. Next, he phoned his employer, and asked to speak to Gordon Shipley.

The HR director came on the line. "Shipley here." His sandpaper voice often intimidated people. Hawksley came to regard him as fair and someone with sound judgment. He gave him a brief rundown of his troubles, asked for time off.

"Sorry to hear about this," Shipley said. "Take as much time as you need. You're also going to need a lawyer. You can set up an appointment through our EAP service."

"Okay, thanks, Mr. Shipley. I should be back in a few days."

In the afternoon a locksmith arrived to deadbolt locks on the front and back doors.

It came as no surprise to Hawksley when three days later a letter arrived from *Garrett, Wilksby and Associates*. The writer, a Steven Dykstra, notified him his client, Darlene Bondar, had filed for legal separation. The lawyer advised him to seek legal representation, and ready himself for any "contested issues." He also asked for an agreed-upon time in which his client could pick up her personal belongings.

The following evening Darlene's brother, Stan, phoned. He made obligatory small talk before he got to the reason for his call—"I'm calling to pick up Darlene's things, man. Hope you don't mind."

Hawksley didn't: the sooner all physical reminders of Darlene were gone, the better. "Nah, s'okay. I get it."

"Cool. So what's a good time to come?"

"Saturday morning, say ten. But listen, I don't trust her, so have her make a list of everything she wants, and bring it with you. If I agree, you can take it away. You, not her. She doesn't step foot on *my* property."

Hawksley ended the call, and phoned his buddy, Rick Mikita. He explained his situation. "I need you and a couple of the guys to come over, you know to hang around in case something goes wrong. I'll call the others."

"You expecting something to go wrong?"

"Not really, but, uh, you know? Just play it cool, like you're there to, you know, lend a hand or something."

"So what happened with you two?"

Hawksley hadn't planned to say much, but his resolve fell to the wayside. He detailed the events of finding Darlene and his neighbor. When he finished, the line went silent for a moment.

"Wow. Hot. Two chicks."

Hawksley couldn't hide the agitation in his voice. "Jesus, Rick, a little support here, and stop thinking with your dick."

"Ah, sorry, dude. Can't stop the blood from flowing south."

"Yeah, yeah, whatever."

"Okay, I'll try again. Sorry, Hawk. What a douchebag. Always knew she was a ho."

Maybe, Hawksley thought, but a ho he'd miss, in spite of everything.

"So you'll come?"

"Count on it. Be nice if your neighbor makes an appearance. Say, those pictures you took; any chance I can get a look at them?"

Hawksley placed the phone back in the cradle, certain he heard Mikita chuckle.

The lantern-jawed Stan and two friends arrived in a five-ton truck.

Hawksley neither liked nor disliked Stan; he hadn't had much chance to know him. They shook hands. Hawksley made a fast excuse about the presence of his friends. "Thought they could help loading her stuff."

Stan's eyes narrowed. "Huh. Okay…I guess."

He's not buying it, Hawksley told himself. To remove himself from his awkward situation, he quickly introduced everyone. Stan in turn introduced his two companions. Introductions over, Hawksley said, "Okay, let's get started. Darlene's personal belongs are in a pile on the dining room floor. Got the list?"

"Yeah, here."

Hawksley and Stan negotiated items on the list while the others listened in. None of Hawksley's earlier worries about awkwardness came to pass.

Both sides helped to load the truck. Darlene's grandmother's oak bureau at last hefted onto the truck, Stan jumped down and approached Hawksley. "Sorry about all this," he said. "Shit happens, huh?"

"Sure does," Hawksley said. "Don't worry about it. See you around."

"Yeah. Maybe we can go grab a beer sometime."

"Yeah, sure. Let's do it." Hawksley knew it wouldn't ever happen. A deep melancholy settled on him when the truck pulled away.

Mikita saved him from further gloom with a slap on the back. "Get some pizza? We already got the beer. "

Hawksley turned and smiled. "Good idea."

They moved toward the house. Mikita cast a glance at Nancy's house. "Haven't seen your neighbor yet, the one with…"

Hawksley made a face. "Why? What're you gonna do, ask her for a date? You're unbelievable."

"Well, you know, if she was getting it on with Darlene, she musta been hot. Sure you won't share those pics?"

Hawksley answered with a cuff to the back of Mikita's head.

The four friends sat on the floor, ate pizza, and drank beer. Bill Allen roamed the near-empty house before he sat and put his beer bottle on the floor. "Kinda empty now."

Hawksley nodded. "It is, but at least I get to keep the bed. I got rid of a lot of my things when she moved in. Big mistake. Ah, well; it's only stuff. I'll get more down the line."

"Think she'll take you to the cleaners?" Mikita asked.

"Nah. I had a pre-nup, and, we didn't have a lot by way of cash. We'll sign the paperwork, and in a year from now I'll be free again."

The others left. Night arrived and Hawksley had the house to himself. Alone in the world, he sat on a rug and leaned against the living room wall. He reviewed his life during these last few days. His unresolved pain welled up behind his eyes. The first tear broke loose down the side of his face, close to his ear. Other ones took a more direct path down his cheeks. His chest rose and fell, and he let loose his anguish. At last, with the last tear shed, he rose, unsteady, and made for the box of tissues in the bedroom.

Chapter 4

Over the next few days Hawksley flipped between bouts of anger and despair—anger at Darlene and Nancy, anger at himself for playing the cuckold fool, and despair at the sudden, unwelcome emptiness in his life.

The situation, the emotional aftermath, it all defied understanding. She's gone, he told himself, and there's nothing he could do about it. Focus on something else, anything. Okay, what about his family? He'd better tell them before they heard the news elsewhere. Shame and wounded pride favored hiding the truth, but he knew he couldn't. Still, how would he begin, what would he say? Didn't matter: call and tell them.

Two long, deep breaths and Hawksley picked up the receiver. "Get it over with," he whispered and dialed his father. A wave of relief washed over him when the answering machine kicked in. He wouldn't have to listen to a lecture. For now. He left a message.

His mother and her new husband, Alex, would still be in Arizona. His sister, Maddie, kept in closer touch with them. He'd ask her to relay the news. No point calling now. Logan, his younger brother, sat on the other side of the world, guarding some outpost in the mountains of Afghanistan.

He phoned Maddie in Hobart.

Ever the Earth Mother, his sister cooed and offered kind support. Did he need anything? Did he want her to come to New Albany?

He assured her he'd be fine, not to worry. "I'll get through it. You did warn me about rushing into the marriage. Well, nothing I can do about it now. Anyway, tell Mom, and say hi to Earl and the kids."

At eight p.m., he laced on his old grass-stained Adidas, stepped into the garage and pulled out his lawnmower. His muscles felt coiled, tight; the three quarters of an hour to mow front and back might help loosen them.

He cut the front in a diagonal manner.

On the fifth swipe toward the house, Nancy's red Monte Carlo pulled into the driveway. From habit, her eyes found Hawksley's. He held her gaze. She whipped her head forward, perhaps embarrassed they'd made eye contact.

He took pleasure in her reaction. *Go on. Pretend you don't see me. Hope your guilt or whatever eats away at you.*

Her presence roused memories of her ex-husband, Tony Picton, with his import-export business. The man who once drove a Ford Focus now had an addiction to luxury cars, and lived in an upscale gated community. From time to time Hawksley got a glimpse of Tony tooling around town in his latest car, his younger, trophy girlfriend, once his secretary, bedside him.

Nancy had walked in on Tony servicing the secretary. When he arrived home, she issued an ultimatum: her or me.

The secretary and her model's body, won out. Tony left the house.

In spite of the bitter split-up, Nancy did all right. She kept the house and leased a new car every year. From time to time Hawksley saw her carry shopping bags home with high end names.

Something new came to Hawksley: this *Garrett, Wilksby, and Associates*, were they Nancy's lawyers? Did she tell Darlene to sic them on him? Ah, who cared?

Hawksley mowed over by Lindsay Hadden's driveway, or more accurately, now Kimball's house.

Three weeks before Kimball took possession, Hawksley found himself in a sidewalk discussion with Nancy and Phil Lofton, a 9-1-1 dispatcher who lived on the other side of Nancy. Phil knew something about everyone on the street, and broke the news about Kimball.

"Drug dealer," he said. "The cops have him on their radar. Word is he deals in quaaludes, weed, LSD, ecstasy, crystal meth, oxycodone, and crack."

"No," Nancy whispered. "He's going to live here, on our street? How do you know all this?"

Lofton gave her a long-suffering look. "Where I work, Nance. Anyway, he's a dealer, not a pusher."

"What's the diff?" Hawksley asked.

"Big one," Lofton said, pleased with himself. He shifted his gaze to his daughter, on the sidewalk. "Bethany, let your brother have a turn." He gave his attention back to his eager audience.

"Pushers can make anywhere from eighteen to twenty-five thou a year—as a rule they're good at avoiding jail and being murdered by rivals or unsatisfied customers.

"The guess is someone like our new neighbor takes in anywhere between one and two hundred thousand a year. Dealers never keep drugs in their house. And they don't sell directly to customers. They rely on bottom feeding pushers to move the product."

Hawksley slowly shook his head. "Doesn't matter. None of this is good."

Nancy put out a well-manicured hand, and patted his arm. "Maybe it won't be so bad." She pointed to Lofton. "Phil's already said the police know about him. They'll keep him in line."

Hawksley shook his head. "I don't want him kept *in line*. I want him in prison. Definitely not here."

"Might not be as bad as you think," Lofton said. "We live in New Albany, Indiana, not South Central, L.A. or Washington Heights, New York. New Albany isn't exactly a killing field of drugs. Doesn't mean there isn't cause for worry. Maybe we can get up some kind of petition to stop him from moving into the neighborhood."

"Maybe," an unconvinced Hawksley replied. "I hope you're right, about not having cause to worry."

He later thought about his new neighbor. If Kimball had wealth, he didn't show it. He owned a seven-year-old pickup, a Mazda 3, and a vintage Kawasaki motorcycle. He didn't hold wild parties, and hadn't drawn any attention to himself. Little about his dress or lifestyle set him apart from most males his age.

Hawksley shut off the mower and pushed it into the garage. *Maybe I should sell the house. Start new somewhere else.*

The phone shrilled while he washed his hands. He shook the water off, grabbed the hand towel, and raised his shoulder to place the receiver to his ear.

"'Lo."

"I warned you the marriage wouldn't last," the dry, hoarse voice at the other end said. "You wouldn't listen to me. Had to rush off to city hall."

A heavy smoker much of his adult life, Daryl Pardee suffered from emphysema, and took early retirement.

Hawksley moved the phone to his hand. "And hello to you too, Dad. Thanks for the advice. Real helpful, yeah. Guess the apple didn't fall far from the tree."

"Don't be a wiseass."

"Fine. I left the message to give you a heads up, is all."

Brash, fractious, the senior Pardee's relationship with his wife and children could best be described as troubling. He worked as a garbage collector, and always provided for his family. But he drank; drank, smoked, and chased skirts. He once joked he couldn't make up his mind what would kill him first—lung cancer, liver failure, or a jealous husband.

So far none of them. No longer able to work because of his health, Daryl Pardee applied and received long-term disability.

Hawksley's mother had left him long ago.

"Who filed first?" Hawksley's father Pardee asked.

"Nobody's filed yet. You have to get separated first. *You* oughta know."

His father ignored the jibe. "Well, don't let her stick it to you. Your mother…" Hawksley stopped the rant before it picked up steam. "Okay, listen, gotta go. Talk to you another time. Bye."

At work Ellen Maythorpe pulled him to her buxomly chest. Arms by his side, held in a tight bear hug, she whispered in his ear.

"We heard, Hawk. We're all pulling for you. What's the saying, 'this too shall pass?'" She released him.

"Thanks, Ellen," a somewhat embarrassed Hawksley said. "Anyway, yep, it's done. Onward and upward."

She mock-punched him in the chest. "Atta boy. If you want, I can introduce you to some nice girls."

"Uh, no. I'm good. Time to get to work."

He received well-meaning support and unwanted advice from many of his co-workers. Behind his back he also became the subject of speculation about what went wrong with his marriage.

By the end of the work week life returned to its usual, monotonous rhythm for Hawksley. Almost. The breakup resulted in him dropping weight, and in inability to get much sleep.

Chapter 5

In the sticky, mid-July heat, Hawksley arrived at Dominic Artino's law office to sign his separation agreement. The lawyer had phoned two days earlier. Now Hawksley sat in the reception area of Artino's restored Edwardian house, grateful for the modern arctic-chill air conditioning. He listened to the soft, soothing voice of Artino's secretary on the phone, and ignored the other three clients. Bored, he at last picked up and leafed through an old Time magazine. Forty minutes later, suit coat off, and a stomach big enough to rival Santa's, Artino called him. Hawksley rose and approached.

"Nice to see you again," Artino said. He extended his hand. They shook. Social niceties satisfied, Artino spun and headed down a narrow hallway with an expensive runner over the stained, wooden floor. Hawksley followed.

They entered an office right out of some Hollywood movie, replete with an enormous oak roll-top desk with drawers, nooks, and a leather top inlay. A swivel chair sat in front of it. Two similar chairs faced it. A credenza and two bookcases, both of some kind of dark wood, claimed space against walls.

Artino dropped into his chair, his back to the desk. He reached for a file.

"So, you mind if I call you Hawksley?"

Hawksley shook his head. "My guest."

"Interesting name. How'd you come by it?"

"My Mom. She's a local history buff. Thaddeus Hawksley, a Colonel in the Union Army, led the 6th Light Artillery at the Battle of Jenkins' Ferry, Arkansas. I got named after him."

"So you're not related to him?"

"No. My Mom liked the name, Hawksley."

"Huh."

The subject exhausted, Artino opened the file. "Okay, as I said, I have some papers for you to sign. Then you're done."

"Good enough. Let's do it."

"As I told you on the phone," Artino said, "you and Darlene have sorted out your liquidity, haven't got kids, and there's no issues about the house. It's pretty straight-forward."

Thumb and forefinger under his eyeglasses, Artino rubbed his eyes and opened them.

"Splitting-up's always difficult, but there is a silver lining." He halted, perhaps to let his words sink in. "Darlene's side's picking up the entire tab for the divorce. It'll be uncontested. So, all I need is for you to sign the separation papers."

Hawksley nodded. *How'd Darlene come up with the dough for this? Maybe she decided to pay for it to get on my good side, in case I flashed the pics around. Ah, doesn't much matter.*

Ten minutes later Hawksley unlocked his car. Car door ajar, he plunked himself behind the wheel. *Well, I'm divorced. I guess I should feel happy, but I don't. Truth is, there aren't enough adjectives to describe how I feel. Empty, depressed, alone, those would be a good start.*

He ran a hand across his lower face. No point going back to work now. Shift would soon be over. Might as well head home.

He started the engine and powered down the windows to let out the heat. Seconds later he turned the air conditioner on to high, and directed the windows back up. He stayed in the car and considered this second-last step before divorce. No muss, no fuss, yet the finality of it…

A long, wistful air of disappointment escaped him. Why did he somehow feel responsible? He hadn't engaged in an affair. He hadn't slunk out of the house like she did. Still, the memory of her betrayal hurt in ways no language could describe. Not only had she betrayed him, but she did it in a cruddy way—with another woman. Guys like Rick surfed the net for this kind of porn, but he found it disgusting.

His eyes filled. He glanced about to see if anyone noticed him. No, all by himself in the small parking lot behind his lawyer's office.

He swallowed several times, swiped at his face with his fingertips, and put the car into reverse. It's done, he told himself. Get over it. Bring yourself under control. All right. And do what next? Should he go have a beer? Be perfect in this heat, but… He talked himself out of it. Booze and raw emotions: a bad mix. Yet he didn't want to go home to his empty house. What about *Has Beans?* Nobody ever got pulled over for a DUI from drinking coffee.

On his way, a strange sensation overtook him, one he'd never had. For a brief moment he experienced himself as two separate entities—the first sitting behind the wheel, the second a distance off, watching. The entire process lasted but a few unnerving seconds, long enough for his heart to race. He gasped and took in several deep breaths. "What, what happened?" he asked aloud when he pulled into a parking spot of the strip mall and shut off the engine. "What's happening? Am I going nuts?"

Nothing in the temporal or spiritual world answered. He sat in the car and considered what he'd experienced. Was it—whatever *it* was—the result of stress? If so, how come he'd never had anything like it before?

Unable to reach any conclusion, he dismissed the whole matter and entered the cafe. Daily papers well thumbed through, the news outdated already, he took his coffee and sat by the front window. Once more he thought about his separation and everything before and after it. He stared out the window.

"You all right?"

He turned his face up to a girl with large eyes. "Huh? Oh, yeah, sure. Fine."

She smiled down at him. "Good. You look like you lost your last best friend in the world."

He gave her a tight smile, and she moved off to clear dishes at the next table.

Hawksley left the café and walked past a health food and a party store. In a shadowy alleyway between the party store and its immediate neighbor, a pizzeria, his eyes caught something move. Probably a rat foraging.

At sixteen Hawksley had worked part time as a tray boy at the A&W on Gaynor. At the end of his evening shift, he'd throw out bags of garbage with leftover burgers, fries and other food. Nocturnal creatures—rats, mice, skunks, raccoons, and feral cats—scavenged there. They ignored each other and concentrated on the free plunder.

For fun, Hawksley and two tray girls sometimes tossed food toward a rotund rat. They'd laugh as it lumbered toward the temptations.

Unsure why, Hawksley now stepped farther into the alleyway. His eyes adjusted to the lack of light. Uh-uh, no rat. Too big, and the wrong shape.

He didn't think it to be either a cat or bandit-masked raccoon. With caution, he stepped closer. The puppy noticed him and released its morsel of food. It spun about and made for the back corner of a dumpster, its back to a wall. The terrified, dingy puppy with sad eyes, pointed ears, and light-colored brown fur, did its best to hide.

Hawksley approached and held out a hand. "Not gonna hurt you, little guy," he said in a soothing voice. He bent and advanced. "You don't have to be frightened of me."

Unconvinced, the puppy backed further against the brick wall. A stuffed and torn teddy bear lay next to it. Hawksley took in the sight. "Oh, beyond sad. The little bear is your only friend."

The puppy mustered enough nerve for a last-second escape. It made a dash past him. He caught it. It yelped in fright. He picked it up, and cradled it. It buried its face in the crook of his arm, it's tiny body shaking.

He rose and spoke to it. "Where's your mama, little guy? By the looks of your situation, I'd guess she's not coming back. Aww. Don't worry. I'll make sure nothing bad happens to you."

The side door to the party store flew open. An older Asian woman stepped out with a garbage bag. Startled, her gaze took in Hawksley, perhaps unsure of any possible threat.

She found her voice. "What you do here?"

To Hawksley, her statement sounded more like an accusation than a question. He offered his best smile, and dropped his gaze to the puppy. "Nothing. Didn't mean to scare you." He pointed. "I saw this little guy here. Is it yours?"

She shook her head with strong conviction. "No. You go away."

Somewhat intimidated by the petite woman, Hawksley nodded. He bent, picked up the tattered bear, and moved past her.

Out of the alleyway, he considered his catch. "I think she answered my question. You don't belong to anyone. Your mama's gone, and nobody wants you. You deserve better."

In an instant, a firmness of purpose overtook him: he'd keep the pup. Scruffy, smelly, in need of a good meal or two, to say nothing of a bath, but it now belonged to him.

Hawksley unlocked the car, again let out the heat of the day before he shut the doors. "Get you home, something to eat, and then clean you up. And then I've got a lot of reading to do about dogs." His eyes moved to the bear on the seat. "I'll wash it, little fella. Will have to mend it as well, but I don't guarantee how good a job I'll do.'

Perhaps responding to his soft voice, the puppy ceased its trembling.

He put the car in reverse. Little puppy nails tried to make purchase with his shirt, to climb up toward his shoulder and head to who knew where? He pulled the puppy into his lap again. Who could blame it, taken away from the one place it probably knew as home—an alleyway.

The car in his garage, Hawksley took the pup inside and let it explore. It sniffed the entire interior, eager to get a sense of its new surroundings. It wandered from room to room. At last it moved into a corner, squatted and peed on his dining room rug.

He rushed over, scooped it up and carried it outside. "Okay, this is where you go from now on."

Dark, sad eyes stared up at him. He picked it up and held it high. "Ah, you're a she, not a he."

Chapter 6

The puppy gave Hawksley a new sense of focus. He set aside his episodes of gloom, doom, sadness, and gave himself over to enjoying the dog.

He picked out a name, Torchy. Next, he plunked her in the kitchen sink for her first bath. Frightened he might drown her, she fought his efforts. Tiny nails on fast-moving paws worked to free themselves from his grasp. As too did her snake-like moves. He endured. His voice calm, he said, "Hold still, little one. Not looking to drown you. Be over soon, and you'll be clean."

Finished, he placed her on the floor, and failed to step away when Torchy shook the water off her. Hawksley laughed. "Lesson learned. Okay, time to wrap you in this towel."

Minutes later he said, "You were going through garbage when I found you, so I guess you can handle solids. Let's see what I've got in the fridge."

He cut up some bits of chicken and set it down for her. Later he brought Torchy to his desk while he searched for the closest pet store. Tomorrow he'd get some supplies.

Fast enough, the puppy lost her fear of him. Lively and ready-to-please, her bushy tail fanned the air every time he spoke to her. He stared down at her. Excited yellowish-brown mammalian eyes stared back at him. The tail wagged again. She'd forgiven him for the bath.

He crouched and touched her black button nose. "You know, Torch, I was meant to find you. The universe planned it."

She slept on the bed with him. He hoped she wouldn't have an accident, and she didn't. A different story the next day; three times, around the house. Still, he remained patient, and hurried her outside each time.

From the internet he learned dogs were social animals. They needed company. He frowned. Not good. He couldn't leave Torchy alone. He searched for solutions. Not many. The best might be a dog sitter.

A flurry of phone calls followed.

"Ouch," he said after he hung up with the last number he called. "Pricey. Another dog, maybe? No, too much work. A kitten? Cats were said to be low maintenance. The more he thought about it, the more he liked the idea. He'd get a kitten to keep Torchy company. The two could grow up together. He'd check the shelter to see what they had.

A minute later he retrieved his keys and put her in the utility room. "Be a good girl, Torchy. Back as soon as I can."

Kind eyes stared up at him, her tail wagging.

In his car he marveled at the suddenness of events. Within twenty-four hours he'd have one, maybe two live-in companions.

He stopped at a large pet supply store to buy food, dog collar and leash, and a bed. To his delight they had kittens up for adoption. He studied them, and liked the look of a calico with a white stripe down its chest.

He spoke to the attendant and discovered the kitten was also female. Meant to be, he told himself, and filled out the adoption papers.

He placed the kitten, two beds and animal supplies in the car. "Okay, then, kitty," he said slid and behind the wheel, "let's go home so you can see your new digs and meet Torchy."

One small piddle when he returned. Not bad, all things considered.

He cleaned up while the two animals inspected each other. Neither showed hostility. Torchy made the first playful lunge. The kitten reacted with a frisky sideward bounce.

Hawksley watched. "Good. I think you two are going to be friends. Now, what will we name you, kitty?"

Once more he consulted the internet. He found a name to his liking.

"Vesta." He sounded it out again. "Goddess of the home." He tickled her under the chin while Torchy sniffed her. "How do you like the name, Vesta?"

If she had an opinion, Vesta held it back.

Lights out, Torchy slept next to Hawksley, and Vesta on his chest. Both stayed clear of their beds.

Hawksley delighted he didn't have to house train Vesta. She took to the litter box from the start. She did like to roam outside, but always came when he called her.

The pup on the other hand proved more of a challenge. Hawksley came home to more than a few accidents. He never over-reacted, cleaned the mess, and took her outside for "last call" before he settled in for the night. Eager to please, Torchy caught on several weeks later.

Trouble with Hawksley's new neighbor arrived in mid-September.

Kimball liked heavy metal, and liked it loud; loud enough to break any noise ordinance bylaw. Hawksley on the other hand hated the all-bass, talentless two-chord playing rebels-without-clues bands. Aside from poor musical taste, he couldn't understand why Kimball drew this kind of attention to himself.

On a particular hot Sunday afternoon, Hawksley had fallen asleep during a Browns-Lions game. Overloud, aggressive bass from Kimball's stereo woke him. It took him a second to get his bearings. Naps always disoriented him. He groaned. "What is it with this asshole?"

He puzzled out what to do about the racket. Should he call the cops and ask them to go visit Kimball, maybe give him a citation? No, take too long. "I'm already half-deaf. Imagine what I'll be by the time they get here?"

No other solution came to him. With reluctance, he left his house the same moment Kimball backed his pickup out his driveway and drove away.

Hawksley spied Kimball's wife or girlfriend out front. "Get this over with," he mumbled to himself. He walked across his lawn and made for the tall, attractive, ponytailed woman in skin tight jeans at work in her flower bed. He had little interest in engaging the unfriendly, peroxide-blonde, bed-warmer—or whatever she was—in conversation or anything. If anyone gave off major bitch vibes, she did. He noticed the bangles on her wrist. Who wears bangles while they're gardening, he asked himself? Dumb blondes, that's who.

Satisfied with his put-down, he stopped next to her. She raised her chin and gave him a deadpan expression.

"Hi. Your music. It's loud. Really loud. How 'bout turning it down?"

Unable to see his own at-rest face, or heed the tone of his voice, he only took in her annoyed response. A shadow crossed her face. Without a word she rose and entered her house. A few seconds later the speakers no longer put out their head-aching noise. He waited, ready to thank her. She failed to return. He shrugged, spun around and crossed back onto his property.

When long evening shadows played across his lawn, Hawksley started up his lawnmower. Two swipes near his driveway and he caught sight of Kimball stepping onto his property. Everything about the man's long strides said aggression. Hawksley's brain and body readied for the possibility of threat. Angst and energy of distant football practices charged his muscles.

Kimball stopped and pointed to the lawn mower. Hawksley understood the command, and released the stop bar of the mower.

"Yeah."

"Your mower's noise is bothering me."

At once Hawksley heard the blood rushing in his ears. His mouth ran dry. "What?"

Kimball jutted out his chin. "You heard me."

Unlike Logan, Hawksley coasted through middle and high school without a single altercation. He got on well with his schoolmates, a skill he carried into his workplace. Now he found himself up against naked aggression. Thousands of years of biology came to his aid. In an instant his face reddened and his lips thinned. "You're on *my* lawn, asshole. What the fuck is your problem?"

Clenched fists by his side, eyes narrowed, Kimball moved closer. Hawksley smelled the alcohol. "*My* problem? Where you get off ordering my girlfriend to turn down the stereo?"

"What? You making this up as you go along? I didn't order her to do a thing. I asked nicely. Too deep a concept for you, peanut brain?"

The words no sooner out, than Kimball charged. The former safety of the Bulldogs anticipated it and sidestepped the rush. Kimball flew by. Hawksley stuck out his foot. Arms out in front, Kimball fell forward. Down, unable to protect himself, Kimball received the first kick to his ribs. Hawksley kept kicking. Kimball rolled away and curled into a fetal position.

The kicks stopped. Huffing, out of breath, Hawksley glared down at him. "You get up before I tell you, you sonovabitch, and your next stop's the hospital. Understand?"

"Yeah," a dejected Kimball repeated.

"All right. Up and off my lawn. This better be the end of you getting yourself all liquored up and coming over here to pick a fight. Got it?"

Kimball rose, unsteady on his feet. He winced and hobbled toward to his house.

His girlfriend rushed onto Hawksley's lawn and spoke to Kimball. He answered something. She in turn turned venomous eyes on Hawksley. She screamed and swore at him before she led Kimball away.

A few neighbors stood on their lawns and watched in silence. Still full of adrenaline, yet embarrassed, Hawksley restarted his lawnmower. Careful not to look at anyone, his mind raced at what he might have unleashed. Revenge, guns, all sorts of unwelcome possibilities.

In his house he paced his living room, smacked his forehead, and threw himself onto the couch. "What's going on with me? First Darlene, now this. Stupid, stupid, stupid."

In bed, sleep wouldn't come for much of the night. When it did, he had the worst sleep. Frightened images of violence flooded his mind. Torchy and Vesta grew tired of him thrashing about, and jumped off the bed.

Chapter 7

Word of the fight tore through the neighborhood. Hawksley become something of a local celebrity. People left messages on his voice mail. Anonymous supportive notes found their way into his mail slot.

He drew no comfort from any of it. He wished the whole thing hadn't happened. If only he'd kept his cool...

"You serious, bro?" his square-jawed brother said during their video call. "You got into a dust-up with a drug-dealing neighbor. I gotta say this—are you out of your fucking mind?"

Hawksley moved his face closer to the screen and grimaced.

"I know. I know. Played it over in my head a hundred times. Guy stomps over half pissed and all attitude-y. Next thing I know he's rushing me. Law's on my side. *He* was on my property; he started this."

"Yeah, and *he's* got guns."

"Neighbor says he's a felon, so can't own weapons."

Logan's mouth twisted. "Uh, bro, he's a criminal. *Crim-in-al*. He deals drugs, remember? Bad drugs. Think a little thing like getting a piece will slow him down? And how do you know he won't send someone over to visit you?"

Hawksley groaned. "Thanks for cheering me up. So far no one's shot up my place yet. I'm hoping the whole thing blows over." He closed his eyes for a second, opened them and blew out his cheeks. "Funny–not funny as in hah-hah, but funny as in weird. I got two neighbors, and I avoid eye contact with both."

"Well, keep clear of the drug dealer. And this Nancy chick—she the one I saw before, right?"

"Yeah."

"She's hot, bro. If you don't make a move on her, send her here. I'll make lots of eye contact with her."

Hawksley shook his head slowly. "Yeah, I'm sure your platoon would be more than happy to share her in your sandbag post. Now would you like her in Western clothes or in one of those whatchamacallit head-to-toe thingy?"

"Hijabs, and no, I want her in a mini skirt and killer heels, looking as sexy as she can. Here, after a while, even the Hijab women start looking good. Saw a bare-footed one flashing her toes. Got all excited."

Shared brotherly laughter drew the two closer, despite the physical distance.

Logan spoke again. "How're you doing with the Darlene thing?"

"Bad days and good, but mostly getting better, I think," Hawksley said "Sleeping okay, well, except for the last few nights." He offered up a self-mocking laugh. "The worst is being lonely, but Torchy and Vesta really help with out there." He brightened. "Say, wanna see 'em?"

"Yeah. You bet."

"Okay. Sec."

Hawksley returned with the pets in his lap and held them up for inspection one at a time before he set them down.

"Aw, really cute, man. *Really* cute. And you found the puppy in the alley?" "S'right."

"Who'd dump a helpless puppy in an alley? Idiots. Well, I'm glad you found her. You got her to the vet, right? Check-up, shots, dog tag, all the things they need?"

"I did, yep. The full nine yards."

A short break in the conversation. Two brothers grinned away at their monitors.

Hawksley took a breath and said, "How's it going at your end?"

Logan pulled back from the monitor, looked left, right, and behind him before he fixed his eyes on the screen.

"Good to be back on base again, but gotta be careful what I say. Tent flaps have ears. Afghanistan has always been a desert shit storm. National sport here is them killing each other and growing heroin. Tribal fighting alla time. They only stop for Mongols, Persians, Greeks, the Brits, Russians, and now us. Unites them until the foreigners are gone. Then they go back to growing opium poppies and killing each other."

"Looks like you seem to know a lot about it," Hawksley said.

"Hard not to, being here."

"I bet. When are they sending you back out?"

"Couple days."

"Well, be careful, Sergeant Pardee. Folks here, including me, want you back alive, safe, and in one piece."

"Do my best. And you too. Especially you. I'm not doing any re-up. Done the end of September. Got contacts in Chicago for security work. Make some serious coin. Okay, listen, gotta go. Somebody behind me wanting his turn on the computer."

"But I'll talk to you before then, right?"

"Yeah, oh sure. Hi to Maddie and Mom, and don't forget, if you send your hottie neighbor here, I'll pay the freight."

Hawksley threw back his head and laughed. "I'll go ask her." He turned off his laptop, grateful technology allowed him instant access to the other side of the world.

Conversation with Logan brought him back to his childhood. Difficult because of his father; difficult for them all. But the kids and their mom got on well and formed a unified front against Daryl Pardee.

Neither Hawksley, Maddie, nor Logan blamed their mother when she walked out on the marriage. In private conversation, they wondered what took her so long.

Chapter 8

Thursday Hawksley arrived home from work, greeted by a happy Torchy and Vesta, both eager for their dinner.

"Go do your business," he said to the pup, and opened the door for her.

She dashed out. He looked down at a meowing Vesta. "Okay, okay, it's coming." He moved into the kitchen, Vesta close behind, rubbing herself against his legs. He bent and scooped out the remains of a can of cat food into her bowl.

"Boy, kitty, you'd think I never fed you. Better get this down before Torchy comes back."

Head down, eager to enjoy her wet food, Vesta ignored him.

"I better go get Torchy," he said to himself, picked up a disposable waste bag, and hurried out to fetch the dog.

After dinner he read the next chapter of his textbook, *Introduction to Chemistry.* He liked the instructor and small class at U. of L. She knew her stuff, and interacted well with her mostly older, male students.

Torchy distracted him halfway through his overview of organic chemistry. She repeatedly arched her head and back, and made loud breathing noises. He turned from his textbook and gave her his full attention.

"Torchy. What's wrong?" In reply, she retched.

He bounded out of his chair. "Oh, gawd." He tore off for the kitchen and returned with a roll of paper towels and the garbage can. Cleanup done, he washed his hands and waited. Maybe she'd be fine.

She continued to retch. She needed help. Hawksley checked the internet for emergency veterinary care centers open. He found one close by; keys in hand, he scooped up the sick dog, and made for his car.

Two days and five-hundred-and-sixty dollars later Hawksley brought a still feeble Torchy home. His conversation with the vet played itself over and over again.

"Poisoned?" he'd said while he held Torchy. "She stays on my property. Where would she eat poison? And who poisons harmless puppies?" He slowly shook his head. "My cat goes out too. Good thing she didn't find whatever Torchy got into. Wonder if I should keep her in from now on?"

The middle-aged vet with the high forehead and downturned eyes shook her head.

"I can't say what happened. The poison could have been left out for rats. Not the kind of a thing a cat would be attracted to. You know, our experience with this tells us there's a good chance somebody doesn't like you, or Torchy here."

She reached out a hand and stroked the puppy. "Who wouldn't like you?" she cooed in a soft voice.

"And you're sure it was poison? Not something not agreeing with her?"

"Something didn't agree with her, all right," Dr. Kantor said. "Strychnine. We found it in her blood. Good thing you brought her here fast. I'd like to see her again in a week for a follow-up. And of course call if anything changes."

At home Hawksley moved Torchy's bed next to his desk. He placed her down gently. "May be a while before you're up and at 'em again, Torch. Why don't you lie down and keep me company."

Vesta, stepped into the dog's bed, craned her neck and sniffed Torchy. Done, she stepped out of the bed.

"See," Hawksley said. "She missed you too." He returned his attention to the conversation about the poisoning. Rats? No. He dismissed the idea. He'd never heard of anyone in the neighborhood having problems with rats. So how else did strychnine find its way into Torchy? Did her barking cause this? He doubted it. Besides, he kept her indoors most of the time. Problems with his neighbors? He got on well enough with the Patels and Freys behind him. With everybody—everybody but Kimball and Nancy. It had to be one of them.

Of the two suspects, he considered Nancy first. Poisoning didn't fit with what he knew of her. She liked animals. He recalled a time when she took an injured bird to a local animal rehab center.

Not Nancy.

The spotlight fell on Kimball. Hawksley examined the evidence against him. "Couldn't let it well enough alone after the beating, huh?" he said under his breath. "Had to get payback. Okay, pal, my turn."

He hadn't formed a solid plan when he visited Phil Lofton. They sat at a picnic table in Lofton's back yard, drinking beers.

"So what brings you knocking on my door?" Lofton asked.

Hawksley took a pull on his beer. "Not subtle, am I?"

Lofton tossed a shoulder. "I don't know. What?"

"Somebody poisoned my dog. I'm pretty damn sure it was Kimball. I can't prove it, so there's no point calling the cops. And I can't go over there and duke it out. If I do and he presses charges, I'm the one standing in front of a judge."

"Yeah, and he'll say you continued your beef with him."

"True, but he's not getting away with this."

Hawksley paused and took another pull on his beer. "If I'm going to do something, it needs finesse. Listen, you work at police HQ. Tell me what kind of trouble I'm looking at going up against him?"

Lofton stopped peeling the sweating label off his bottle. He met Hawksley's gaze. "You sure you want to ask?"

Hawksley nodded. "Like I said, I have to do something, so yeah."

The label off, Lofton set it down and picked up his beer. A long pull later he returned the bottle to the table.

"All right, first, revenge, especially this kind, is never a good idea, for a lot of reasons."

"Got it, but give me something to work with."

Lofton pursed his lips. "Your funeral. I've said enough about it, so let's move on. Kimball's settled into the neighborhood, keeping. From what I hear, he likes it. Last thing he'll want is publicity. I doubt you'll draw any comfort from this, but I'm guessing he's kicked himself for getting into it with you."

Lofton rolled his shoulders. "New Albany's not some ghetto neighborhood where street cred is everything, where every slight, real or imagined, is met head-on. We're a small, white Midwest city. We don't wear do-rags, don't have street gangs, and don't flash gang colors. There's no upside to Kimball living on our street, but his pushers aren't here, or hanging around our school yards either. His customers come mostly from white, middle-class professionals."

He broke off and took another sip of his beer. "What I'm getting at is he's not likely to 'pop a cap' into you. He's a drug dealer. A Midwest version who reflects the values of our Midwestern city." He twirled his beer bottle. "Strange, huh? A drug dealer with values? But it doesn't mean he's a pussy either."

"Okay, so I'll definitely have to remind myself of all this."

"Yes, you do, and think twice who you're up against." Lofton shook his head and stared at the grass. "Oh, and if what you do brings you to the attention of the cops, remember I work for them. I gave you no advice, right?"

"Right."

"Good, and to quote John Wayne, 'A man oughta do what he thinks is best.'"

Hawksley finished his beer, and set it on the table. "Thanks, Phil. Given me a lot to think about. So, I wasn't here, and we never had this beer."

He rose, Lofton with him. They shook hands. "Exactly," Lofton said. "Take care."

"You too."

Back in his house, Hawksley played back his conversation with Lofton. Made sense, everything the man said. In particular about Kimball not relying on gun violence.

The memory of Torchy's suffering came back to him. The more he dwelled on it, the angrier he became. Bit by bit his earlier logic surrendered to his emotions. He made up his mind to right the wrong.

What's Kimball's Achilles heel, he asked himself? What's the one thing he doesn't want?

The answer came as fast as the question: attention. His business depended on staying on the down and low.

A plan took shape. He'd bring Kimball into the limelight. Over the next few days Hawksley fleshed it out. At last satisfied with his scheme, he drove across the river. He entered a printing shop and ordered dozens of flyers for a house party at Kimball's house on a Friday evening.

It took several hours to get the flyers ready. Hawksley next hired a distributing company. They plastered flyers all over New Albany city core and the UI satellite campus. Bold, colorful, the flyers advertised free food, drink, and lots of wild music.

Three days later, past sunset, scores of young people showed up at Kimball's house. They filled his driveway, parked across his lawn. A few even parked on Hawksley's lawn. He accepted the encroachment, and told himself the end result justified the sacrifice.

Young people knocked on Kimball's door and demanded to be let in. Kimball, incensed, swore yelled, and even got into an altercation with several party-goers.

Realizing they'd been deceived, the revelers took their fury out on his property. They damaged his pickup and pelted his house with beer bottles and anything else within reach.

The commotion brought out a small collection of neighbors, including Hawksley. He caught a pungent whiff of marijuana. Hawksley guessed it had to come from the students. Kimball wouldn't chance having any at hand. He looked on with satisfaction. *Oh God, this is going better than I imagined.*

New Albany's Finest arrived. Soon enough charges of disorderly conduct, drinking underage, possession, criminal mischief resulted in half a dozen revelers arrested.

The civil disturbance caused a firestorm of media attention. *The New Albany Gazette* arrived first, followed by a van from a local TV station.

More news outlets arrived. Reporters and cameramen approached Hawksley and nearby neighbors for comments.

Two cops spoke to Kimball and gestured toward the interior of his house while film crew cameras rolled.

Hawksley, too far away, couldn't hear the conversation, but watched an agitated Kimball wave his arms around. The cops said something in return. Kimball dropped his arms and in resignation motioned for them to come inside.

Phil Lofton sidled up to Hawksley. "Wow. Any idea what stirred up this beehive?"

Hawksley played along and shook his head. "Dunno. I've never seen so much action on our street."

"You think this whole thing was planned?"

Hawksley raised a shoulder. "Planned? By how, why, and who? If it was, somebody went to a lot of trouble."

"Yeah, my thinking too."

At last the police brought order back to the street. Students drifted off. Kimball and his girlfriend barricaded themselves in their house.

"I better split too," Hawksley told Lofton. "More than enough excitement for one night."

"Hear ya." Lofton tossed off a casual wave and walked down the street.

The next few days Hawksley's stomach and muscles suffered from nervous tension. Would Kimball make him to be the instigator behind the disturbance? Should he have waited longer before he launched his counter-offensive?

A new thought chased out the old. Should he have cooled down, not rushed to get his revenge? Too late now, he told himself. Nothing to do but wait and see what—if anything—might happen.

Nothing happened. The dealer kept the blinds of his house down and became something of a hermit.

Hawksley allowed himself to relax. The world spun on its same orbit. Everything would be all right. If Kimball fingered him for this commotion, maybe he'd get why and leave well enough alone now. *We've both had our fun,* an inner voice said to Kimball. *Now let's leave it there.*

Chapter 9

Fall arrived, but summer wouldn't release its hold; hot days lingered.

Hawksley hadn't used his vacation days yet, so contemplated a week of hiking somewhere. He settled on *Daniel Boone National Forest*, a three-and-a-half hour drive into Kentucky. He liked to hike, and Torchy would enjoy herself.

At work he asked Ellen Maythorpe if she would look after Vesta.

She nodded. "Sure. Happy to. Bring her over. Want me to keep an eye on your place too?"

"Yeah, sure. Stop by once in a while and see if everything's fine."

Hawksley next searched the internet for accommodation near the park. He found a motel advertising itself as dog friendly.

"It's an extra fifteen dollars a day," the woman on the phone said. "Because of the time of year. You're lucky you found anything. People like to come and see the colors."

"A bit early yet, isn't it?"

"It is, but it doesn't stop folks from coming anyway. Would you like to make a reservation?

"Yes."

He hung up and spoke to Torchy. "Well, little one, this is going to be a whole new experience for you. We're gonna hike, explore some caves, have a really nice time."

Wednesday morning before he left for holidays Hawksley stepped out his back door. Plastic garbage bag in his hand, he dropped it into his trash can.

A noise from Nancy's garage door rising caught his attention. Seconds later, car keys in hand, she stepped out of the back of her own house. Clad in tight jeans and a red T-shirt with *"Coffee before talkie,"* written on it.

For an instant she froze at the sight of him. Mutual eye contact between the once-friendly neighbors didn't last more than a second.

Move, Hawksley ordered himself, unwilling to even acknowledge Nancy's presence.

Her words stopped him. "Can I talk to you, Hawk?"

Talk? He'd vowed he'd never say another word to her. And yet her face held something, maybe a pleading look.

"About what?"

Whether the gruffness of his voice, her possible loss of confidence, he didn't know, but her hand jerked. It moved up toward her neck, stopped, and fell again. Her voice squeaky, she said, "Um, I know I can never undo what I did. I'm the worst person in the world, and I wanted to tell you how sorry I am for betraying you, and causing your marriage to fall apart."

She paused, released a rush of air and pressed on. "My therapist said I should talk to you. I agreed, but always lost my nerve." She exhaled with force. "And here I am."

Something in her confession, her willingness to make herself vulnerable caused a shift in him. His stored-up bitterness relaxed its grip. Even so, his response surprised him.

"Truth is, *you* didn't betray me. Darlene did. You have some responsibility in this, especially since you ended up in my house."

Nancy studied the ground before she allowed herself to meet his gaze again. He took in the damp glistening eyes, and heard the catch in her voice.

"I know. I could offer any number of excuses, but none of them work. All I'll say is I didn't do well after Tony left. I should have gone to see a therapist then, but I didn't. Instead, I got caught up in something with Darlene. I'm not even a… you know, lesbian. Anyway, what does it matter now? What I really wanted to say, I said it. My deepest regret. If there's any way—any way at all—I can ever make it up to you…"

Hawksley wasn't sure he could absolve her. Images of her and Darlene still vacated his dreams. "Never mind. It's done. What's past is past."

She sniffed. "Can we work to be friends again?"

Friends, he asked himself: were they ever friends? Friendly, at best, but not much more. Still, she did want to repair the damage. Fine. Where was the harm now?

"Uh, sure. Why not? Be nice to be on good terms with at least one of my immediate neighbors."

"Oh, you mean…?" She pointed to the east side of his house.

He nodded. "Yeah."

Neither said anything more about Kimball. A quick nod from her, and she said, "Thanks, Hawk. I'll work to be a better neighbor."

"No problem. Um, do you mind my asking if you still see Darlene?"

She responded with a fast shake of her head. "No, never. Last time I saw her was when, well, you know… I stopped by where she worked once. Wanted to talk to her." She broke eye contact for a second. "It didn't happen. Now I'm sure if she spotted me on the sidewalk, she'd probably cross to the other side."

Nancy offered Hawksley a lopsided grin. "Anyway, I'm grateful to you for talking to me, and forgiving me. Can I ask, how are you holding up?"

"Better now. Got two housemates—Torchy and Vesta. They make good company."

"Yes, I saw them. Adorable." She moved onto a different topic. "Seeing anyone?"

The words no sooner out of her mouth, than she said, "I guess it's way too early isn't it? Anyway, none of my business, really."

He shook his head. "Not since Darlene. Don't want to go to clubs in case I run into her. Even then, haven't had much interest. Someday, maybe."

"Well, don't let yourself get too down. So we're good now?"

"We are, so don't worry about this anymore."

Thrilled yet surprised at this sudden, unexpected encounter with Nancy, Hawksley backed his car out of the driveway. He went over the encounter for much of the trip. He almost passed the cutoff to the motel.

At the front desk, Torchy received considerable attention from three kids. "C'mon, Torchy," Hawksley said, time to go. Say goodbye." He took her to the room, placed a bowl of water and her food in front of her, and left her to find something to eat.

Early the next morning Hawksley made for the national park. Warm temperatures still allowed him to hike in khakis shorts. He sprayed himself with DEET, careful to apply the repellant to his bare legs, arms and neck.

Each day Hawksley followed the trails and moved deeper into the dense woods. Hawksley took deep, glorious inhalations of the forest's natural fragrance. "Wish I could find some way to bottle this."

Torchy too loved the hikes. When Hawksley guessed it safe, he let her run off-leash. On occasion they arrived at large openings. A few times he scolded her for leaving the trail.

On his second to last day Hawksley readied for a Class 2 trail. At the parking lot he searched his backpack for his DEET. Where was it? It came to him—on the bed in his room. Should he waste the twenty minutes and go back to the hotel?

He weighed the advantages and disadvantages. Not many mosquitos left, he told himself. He guessed he'd be safe.

They set off on the high-stepped trail. Loosening and fussing with the straps of his backpack, Hawksley failed to note a warning poster—a drawing of a tick, against a white background, surrounded by a red circle.

A few minutes later Torchy charged up ahead. Winded, Hawksley arrived at the summit, but lost sight of her. He hollered. No response.

"Dammit, dog, where are you?" he shouted.

A rustling on the other side of a shrub caught his attention. A wild animal? A bear? Coyote? Should he chance it and find out? Maybe something happened to Torchy.

Careful to make noise, Hawksley advanced into the tall grass, and saw the carcass of a doe, and a curious puppy sniffing around it.

"Torchy," he called to the dog in a stern voice. "Come."

She obeyed.

He clipped his leash on her. "Let's get out of here before some four-footed diner comes back to claim its meal." He took a fast and final look at the maggot-infested body.

Man and dog turned and made their way back down the trail. "Hope you didn't eat anything we'll both pay for later," Hawksley said to Torchy.

Back in his room, drained from the strenuous hike, Hawksley undressed and stepped into the bathroom. Rain-shower spray kept him under the water longer than he'd intended. Glorious. He had to force himself to turn off the tap.

He dried himself and paid no heed to a small red dot at the back of his calf.

Showered, changed, he filled Torchy's water and food bowls.

"Be a good girl while I'm gone," he said while she ate. "No barking. I'm going to get my dinner too. And maybe a few beers."

*   *   *

"Did you have a good stay with us, Mr. Pardee?"

Hawksley made eye contact with the blue-eyed receptionist. "Sure did. Good weather, good hiking. I'll come back."

"Pleased to hear it." She smiled across the counter. "Have a safe trip home."

"Thanks, and see you again."

Close to four hours later he pulled into his driveway.

Ten days later Paul Inkster pulled into the company parking lot about the same time as Hawksley. Both stepped out of their vehicles.

"Another day, another dollar," Inkster said. He studied Hawksley' profile. "You look like shit."

Hawksley blew out his cheek. "Yeah, feel like crap. No energy. Achy, run-down."

"Maybe you should go see a doctor."

"Intend to after work."

"Well, hope you get better fast."

"Thanks."

Since he'd returned from the national park, Hawksley couldn't shake the nagging suspicion he'd contracted Lyme disease. The large itchy rash on his calf, headaches, followed by bouts of chills and sweats, everything pointed to it.

He'd checked the internet, and diagnosed himself. Like a detective, he sifted through evidence of how he might have been bitten. It had to be near the doe. He hadn't noticed anything at the time. Common enough, this not knowing, according to internet message boards.

In hindsight he should have gone to see Dr. Gurpal as soon as his suspicions grew. Everything now hurt. And he tired fast. Twelve hour shifts felt, never easy at the best of times, now felt like small eternities.

Four hours after he clocked in, Hawksley clocked out and asked to see Shipley. The HR manager invited him into his office.

"You all right?"

Hawksley shook his head. "No, sir, and it's why I'm here. It started with my neck, and then the headaches. They got worse and worse."

He went on to detail his symptoms, and his suspicion.

The bespectacled Shipley ran a palm over his brush cut and shook his head. "No, you're smart. Get tested. Right away." He opened a drawer and pulled out a form. He handed it to Hawksley. "Call and let us know what's happening. If you think you'll be off more than a couple of weeks, have your doctor fill out this form and send it to us. So, good luck. Sorry to hear about this."

He shook his head in sympathy. "Hasn't been a good year for you so far. Get well fast."

Hawksley rose. "Thanks, sir. I'll stay in touch, and let you know what's happening."

Outside Hawksley unlocked his car. He'd stop at a walk-in clinic. Gurpal wouldn't be able to see him until later in the week. Buckled up, he started the engine and drove off. He cursed himself for his recklessness, leaving the DEET in his motel room. "If only I'd gone back to the motel," he said aloud, "I wouldn't be in this mess."

He snorted. "Ironic. Torchy sniffs around the dead animal. I'm only there for a few seconds, and guess who gets sick? Damn."

Chapter 10

He arrived at the walk-in clinic. Fifteen minutes later a receptionist escorted him to one of the examination rooms.

"Hello, I'm Dr. Payne," the genial-sounding physician with a fleshy nose and wide-set eyes said and entered. "What brings you here?"

Hawksley told him, and showed him the rash on his leg.

The examination took less than ten minutes.

"You can get dressed now," the middle-aged physician said, and tippity-tapped on his desktop computer. He turned from the monitor to Hawksley.

"You have definite symptoms associated with Lyme disease. The blood tests I'm setting up will tell for sure. We'll forward the information to your primary care doctor. In the meantime I'll start you on Prednisone, an anti-inflammatory, and some other antibiotics. If your joints hurt, take over-the-counter meds like ibuprofen with them. But not too many." He paused, drew in a breath and said, "Have any questions?"

Distracted by worries and aches in his body, Hawksley nodded and rubbed his neck. "I do, and I should have written them down. Kind of out- of-it."

"Well, write your questions down for your doctor." The physician followed with a fast nod. "Now, before you go, a word of caution: good chance the antibiotics will increase your fever in the next twenty-four hours or so. And your rash could get angrier-looking. It doesn't mean you're getting worse, but it might feel like it. It's your virus saying it's not happy with what you're doing to it."

"*My* virus? It's in me, but sure as hell isn't *my* virus." Hawksley closed his eyes, opened them again. "Sorry. Got carried away there. Doesn't sound like something to look forward to."

"No, but short term sacrifice for long term gain. Get to your doctor as soon as you finish the meds"

"Right. I'll drop by to make an appointment before I go home."

The doctor's advice about a ratcheting-up of the pain turned out to be an understatement. Hawksley's joints and muscles hurt beyond belief. So too did his pounding headache. His misery consumed him. He moaned and rolled around on the bed. Desperate for relief he swallowed far too many ibuprofen. It only caused him to rush to the toilet and throw up.

He groaned and begged some unseen deity to free him from his suffering.

Unable to do little but suffer and moan, he remained on the bed and wished for death. "I have to do something," he whispered through dry lips. "Something. I can't manage, and Torchy and Vesta need looking after."

But who should he call? His mother and siblings were too far away. His father? No. Out of the question. Ellen? She'd be at work.

A possibility came to him. He dragged himself out of bed and to the phone. Dizzy, he picked up the receiver and hit the speed dial number for Nancy. Darlene had put it in long ago.

Hawksley couldn't explain the need to call. He craved warmth, compassion, and some generosity of kindness.

She picked up on the third ring. "Hello."

"Nancy, it's Hawk next door. Sorry to bother you, but I've got Lyme disease, and am in so much pain. Everyone I know is at work, and I can't look after my pets. I'd be grateful if you could come over and help. Any way you can."

The line went silent for a second. "I'll be right over."

A latter-day Florence Nightingale, Nancy cared for his pets, and ministered to Hawksley. She aired out his house, made tea and honey, and encouraged him to take in more liquids.

Twice she urged him to go to the hospital. "You look terrible," she said. "You're gray, and in great pain. I'll drive you."

He shook his head. "What are they going to do? They can't give me anything more than I already have."

She surrendered after several tries. "All right. So we go with more liquids. And food." She pointed to his bed. "Those sheets need changing. Where do you keep fresh ones?"

He sat while she re-made the bed. *Ironic, she's making my bed, the bed Darlene shared with her.*

He kept the opinion to himself.

She examined her handiwork before she turned to him. "I'll ask again. Sure you don't want me to take you to the hospital?"

He shook his head. "Got an appointment with my doc tomorrow morning."

She helped him back into his bed. Once he settled in, she asked him where he got the bite.

Hawksley considered himself a private person, not overly given to talking about himself. For some reason, whether the way she asked, how she pulled a chair closer, ready to listen, her question touched something in him. He felt his eyes moisten, blinked rapidly, and cleared his throat. In the moment he also experienced a connection to her. He told her all he knew.

"I'm on the low end of the learning curve on this thing," he said and finished his tale. "Doing things wrong, I took so much ibuprofen last night to get rid of the headache. Made it worse. Threw it all up." He folded his hands together. 'I'll know more as time goes by."

Nancy shook her head. "You should thank your stomach. It became your best friend by throwing up. Ibuprofen damages the lining, to say nothing of what it does to your kidneys and liver. Did it help your headache?"

"No."

"Sorry. Look, let's get some food into you. It'll help what you're taking."

She made him a light meal of two soft boiled eggs, slices of cheese, and dry toast.

Vesta bounded up on the bed and sniffed at his meal. His back against the head board, Hawksley stroked her.

"Will you be all right?" Nancy asked and watched him eat.

"Better now than before. You've been my life-saver. I think I'll make it through the night. I can't thank you enough."

"No need. I'm a phone call away. I'll stop in tomorrow morning. You mentioned a doctor's appointment. When?"

"Tomorrow at ten."

"I'll take you."

"You don't have to."

"I *know*, but I want to. You're not in the best shape to do anything."

Hawksley stared into her eyes. Kind eyes, he thought. Had he forgotten, or did he even know she had kind eyes? She'd been a good-enough neighbor, and then the thing with Darlene happened. Afterwards, well, he wanted nothing more to do with her. And now?

Hawksley blew out his lips. Doing a bad thing didn't make someone a bad person any more than doing a good thing made them good. The thought brought him to Darlene. Would he ever get past her betrayal and forgive her?

He pulled out of his rumination. "I'm sorry about what happened between us." The acknowledgement came out in a half-whisper.

Nancy tilted her head and studied him. "Where did this come from?"

Hawksley raised a hand and let it drop next to the tray. "Thinking of things, is all. I'm sorry for any trouble I caused you."

Nancy leaned to take his tray. "Wrong way around. I'm the one who caused it. I'm honored you reached out to me. What say we not bring this up anymore, leave it where it belongs—in the past?"

"Deal. And thank you again."

"Welcome. I'll take care of these dishes and lock the door behind me. Try to sleep."

Easier said than done, he knew, but somewhere in the night exhaustion claimed him. Even so, his throbbing headache intruded into his sleep.

He woke past dawn, rubbed his temples, and checked in with himself. Better? Maybe. Hard to tell. Then again, his stomach didn't feel as bad as before. Had to be a good sign. His headache and general achiness still hung around. Hot and cold flashes hadn't returned. Counted for something.

He rose, put on his old housecoat and trundled out to the kitchen. "Look at me. I'm walking like an old man."

He let Torchy out the back door and watched while she did her business. "Torch, c'mon," he called. "Come on, girl, get in."

Hawksley shut the door and followed her. They'd been great, his pets. They'd stayed on the bed with him for much of the time, and made few demands. He vowed he'd give them more attention throughout the day.

He was spreading butter on his toast when the phone rang.

"'Lo."

"How are you feeling?" Nancy asked.

"A little better, I think."

"A good sign, maybe. Listen, I'll be over in a bit."

Hawksley unlocked the back door.

Nancy let herself in. Pressed jeans and a pink blazer over a white T-shirt gave her a casual, relaxed look.

She approached and studied him while he drank his instant coffee. "Still look pale, and the tightness around your eyes shows. Can you get washed-up and showered before your appointment?"

On the way to his doctor, Hawksley looked at his list of questions. He hoped he wouldn't get distracted with other things.

Nancy waited while he met with his physician.

Gurpal sat at his desk and gestured for Hawksley to sit in the chair. Soft-spoken, the physician enunciated every word with care.

He tapped Hawksley's file. "Your tests are back. You won't be surprised with the finding. A black-legged tick found you." He stopped and let his words settle on Hawksley. "Lyme disease."

In reply Hawksley pressed his lips into a tight line of disapproval, and again cursed himself for the fateful day in the forest.

Gurpal intruded into his thoughts.

"Right, then, take off your shirt and pants, and climb up on the table."

He took his time examining Hawksley and asked his own questions about where Hawksley thought the bite had happened, and if he guessed his symptoms to be severe, continuous, or only coming on at times?

The question of his symptoms annoyed Hawksley. *How the hell would I know the state of them? I've never had this before. You're the doctor. You tell me.*

His first impulse was to blurt out his inner thought. He managed to hold himself in check. *Chill. He's only doing his job.*

The physical completed, Gurpal invited Hawksley to dress again. "So, Lyme disease," he said when Hawksley took a chair next to the desk. "Now, knowing you as I do, I'm sure you've done a lot of reading about this. I bet you can teach me a thing or two."

Hawksley shook his head. "Doubt it, but I've written down some questions."

"Good. Let's hear them."

The physician answered all of Hawksley's questions before he suggested a treatment plan. He finished with, "It's tough, real tough, what you're looking at, but we'll be hopeful you'll get the better of this."

"'Tough?' I can give you a different word. I've got sweats, headaches, a sore throat, and feel like throwing up. I'm not sure I can handle what my body's doing, 'specially since I've been on this, this um, Herxheimer thing." His eyes darted from the table to the physician and back. "What the hell is it with these drug companies? Can't they come up with simple, pronounceable names?"

Gurpal furrowed his brow, glanced at the file, and turned his attention back to Hawksley.

"You're not alone in your complaint. As for the drugs, you're on powerful ones, including a tetracycline antibiotic. They can feel like they're making things worse—in the short run."

He threw a hand into the air. "Maybe the worst is behind you. Let's give everything a chance. If the headaches persist, and over-the-counter medication won't help, come back. We'll try something else. Now, one other thing. Some of these drugs wreak havoc with gut and blood stream. They kill good bacteria, which you need. The way to counterbalance is with probiotic supplements. I'll write it down for you. Go to the drug store and get them. Oh, and yogurt from the supermarket."

Hawksley nodded. "Lots to remember."

Gurpal nodded his agreement.

"Getting back to health is often trial-and-error with Lyme disease. You might be fine after you finish your medication. Then again, you might be part of a group with chronic symptoms. Let's hope not. Time will tell."

Hawksley eyebrows shot up. "Chronic? As in it won't go away?"

"Yes, but let's wait and see."

"Oh God, this gets worse by the minute." The words no sooner came out than Hawksley lectured himself. *Grow up. Stop whining. Face your troubles head on.* A fast glance at the floor, he returned his gaze to the physician.

"Sorry Dr. Gurpal. I'm upset, is all."

"It's all right. I understand. We don't know for sure yet how your body will react over time. "Let's go one step at a time."

"Yeah, let's." Hawksley crossed his fingers and held them up.

Gurpal responded with two fast blinks. "Set up a follow-up appointment for next week."

Nancy's head shot up when a dejected Hawksley returned to the reception desk and made another appointment.

"How'd it go?" she asked when they stepped out onto the sidewalk.

The side of Hawksley's mouth drooped. "All right, I guess. Have to finish the meds and come back in a week. Later, who knows…?"

Hawksley improved. It took weeks. Night sweats and general numbness at last left him. Not lightheadedness, shortness of breath or diffuse pain.

In time he came to terms with his new reality. He also discovered a new truth: his symptoms worsened whenever he placed himself under stress.

"If it's possible to have a dialogue with your body," he told Nancy, "my body's says, 'okay, if you do that, then this will be the consequence.' If I push it too hard, guess what—my joints get sore. My thoughts also race like crazy, and I get this thing they call 'Lyme Fog.' You ever heard of it?"

She shook her head. "No."

"Me neither. Until now. Words I know I know, can't pull them up. The kind of thing you hear with seniors."

"Aw, sorry. Anything else?"

Hawksley nodded. "Yeah. Still have headaches, and still have trouble sleeping."

Nancy inclined her head. "Maybe you should make a list of what you're learning about your body—what helps, what doesn't. What makes you extra achy, what makes headaches worse, if anything?"

"Not a bad idea. I've already learned showers are a no-no. Feel worse every time I take one. Baths aren't easier, but I can manage better. And I'm beginning to suspect I should stay away from certain kinds of foods."

"It's to your credit you want to learn. And the more you learn, the better you'll be."

Gurpal adjusted Hawksley's medication. He put him on stronger pain relievers, as well as antidepressants and anticonvulsants.

Hawksley took Nancy's advice. He spent considerable time reading and researching his disease. He shared them with the open-minded Gurpal.

"Be careful," the physician cautioned Hawksley when he told him about something he saw on the internet. "Read everything with a note of skepticism. There's a lot of quackery out there. Science-based investigation is still your best bet."

Nancy agreed. "He's right, you know?" she later said and poured them more rose hip tea. "You have to be careful, but I read something I want to tell you about. Interested?"

"Sure."

She set her cup down in the saucer. "Okay, hope I get this right. You got a bite from a tick. It releases free-ranging parasites. Nothing in your body is the same once they're in. It gets a little complicated, but even after antibiotics and your immune system kill parasites, the parasites release poisons before they die. And those poisons are responsible for making you feel extra lousy."

Hawksley nodded. "Now you mention it, I do remember my doctor telling me something along those lines."

"Anyway," Nancy said, "everyone who's bitten is different. There's dozens of symptoms, but the point is everyone has to manage what hits them in their way. Most important is how you handle general stress, and what the stress does." She took another sip of tea, set it down and said, "Thus endeth today's lesson. Be careful what you hear and see. There's all kinds of nut bars giving advice about things they don't know. Like Jenny McCarthy."

"Who's Jenny McCarthy?"

Nancy made a dramatic show of shaking her head. "You don't get out much, do you? Jenny McCarthy—the, bleach-blonde who claims vaccinations are linked to autism?"

If asked, Hawksley might have dismissed the claim things happen for a reason. From his experience, life offered tremendous evidence to the contrary. All the same, it amazed him, his re-purposed relationship with Nancy.

One night at her house she made dinner. Later they moved to her living room.

"Interesting," she said, "how we've really got to know each other now Tony and Darlene are gone."

Hawksley set down his spiced tea. They'd agreed he wouldn't feel offended if she drank in front of him. "You ever watch 'When Harry Met Sally?'"

"I have. Loved it. Why?"

"There's a scene where Harry says no man can have a friendship with a woman without wanting sex."

Nancy curled her legs under her. "Yeah, I think I remember it, but look at us. We've managed it. Other than you."

"And I don't have female friends. Well, I had one in high school."

"What happened?"

"Life. She left for college out West, and I got a job at Houghton. Anyway, now I have a new female friend."

"Thanks, Hawk. I'll never sell out our friendship again." She raised her glass of white wine in toast. "Here's to us."

He picked up his tea. "To us." He drank. "One thing, I'll say it now, and never refer to it again." He paused. A grimace followed. "Those pics I took. I erased them. You never have to worry."

In reply, her eyes glistened and held his. "I'm glad," she whispered. "I mean I brought it on myself, but I have to admit this takes a small weight off me."

Chapter 11

Two weeks before Thanksgiving Hawksley sat hunched over his desk, his brow furrowed over the chemistry assignment.

The phone rang and jarred him out of his concentration. He rose and answered it.

"Lo."

"Hi, Hawk," a buoyant, chirpy Maddie said. "How are you?"

"Maddie. Fine, sis."

"Are you, or just saying?"

He put a smile in his voice. "Can't fool you, huh?"

"No, you can't, so don't try. How are you really?"

"All right, mostly."

"'All right' as in how?"

"All right, as in I'm fine, Grand Inquisitor. More good days than bad."

"You'd tell me if you weren't, right?"

"Yes, I would. So, what's up?"

"Nice topic shift, Hawk. Smooth. Anyway, I'm calling to invite you up for the Thanksgiving weekend. Mom and Alex are coming. You like him, don't you?"

"Yep. What I know of him."

"Me too. Anyway, Logan's in Highland Park. About an hour-and-a-half away. We see more of him now. Do you want to come, or have you got a better offer?"

"No, no better offer. Who could resist the charms of Gary?"

"You like your little joke, don't you?" his sister shot back. "I may have to report you to the Gary Chamber of Commerce. Expect a Cease and Desist letter anytime soon."

She giggled. "Anyway, we live in Hobart, seven miles southeast of Gary. In any case, glad you'll come. Be wonderful, the family together. Our place will get a little crowded, what with Earl's Mom and Dad coming too. I'll get reservations at a nice family-run hotel for you, Logan, Mom and Alex."

"Great. Give us a chance to gossip about you and Earl."

"Smarty. Can't wait until you're all here."

*   *   *

Frost coated gnarled leaves when he crossed his lawn to Nancy's house. He intended to ask her to look after his pets.

A gray low-riding Hyundai with tinted windows stopped in front of his house. Hawksley couldn't see inside, but something about the vehicle made him stop.

He stared at it and at last continued across Nancy's lawn.

Perhaps to tease, the driver inched ahead.

Hawksley picked up his pace.

The car maintained the same speed to stay with him.

Anger coursed through Hawksley. He drew in a lungful of air, belted out, "Hey," and charged toward the car. It peeled away.

Hawksley watched it disappear. "Shoulda got the license," he muttered to himself.

He returned to his house, heart pounding, palms sweating. Did somebody want to spook him? If so, who? Had to be Kimball. *I should have known better than to poke the hornet's nest. Lofton warned me. Now look.* He wished he hadn't been so consumed with payback. Well, too late now.

All right, he told himself; what's done can't be undone. Move on. Focus. Why would Kimball have another go at him? Maybe he belonged to the revenge-is-best-served-cold club. Could this menacing car be a sign of more things to come? *Hello, you're living next to a drug dealer. What'd you expect, a Dalai Lama response.*

Hawksley's heart raced, his muscles tensed. In turn it brought on dizziness and tightness in his neck and shoulders. He'd lived with the disease long enough to recognize the effects of stress. Stress couldn't be avoided, unless you were dead. For him, stress was like tossing gas onto a flame.

Your own damn fault, his inner voice lectured. Worrying isn't going to change anything. Be careful from now on. *Go take some Xanax and ibuprofen.*

He forced himself to stop thinking about Kimball. What happens is what happens. Think of something else. He rose and walked to his computer. His heels weren't sore, a general problem for him. A good sign, He also found he could read the monitor of his computer without the characters jumbling around. All right, I'm still wired, but it's not as bad as it could be.

He took a few pills. They evened him out somewhat; not one hundred per cent, but enough to focus on things—like being back at work.

He walked to the kitchen. Kettle boiling, he made toast. The phone rang.

He picked it up on the second ring. "'Lo."

"Hey, Hawk," the lilting voice said. "I'm off to the farmers' market this morning to get some apples, and a few other things. Interested in coming?"

He hesitated.

"What's wrong?

He arched his eyebrows. "What makes you think something's wrong?"

She responded with a snort. "What's going on? Gonna tell me or not?"

He gave her a dramatic shake of his head. "What is it with women? They got some hidden gift for seeing things?"

"Okay, I won't even respond to what I just heard. So, gonna tell me or not?"

"All right, all right. I was on my way to see you…"

He recounted his experience with the Hyundai, and the cost to him.   She listened without interruption.

"Weird. Why would strangers want to harass you, or worse?"

He held back for a few seconds. Should he tell her? Why not? She'd proven herself to be kind, compassionate, and capable. She deserved the truth.

He drew in a breath. "Okay, 'member the night all those students and cops came to Kimball's house?"

"Yes."

"Um, well, I'm the one who sicced them on him—the students, I mean. Not the cops."

"Ohmigod. *You*? Listen, I've got to hear about this. Why don't we do it face-to-face? Feeling good enough to come to the market? If you are, we can stop for tea beforehand."

"Yeah, sure. Give me a few minutes."

Hawksley hung up, fed Torchy and Vesta, and ate his toast. Next, he donned faded jeans, a Louisville Cardinals hoodie, and his favorite baseball cap.

*   *   *

Nancy parked a block from the market and pointed to a café. "We can get something here, and walk to the market, if you're up for it."

They sat inside by the large picture window, and enjoyed the morning sun. Both watched pedestrians pick up their pace in the crisp air. Nancy slipped out of her caramel trench coat. She peeled off her printed scarf, and tugged at the sleeves of her cardigan.

"You look nice," Hawksley said. "Always do. Compared to you I look like I'm waiting to get picked for day labor."

"Don't worry about it. We're not going to a gala. We're spending time together, and then the market."

"Ask you a question?"

"Sure."

"How come you're not taken?"

She snorted. "Taken? Now there's an old-fashioned word. Anyway, I could ask the same about you?"

He pointed to himself. "Got too much baggage now. And lost my confidence somewhere."

"I'll say this about you," she said. "You're way ahead of the game of most of the single guys I know. About the confidence thing: takes time, and you have to learn to trust again."

She caught herself. A flush came to her cheeks. "Boy, I put my foot in my mouth." Her eyes moved down to her coffee.

He rescued her. "Nancy Picton," he said in mock seriousness. "We weren't going to bring this up again. Cut it out."

She raised her head, and Hawksley smiled at her. "Like I said before, water under the bridge. Anyway, you stopped in the middle of giving me good advice about trust."

She stirred her coffee again. "Oh, yeah. Takes time, is all. I'm more trusting now than when Tony left. I'll be more trusting in six months. Same'll go for you." She paused. "So, now. Mr. Shit-Disturber, got yourself into a bit of a mess?"

Hawksley made a face. "I think so. Couldn't let well enough alone, me. Can't take it back now."

"You sure it's him behind this scare?"

"Only one who makes sense."

"I suppose. Maybe nothing is coming. Maybe he only wanted to intimidate you some more."

"Succeeded. Dizzy, and my muscles hurt like hell after the car pulled away."

"So the lesson is be super careful from now on." She sipped her tea, set down her cup, ready to say more when the door opened. Her thinly-plucked eyebrows shot north. She nodded to someone over Hawksley's shoulder.

The action caused him to turn. A thick wraparound scarf almost hid her chin, but Hawksley recognized Darlene at once. A male companion stood next to her. Hawksley took in her shorter hair and fiery red lipstick. He also noted her Lycra stretch jeans, heels, and leather jacket, cut high to show off her behind.

Hawksley glanced at her companion, and dismissed him at once. *Pretty boy, all tanned. Trying to be some kind of GQ model?*

For the briefest moment Hawksley and Darlene locked eyes. She gave him an imperceptible nod and turned away. She moved farther into the café, her companion behind her.

A begrudging thought raced through him. *So now we're back to men, are we?* He faced Nancy again.

"Well…awkward," she whispered. "You certainly didn't need to run into her today, of all days."

He did his best to downplay the encounter with a nonchalant shrug.

"There's what, thirty-five thousand people in New Albany? Surprised I haven't run into her 'til now."

Nancy agreed.

"In a town this size, you'd think it would have happened before now. Wouldn't you like to be inside her brain right now?"

"Yeah. Be a load of fun. Darlene lives for gossip. You and me here; this'll feed her for weeks."

He chuckled.

Chapter 12

"Sure you're still up for the market—after Darlene?" Nancy asked.

Hawksley waved away Nancy's concern.

"Yeah, I'm fine. Ready when you are." He put the money on the table, rose, and forced himself not to look at Darlene.

They entered the bustling old building and wandered the aisles, inspecting the offerings in the stalls.

Nancy bought squash, apples and tomatoes. Hawksley bought kale, broccoli, sauerkraut, and some turmeric.

"Trying hard to do the homeopathic thing, and join the ranks of vegetarians."

"Is it helping?"

"I guess…yeah. I take the meds my doctor prescribes, and cat's claws, and herbs. I think I'm seeing some improvement. Now if I can only stay the hell clear of stress."

"Then you'll be dead. What you need is to be a better stress manager."

He stared off into space for a moment. "Easier said than done, but good advice anyway."

*   *   *

Nancy stopped to query a farmer about his eggs.

Hawksley let his gaze move around the aisle. Not so long ago, he reminded himself, crowds didn't bother him. Since the Lyme disease they made him nervous. *Stop stressing about the crowd*, he warned himself. *Watch the people; you're a people-watcher*.

His gaze flitted among the customers in the aisle, and landed on a tall, lean woman in skinny jeans and a black collarless jacket. His eyes widened. Could it be…? The face a bit fuller, more defined, the skin clearer. Her outer clothes hid the slim hips, firm muscular lines, and small breasts he remembered. All the same, he'd have recognized her anywhere.

She held out her hand to a vendor, and took change he handed her. She placed the coins in her wallet and accepted a small plastic bag. It found its way into a canvas tote bag. Her task finished, she turned toward Hawksley, looked up, and found his eyes.

It took less than two steps before recognition flooded her face. Her lips pulled back, and she gave up the smile Hawksley so well remembered. The genuine article, the smile moved all the way up to her eyes. Nothing cheesy, nothing Madison Avenue fake, only joy and delight.

In turn, Hawksley threw back his shoulders and forced a smile with a confidence he didn't feel. She'd gone off to UC Berkley on a scholarship. He stayed to work at Houghton. She aimed for the moon; he aimed for a steady pay check. And now he had a disease.

Here, six years since he'd last seen her, a wide-eyed Katie Maines advanced.

"Hawk." She moved into him and pulled him closer. Seconds later she released him. "Good to see you. Had to look twice to make sure it was you. How've you been?"

He shot her another tight-lipped smile. "Katie. What a surprise. You look great." His once easy-going camaraderie with her now gave way to awkwardness and anxiety. Seconds later the first wave of dizziness hit him. He searched for an honorable exit strategy while he continued to smile.

Nancy joined the smiling marathon. She held out a hand to the new arrival. "Hi. I'm Nancy, Hawk's friend, and you are so pretty."

Hawksley did his best to recover his composure. While Nancy pumped Katie's hand, he said, "Attractiveness runs in her family, Nancy. You should see her sister and Mom. Her Dad—nice guy, but not so much."

The ice-breaker worked. When the laughter died, Hawksley spoke again.

"Nancy, like to introduce you to Katie Maines." He turned to Katie. "And this unsinkable spirit, Katie, is my good friend and neighbor, Nancy Picton."

An evident look of mischief in her eyes, Nancy's voice rose. She pointed.   "*Katie*? Is this the girl you talked about before?"

A red hue appeared on Hawksley's cheeks. He batted Nancy's outer leg with the back of his hand. "Ignore her. She gets like this when she's off her meds." He made an exaggerated pull on Nancy's elbow. "Time to get you home, Nance and wash down the pills with a nice cup of tea."

The other two laughed, yet Hawksley wanted nothing more than to leave. He and made a show of examining his watch.

"Um, listen, Katie, like to stay and talk some more, but Nancy and I do have to go. Need to pick up my car from the garage. If you're in town for a bit, call me. Let's see if we can get some drinks, and catch up on old times and things."

Katie crinkled her forehead. "Okay, but…"

She never finished her sentence. Hawksley jumped in with, "Sorry, Kate. Gotta go. Give me a shout if you're not doing anything."

"You're listed?"

"Course." He tugged on Nancy's arm. "Anyway, cheers. Say hello to your family."

Shoulders hunched, Hawksley exited the market with Nancy. She studied his profile.

"Rude. Did I miss something? She looked like she wanted to talk to you."

Hawksley patted his hair. "I know. Hate to admit this, but got panicky."

"Why?"

"Want the truth or the convenient excuse?"

"The first one."

They stopped at her car. She clicked her fob to open the doors. Groceries in, they busied themselves with the seat belts. Nancy backed up while Hawksley talked. "Doubt it'll make any sense, but it's like I had an inner voice telling me to get out of there. As fast as possible."

"But you liked her. A lot, from what I remember."

"Yeah, but it hit me—we've changed. We're not teenagers anymore. She went off to college, and here I am. I, I don't know. We were talking about confidence earlier, and look, gone. I see Katie, and all I can think of is leaving. Fast." He blew out his cheeks. "Anyhow, thanks for not giving me away, about getting my car."

"Yeah, sure. Want some feedback?"

"I guess. Why not?"

She pulled into their shared driveway. "You're being too hard on yourself. You usually keep it together. And from what I saw, she liked you."

Hawksley dismissed the comment with a shrug. "Doesn't matter. Bet she's only here for the weekend, and then heading back to wherever."

Nancy pulled into her garage and turned off the engine. She turned to study him.

"Say, what are you doing for Thanksgiving? I'm having a dinner party. Interested?"

"Yeah, but I've already accepted my sister's invitation. Up near Gary. Leaving tomorrow, but thanks anyway. Having some guests?"

"Yes, another couple coming. You'd like them. And a new friend."

Hawksley arched his eyebrows. "'A new friend? As in male, female?"

"Male, and don't get ahead of yourself. It's not a date, and we'll see how things work out."

*   *   *

Wednesday morning Hawksley headed off to his sister.

The three hour trip to Hobart cost him a bit of stiffness. He'd do the Cat-Cow yoga exercise Nancy taught him once he unpacked. It would loosen him.

He saw a sign for Gary, glad Maddie didn't live there. Emblematic of the Rust Belt, some of his co-workers talked about Gary in the same way they talked about Detroit. They remembered the Gary in its golden days, when it boasted a thriving middle class, safe streets, good schools, and a vibrant city core.

Carl Winder, a production supervisor at Houghton, who moved his family to New Albany, once said. "Back in the Seventies it all fell apart. Steel mills, the backbone of the city, cut their work force. People like me left. City went broke. Got worse. You go there now—houses boarded-up or deserted. Crime everywhere." He shook his head in disapproval. "Sad, when you think about it."

Nearby Hobart had its problems, Hawksley knew, but compared to Gary, it might be described as idyllic.

Maddie and her family lived by the lake in a leafy, tiny district with plenty of bicycle paths and pedestrian walkways.

Hawksley pulled into the driveway next to an Audi. His aches consumed him enough to pay little attention to the luxury German car. With care he extricated himself from behind the wheel. Tightness in his back and shoulders caused him to wince.

The front door opened. Maddie, his busty, five foot seven sister bounded out, followed by her husband, Ken, and their two children, Caitlyn and Ben. Rufus, their yappy dachshund, raced after them.

Adjectives to describe the Pardees might go from lean and wiry to lanky or slim. Maddie fit none of those. Pear-shaped, she'd joke and say she'd been born in the wrong century. "Rubenesque women were once the rage. It'll come back, you'll see." She pulled Hawksley to her.

He threw his arms around her and glanced at the children. They showed no signs of inheriting their mother's girth.

Maddie released him. "Come in, come in." She pulled him into the house. Inside she cocked her head, stopped, and studied him.

"Uh-oh. Not good. You look in pain." She turned her head and ordered Ben to bring Uncle Hawk's luggage into the house.

Maddie's husband approached.

Hawksley held out his hand to his angular and good-natured brother-in-law. They embraced each other.

"Hi, Ken. Always good to see you."

Hawksley often marveled how Maddie reeled in Ken. Opposite in physical and psychological composition, yet their marriage worked. They adored each other, and their children.

Hawksley thought Ken Wilcott quiet and decent. He held a mid-management position at *Dawson-Stays* in Chicago, a Fortune 500 wealth management company.

"You too, Hawk," Ken said. "Welcome. Come on in and let me get out of your way."

Hawksley stepped into the living room to see Logan. Considerable back slaps and light shoulder punches followed.

"Look at you," Hawksley said and rubbed the top of his brother's head. "You've got hair. Take some getting used to not seeing you with your high-and-tight. Gonna miss it, and doing all your hoo-rah call?"

"It's oo-rah, smartass," Logan teased back, the boyish grin evident. "But yeah, maybe."

Hawksley made an exaggerated point of rubbing Logan's lapel between his thumb and forefinger. "And look at this. From utilities to *J Crew* yuppie suit. You've come up in the world, bro."

"Gotta go with the times."

Equal in size to Hawksley, Logan held himself with a fluid confidence. Whether borne from strength training, the military, or both, Logan commanded attention. He used an economy of hand and arm gestures, and shunned grand sweeps. He shared his sister's round face, his jaw strong, wide and firm.

Unlike Maddie and Hawksley, Logan's eyes might either be described as blue or gray, depending on the light. They had a piercing quality, a hardness able to cower an opponent into silence. Now they beamed with pleasure as Hawksley pulled away, and embraced his mother.

"Hawksley,' she said. "How are you? How's your health? Are you in pain? Do you need anything?"

Alex, his mother's new husband, stepped up.

"C'mon, Yvonne. Give the lad a chance to catch his breath." A broad grin, he stuck out his hand. "Nice to see you again, Hawk." He held out his hand.

Hawksley shook it. "Thanks, Alex," Hawksley said. "Same goes for you."

The man with the ruddy complexion nodded. "Good drive?"

"Not bad."

Hawksley next greeted Maddie's in-laws, always engaging and good conversationalists.

They all played touch football in the backyard the following morning. Maddie left to periodically baste the bird in the oven. She'd turned the dining room table into something from *House Beautiful*. Everyone oohed, aahed and clapped when she brought the carved turkey slices to the table, an eager Rufus behind her.

Hawksley leaned into his mother and whispered. "Taught her well, Mom. You ought to be proud."

She kissed his forehead. "I'm proud of *all* three of you."

Much of the table conversation centered on Logan's experiences in Afghanistan. He kept the table enthralled with his stories of a country over 7,000 miles away.

Questions came, one after the other: how hot is it? Would he do it again? Is it really a desert? Do they hate us? Did he have the chance to meet and talk with locals? Could you walk the streets in safety?

Hawksley thought the response, from Maddie's mother-in-law, odd. "We're only a couple of miles from Gary, and you can't walk the streets safely there."

Or maybe even parts of Hobart, Hawksley said to himself.

*   *   *

After dinner the women cleared the dishes. The rest gathered in the family room. The lopsided score between the Cowboys and Raiders held little attention. While Maddie's father-in-law and Alex discussed politics, Hawksley and Logan drew their chairs together.

"So how's life at Skipstone Security?" Hawksley asked. He noted how much Logan had filled out. Expensive clothes didn't hide the fact. But his face, especially around the eyes, held a tightness Hawksley didn't remember.

"Lots of business in security contracts," Logan said and set down his whisky sour. "Private and government. Couple of guys I did tour with are in it too. Good money." He nodded toward the front door. "How do you think I can afford the Audi?"

"And you like it—the work?"

"Yeah. Most of it. Money, weaponry, travel—it's all there. And how about you, bro? How're you feeling these days? And don't give me the usual 'Okay' shit."

Hawksley rolled his eyes.

"Someone's been talking to Earth Mother. I'm better than some, worse than you. I'm better than when I first got bitten, but don't know if I'll ever get on top of this. I've joined a support group in Louisville. It's helped. The psychologist, Dr. Meissner, told us flare-ups are often caused by stress. I try hard to keep my stress under control."

"Why? You got a lot?"

Hawksley shrugged. "I don't know." He took a second. Should he tell Logan about his day? Why not? His brother could handle it.

He moved into his tale. When he finished, Logan drained the last of his drink and set it down. "Meeting up with Katie Maines is stressful too?"

"What. Did I miss something? I thought she split town. Is in California or something."

"Well, she's back. Or was back for Thanksgiving. I don't know. Bumped into her at the market. Didn't talk much. Running into her kind of upset my apple cart."

"You two always had a thing for each other, didn't you? He raised and lowered a shoulder. "Never did anything for me. Now, her sister, Bailey, she could rev me up. Me and almost the entire male student body."

"Uh, sorry, bro', but can we move from your wet dream back to what you were saying? You knew about Katie?"

Logan smirked. "*Everybody* knew. Ask Maddie. Deaf, dumb and blind not to have seen it. Hey, if Katie's on the market and you still got a thing for her, make your move. You're not in high school anymore. Like they say, get out of your comfort zone."

Easy for him to say, Hawksley told himself. Logan had an unconquerable spirit, and an abundance of confidence. If he wanted something, he'd go after it and not let anything stand in his way.

Hawksley envied Logan, yet considered him reckless too. The military loved and courted soldiers, warriors like his brother. Legends grew from them. Custer, for example, scoffed at danger, at anyone or anything standing in his way, yet his ego and accompanying foolhardiness caused the needless death of his entire battalion.

You couldn't compare fearlessness in the face of danger and being adventurous to affairs of the heart. In either case, Hawksley would win no medals.

"Like I told you," Hawksley said, "probably only here for the weekend. Let's get off the subject."

"...and back to your neighbor." He paused. "Maybe you should move."

Hawksley shook his head.

"Considered it, but decided it's not worth it. I've put roots down there. And the yuppies are moving in. Thanks to them, my property's already worth $40,000 more than when I bought it."

Logan lowered his voice.

"I guess, but if it gets out of hand, don't take this on alone. Get what I'm telling you? If you think you're in serious trouble, call me. *Me*. Not the cops. What are they supposed to do?" He craned his neck. "Swear you'll call me if things get worse."

Hawksley studied Logan for a moment.

"Sure."

His brother picked up on the hesitancy.

"No. Say it like you mean it."

"Fine. I promise I'll call."

Logan whacked Hawksley's arm. "Atta boy. Nobody fucks with a Pardee."

Their mother approached. "What are you two boys scheming about?"

Logan answered. "Nothing, Mom. Guy talk, you know?"

She shot him a suspicious look. "Why don't I believe you?"

Logan rose, threw his arms around his mother and pulled her off her feet. "C'mon, Mom, chill. Your boys are full of turkey. Nothing else."

Their mother tried for her best authoritarian voice.

"Logan Pardee, put me down and watch your language. There are kids here."

Late the following day, golden rays shimmered off the lake when Hawksley carried his suitcase to the car. He returned to the front door. Handshakes, back pats, a few tears, and promises of staying in closer touch finished the weekend.

He buckled up in the car. A final wave and he backed the car out of the driveway.

On I-65 his mind turned to his conversation with Logan about Katie. He did carry a torch for Katie in school. And he suspected she felt the same about him. Yet neither did anything about it. Why? And when he met her at the market, maybe he should have been braver, should have swallowed his anxieties. People didn't have x-ray visions, he told himself. Insecurities only reveal themselves through behavior. *Act like you feel secure, even if you don't,* his inner voice said.

He drew some comfort from the belief. Even so, it didn't much matter: good chance he wouldn't see Katie again in a long time. Or forever.

His mind drifted from Katie to Kimball, and onto Logan's comment. Not for the first time he lamented his actions. If he hadn't given into his impulsiveness, he'd still have a disagreeable neighbor, but maybe not the menace. He should have practiced more self-control.

Maybe the car was only there to spook him, nothing more, he told himself. And yet on a deeper level, he didn't believe his own words.

Chapter 13

"How'd it go?" Nancy asked when he rang her bell to pick up Vesta and Torchy.

"Great. Wonderful weekend. You?"

"Oh, lovely Thanksgiving. A good fit around the dinner table. Everybody got on well. My Mom and Dad came down from Cincinnati. And how are you feeling?"

"All right," Hawksley said. "I've come to the conclusion I better get used to hearing, 'how're you feeling?'"

"Guess so. It comes from a caring place."

Hawksley changed the subject. "And your gentleman friend?"

She smiled with satisfaction and petted Torchy. The dog fanned the air with her tail, vying for Hawksley's attention. He petted her while Nancy said, "Nice. I'd tell you more, but somebody wants to get going."

Hawksley's gaze followed her to Torchy. "Right, right. Thanks again. Talk to you soon." He picked up Vesta, leaned forward, kissed Nancy's cheek and left. Torchy followed him back to his house. Nancy still on his mind, he let his mind drift to seeing her in a romantic relationship. Why not? She deserved someone.

He recalled when he first moved into his house. Tony invited him over for a barbecue. On occasion the two drank a few beers and indulged in a bit of male bonding. When Darlene stepped into the picture, she and Nancy grew close. Tony split. After he caught Darlene, Hawksley vowed he'd never talk to Nancy again. And look—friendship from the last place he ever expected.

Hawksley found Nancy attractive; judging from admiring glances, so did other males. The vibe, chemistry—whatever one called it—wasn't there for him, or her. They'd grown in their newfound friendship, and come to like one another. Plenty good enough.

*   *   *

He checked his answering machine. Three messages: a male voice invited him to an upcoming, life-changing seminar. Good seats were still available. Hawksley erased the message half-way through the spiel. The second call, an automated message, reminded him outstanding Black Friday sales were still available at *Kohl*'s. The last message came from his father left the last message. "And a happy Thanksgiving to you too." Hawksley caught the whine in the voice. "I'll assume you're away," the message continued. "Probably at your mother's. Be nice, don't you think, for a father to have *all* his kids call him and wish him a happy Thanksgiving? Only one who called me was your sister. Says in the Bible you should honor your father."

It's only Dad, Hawksley reminded himself; *he's still feeling sorry for himself, and wants to lash out at the world. Or at least me. I'm not going to take it to heart and trigger a flare-up.*

Never an easy man to like, Daryl Pardee, and worse when he drank. After decades of marriage he at last drove Sharon Natley out of his life. She packed up after his last drunken rampage.

"Okay, let's get this over with," Hawksley mumbled under his breath, and hit the memory button on his phone. Three rings later his father answered.

"Yellow."

"Dad, it's me. Returning your call."

"Returning my call," his father said, his speech slurred from years of drinking. "'bout what?"

"Dysarthria," Hawksley's mother once told Hawksley. "Your father has dysarthria. I had to look it up. It means speech defect. In his case it comes from hard drinking."

Hawksley had no intention of helping his father find the reason for the call.

"Sorry. No idea. Maybe something about your church?"

"Coulda been, but pretty sure it was something else. Damn."

Stone-sober since his last release from detox, the elder Pardee attended AA meetings, accepted addiction counseling, and Jesus through a small charismatic church. Volunteer congregants visited him daily, brought meals, and prayed with him.

Hawksley applauded the transformation—as far as it went. Yes, his father had sobered up and accepted responsibility for his actions. He even apologized to those he wronged. He never considered his father's transformation deep enough. In his opinion, Daryl Pardee simply became a dry drunk, still miserable, still unhappy, and still tantalized by control. Years of abuse left their mark on the man. His appearance suggested someone ten to fifteen years older than his age. His eyesight had failed him; no longer steady on his feet, he'd soon need a cane.

Hawksley waited. A moment later his father said, "I guess that musta bin it. There's a revival meeting this Thursday night at the church. They're bringing in a pastor from Arkansas. He's giving a talk on these women's rights things, and how they're destroying our society. You should come."

"No, no thanks. Not my kind of thing."

"Do you a world of good, and might bring you into the fold of Jesus."

"Nope, sorry, I'm good."

"You're looking at this the wrong way. It's your immoral soul we're talking about."

"You mean immortal. My soul's fine. Had a good talk with it the other day."

"You know what your problem is?"

Hawksley cut him off. "Another time, Dad. Gotta go." He hung up before his father could respond. He turned his gaze on Torchy. "Now let's hope he doesn't call back."

His parent still on his mind, Hawksley entered the kitchen. He shook out food into Torchy and Vesta's bowls. He imagined his father at a revival meeting, raising his hands to the sky with the others, praising the Lord, talking in tongues. Would they pass around a snake? It would almost be worth it to see it. Almost.

Isn't it something, he asked himself? *Guys like Dad sin like crazy all their lives, and then find Jesus. And everything's forgiven. No trail of broken hearts and wrecked dreams.*

"Had a great wife, Dad," Hawksley murmured and watched the animals eat. "A great wife, and a great girlfriend. Loused it up with both."

Chapter 14

The meteorologist got it wrong. Two hours before quitting time, the tinny radio in the drying facility announced a snow burst.

"Not too much of a concern, folks," Tony Stossa, weatherman at KXLT said. "Might affect visibility for a while. We're expecting one to two inches of snow at best. Now... Karen, over at traffic, is going to update us on an accident on U.S. 460. Karen?"

A squall arrived instead. Strong winds accompanied by heavy snow caused whiteouts; slippery conditions worsened the situation. An hour later the radio advised everyone to stay off the roads.

One of Hawksley's co-workers looked out the window. "Make up your freakin' mind," he groused. "Looks like 'a concern' to me."

As fast as they arrived, the winds died, and the snow stopped. People dared to step outside.

Hawksley zipped up his jacket. "Weatherman at least managed to get the amount right," he said to a co-worker in the parking lot.

"Yeah, but they always manage to screw up the forecasts anyway," the other man added. "Have a good weekend."

"You too."

Hawksley cleared snow from his windows, and settled himself behind the wheel. "Careful," he said under his breath. "Drive very carefully. Remember what Dr. Meissner said about accidents."

A few weeks ago the psychologist cited several studies in Hawksley's support group. The studies suggested a strong link between serious accidents and flare-ups of the disease.

He kept to side streets, and at last made it into the safety of his garage. The storm had him thinking: he couldn't and shouldn't handle heavy snows. He'd get on the internet and check for used snow blowers. It might be too late, but you never knew.

As always, Torchy and Vesta met him at the door. He stepped out with Torchy while she searched for a place to pee on the lawn. Back in the house, he scooped dry food into their bowls. "Torchy, behave yourself," he said to the dog, eager to help Vesta eat her food. "Don't be such a pig. Leave Vesta alone."

After dinner, he read the assigned reading for his chemistry class. Finished, he searched *Craig's List* for snow blowers. Not many. He found two possibilities, phoned the owners and left messages.

He settled on the couch to watch a movie on cable, *Love Affair*, with Warren Beatty and Annette Bening, caught his attention. A half-smile came. If Darlene could only see him now, watching a chick flick. Whenever she suggested they watch one together, he'd beg off, go and open his laptop, or do something else. Now… Life's funny.

Vesta jumped up and curled herself in his lap. He stroked her in an absentminded manner.

Something about the movie made him think of Katie. Maybe a love he let slip away? *Love*? The notion surprised him. Or did it? He dismissed the idea with a shake of his head. No. Nonsense. You're either lonely, horny, or both, he told himself.

He'd found comfort with her in high school, but nothing rising to the level of what he saw on TV. Then what explained his rush to distance himself from her at the market, he asked himself? The normal thing would have been to stay and chat for a minute. If the vibes were good, they could have grabbed lunch or something. None of which he did.

Watch the movie, he ordered himself, and get off this treadmill. Yet the theme—the characters denying the inevitable, until the inevitable won them over—impressed him.

The film ended, and left him sad and empty.

He picked up Vesta and rose. "You know, kitty, this is not helping my mood." He set her down. "Why am I even wasting time thinking about something out of reach?" He threw his hands up in the air. "Okay, enough. Got the munchies. Let's get something to snack on." He placed some dry treats down for them, and readied crackers and almond butter for himself.

He at last turned off the TV and prepared for bed. It took a while to fall asleep. When he at last did, he dreamt about Darlene.

He rose at dawn and shook his head to dislodge her image. Wouldn't take a Freudian to know he still had unfinished business with her. But what? He certainly didn't care for her anymore. Maybe it had to be how it all ended. Badly.

He consoled himself with a give-it-time reasoning. Someday it wouldn't matter anymore. Or shouldn't.

*   *   *

The car clipped Hawksley half a block from his house.

Out for some fresh air, he strolled along Delaney with Torchy, careful to stay as close to the lawns as possible.

Snow plows had earlier cleared the street. Ward 9 had for years talked about sidewalks, but so far nothing came of it.

One hand deep in his pea jacket, Hawksley admired the Christmas lights. He'd better get his up, he reminded himself. At this rate, Christmas will have come and gone before he put up any decorations.

The gray Hyundai turned a corner and came up on Delaney behind him. The driver gunned the engine. The noise caused Hawksley to turn. He whipped his hand out of his pocket and jumped to avoid being hit. Almost. The car raced up the sloping curb and grazed his left outer leg and hip. The momentum spun and pitched him into a snow pile on the McMahon lawn.

The driver spun the car onto the street, braked, and put it into reverse. Tires screeched.

Roused by the noise Steve McMahon, followed by his wife and two adolescent daughters, rushed out of the house and took in the scene. At once the Hyundai's reverse lights went off. It braked again. Tires spun again. The car raced to the end of the street, past Kimball's house, turned and disappeared.

An agitated Torchy circled Hawksley, cold nose pressed to his downturned face. He'd never known such intense pain; not even during the first few days of Lyme disease.

"Stay put, stay put," Hawksley heard someone say. "We'll get an ambulance. Kids, run into the house and get a blanket or something warm to put over him. Go. Now."

The pain came in waves. Hawksley almost passed out. Mouth wide open, he pulled air into his lungs. *Mom, mom*, he said to himself. *Make it go away. Please.*

Time lost its meaning. Hawksley felt a hand raise his head and slip something under him. Words, soft, comforting words poured down on him. He sensed a small crowd gather, heard sirens.

"Come on, clear out," a gruff voice ordered. "Let the paramedics through. Okay, now, anyone see what happened here? Anyone?"

Two EMT workers attended Hawksley. They checked his blood pressure and worked to assess his risk factors. Long, dark, wavy hair moved around his face. "Can you hear me, sir?" a woman asked, her head close to his mouth.

"Yes," he managed to whisper.

Hands felt beneath his neck and skull. "Any pain here?"

"I don't think so."

"Okay, sir, we're going to check your pelvis and legs. After we're done, we'll give you something, and get you the help you need. Hang in there."

The EMT woman patted his shoulder in comfort. They placed him on the stretcher and lifted it into an ambulance. He stared up at the interior of the ambulance.

"Doing great, sir," the woman said and patted his chest in comfort. "Doesn't look like anything's broken, so you can be thankful."

"My dog?" Hawksley managed to say.

""Your neighbor, Nancy, has your dog. She said she had a key to your house."

"It's Nancy."

"Yes, right. Sorry. Nancy. Everything's under control. We'll be at the hospital in a few minutes."

*   *   *

X-rays confirmed he hadn't suffered any breakage.

"You're lucky," the ER Resident said. "We get accident victims like you in here, and many times they never walk again. Or they walk with a cane. Surprised your femoral shaft didn't break. But you've definitely got soft tissue damage. You're going to be sore for quite a while."

"Meaning what—about the soft tissue damage?"

"Meaning you've damaged fibrous tissue. Muscles and nerves. And you'll be black and blue as well."

Hawksley groaned. "Don't know if I'm lucky."

The physician folded his arms and licked his lips. "Good thing you've got a medical alert bracelet. Smart."

"My psychologist suggested it."

The Resident replied with a fast nod. "We'll recommend we keep you here. At least for a few days anyway. The Lyme factor makes it even more imperative. We can keep an eye on you and adjust any medication you may need."

He slipped into silence for a moment. "Do we have your doctor's name?"

"Yeah. Somebody else already asked me about it."

They put him in a semi-private room with a man recovering from heart surgery. Heavily sedated, his roommate couldn't engage Hawksley in conversation. Fine by Hawksley. Chit-chatting didn't hold much appeal for him.

He made it through a rough night, though he woke up every twenty to thirty minutes or so. Again and again he replayed the hit-and-run. Kimball. Had his fingerprints all over it.

Hawksley cast his mind back. Kimball had avoided any further direct confrontation, but he'd twice caught him walking past the house, studying it. It had unsettled him, but nothing more.

On another occasion, when he lowered his garage door, he found Kimball staring at him. Caught in the act, Kimball disappeared into his house.

Alone, all these incidents might have been dismissed as coincidence, but put together they made a statement. Hawksley's stomach roiled with anger. *He tried to have me killed. The sonovabitch tried to kill me.*

*   *   *

Past dawn a perky, cute, young nutritionist came around and asked him what he wanted for breakfast.

He shook his head. "Nothing. Can't eat. I'm too wound up."

"You should eat something, Mr. Pardee," she said. She followed up with a winsome smile, her ponytail bobbing around behind her.

He closed his eyes. *Oh gawd. Suzie creamcheeze.* Last thing he needed.

He opened his eyes again. "Goddamn, you're not listening? I don't want a fucking thing."

Her face blanched, her mouth opened and closed.

He recovered. "I'm sorry," he said and lowered his voice. "I've been in a hit-and-run, and I've got Lyme disease. It's no excuse, other than to say it's affected my emotions. You're right, I should eat something. My stomach's doing flips. What do you recommend?"

The Percocet they gave him helped with the pain, but only for a while.

*   *   *

Nancy came with clothes and flowers. "I'm so sorry this happened to you, Hawk."

"Thanks. You're a good friend. Will you please look after Torchy and Vesta until I get home? I'll pay you for your time."

"Yes, of course, and no charge."

"Can I ask one more favor: could you call work and my family? I'll give you the numbers."

Two cops arrived next. They asked lots of questions about what he saw, what he remembered, did he think someone had targeted him?

"Yeah, I do, and I know who—Brian Kimball, my next door neighbor." He told them about the Hyundai's previous suspicious drive-by.

They listened with interest. One pulled out a notebook from his breast pocket. "So, a low rider—the car?"

"Yeah, you know, those tacky cars with small wheels."

The cop wrote in his notebook. "What color?"

"Gray. I remembered it from before. Pretty sure it was the same car."

"Okay, good, good. Might help us find it."

They continued with their questions.

"So, you can't think of anyone else who might have wanted to do this: a jealous lover, girlfriend, wife?"

"No. I was married. My ex has faults, but she wouldn't stoop to this. Her brother and a couple of buddies came for her belongings after we split up. I helped him move her stuff onto the truck. Everything went fine."

"But you have nothing to prove your claim of this Kimball being behind this," the younger of the two said. "Just this Hyundai?"

"Uh-huh."

"Manage to get anything more about the car? A license number maybe?"

"Sorry. First time I wasn't thinking, and yesterday it came at me from behind."

"And no witnesses?"

"The neighbors, but I don't know what they saw."

The cop flipped his notebook shut.

"Okay, then. We'll see what we can do about tracing the car with what we've got." He fell silent for a moment. "We'll go talk to your neighbor." He opened his mouth, ready to say something, but shut it again. He gave Hawksley a long, considerate look, and said, "Be careful, Mr. Pardee. Real careful."

Hawksley and Nancy watched them leave.

"He's right, you know," Nancy said. "You have to be extra careful now." She lifted a brow. "I never thought I'd say this, Hawk; I despise guns, and all they stand for, but maybe you should either move or get a gun. I'd hate to lose you as a neighbor, but hate it more if I lost you as a friend."

He waited for a few seconds.

"My emotions are unreliable, Nance, and I know I've got a shitload of pain coming my way because of what happened last night. I hope I can get through it, but hear me—I'm not moving, and I'm not getting a gun ... I'll come up with a way to beat him once and for good."

"And this will go on."

"Uh-uh, not like this. This is no more Hatfields and McCoys. I'm gonna win. I'm coming out on top of this."

An unconvinced Nancy gave him her best not-believing-this look, but said no more.

On his second day he received visits from a few of his co-workers, several neighbors, his father, mother and sister.

Daryl Pardee, lumbered in next, strong tobacco smell trailing him. His open leather coat revealed a wrinkled black shirt and brown sweat pants in need of washing. Discolored sneakers, once white, finished him off.

Hawksley remembered a time when his father took personal pride in his dress. Now this detritus of a man long gone could well pass for any skid row bum.

His father sat and took long seconds to indulge in a serious smoker's cough. Finished, he shunned any attempt at social nicety, and said, "What's going on with you, boy? Somebody tries to run you over. You musta done something to get somebody worked up."

Hawksley took a deep, nostril-flaring breath and set his Dixie cup on the bed tray before speaking. "What's going on with *me*, Dad? You wanna know what's going on with me? I'll tell you—the hospital is what's going on with me. I've been hit by a car, I'm suffering from Lyme disease—you know, the disease I told you about, the one you said would go away if I went to your revival meetings?"

He gave his father a long, hard look. "This hit-and-run makes everything worse in me. You raised me, so you know I'm a pretty even-keeled kind of guy. Not these days. I'm ready to tear anyone's head off at a minute's notice. So let me put this to you in words you can understand: either be nice or fuck off. And don't call me boy anymore."

The outburst winded him. Several seconds passed before he evened his breathing.

His father spoke in a softer tone. "Sorry, b…son. It come out wrong, I know, but I didn't mean it so. I've always been this way. It's why your Mom left. Sharon too."

Hawksley held back from saying anything. No point bringing up old stuff.

"Wished I'da known more about your situation," his father said. He readied to say something more when another bout of coughing occupied him. He finished, drew in air, wiped at his eyes and said, "Lemme try again. I hate to see you like this. Hospitals are no place for young people."

The entire Pardee family knew all too well Daryl Pardee blew hot and cold. He could, when he put his mind to it, be charming, a raconteur with engaging stories about life.

Hawksley's father made the effort, and asked about the previous night's incident. "They ain't gettin' away with this."

Hawksley's eyebrows rose. "What are you talking about?"

Daryl waved his hand with marked energy. "This, this—what they did. I haven't been the best parent to you, any of you, but let me see what I can find out about this car."

"No, leave it, Dad. Besides, what can you do?"

"You might be surprised. You forget who I worked for. When the city outsourced garbage collection, they gave the contract to the Mantachie Brothers." He let his words sink in. "They ain't exactly choir boys. I get on good with Victor. Have a little talk, is all."

"Well…yeah, I guess, but let's say you can do something, what about your religion, you know, not doing the eye for an eye thing?"

"Good point. Our Lord and Savior, Christ Jesus, tells us to turn the other cheek." He stopped, leaned forward and whispered the next few words. "Then again, nobody fucks with a Pardee."

Hawksley blinked and stared at his father. Where had he heard those very words? It came to him—Logan, on Thanksgiving.

The similarity made him smile and then chuckle. The chuckle turned to laughter, and then to a full belly laughter. It hurt, yet Hawksley couldn't stop.   At first, the laughter resulted in a confused look on the part of his father. He then joined in.

Both men were deep in laughter when Hawksley's mother and her husband stepped into the room.

Laughter doused, an uncomfortable Daryl Pardee rose and glanced at his ex-wife. No sooner had he made eye contact, then he shifted his gaze back to his son. He moved closer to the bed, patted Hawksley's arm.

"Okay, gotta go. I'll call you soon. Stay strong." He, turned and without a word walked past the other two.

The new arrivals followed him with their eyes until he disappeared. For a second or two Hawksley's mother stared off into space, perhaps lost in another time and place. Her husband brought her out of her reverie. "Yvonne," he said in a low voice.

She blinked twice and shook her head as if to dislodge some memory or notion. Her eyes settled on her son.

Daryl and Yvonne Pardee's marriage ended with a whimper, not a bang. Yvonne walked out. In time the adult children adjusted to the new reality. All the same, the presence of his parents in the same room always unsettled Hawksley. He'd find himself in a blue funk after they left.

Yvonne Hildebrandt approached Hawksley and pulled him forward. "You poor boy. You had us scared. Are you all right? Do you need anything?" She released him and searched his face.

"I'm all right, Mom." His eyes left hers and found the thin features of her husband. "Hey, Alex."

"Hi, Hawk."

Hawksley's mother and Alex offered up a different kind of visit. Easy laughter, pleasant chit-chat almost made him forget his woes. Until the pain returned to his joints, and a heavy tiredness came over him. He found it hard to concentrate on his visitors, their words. A cold sweat formed on his forehead.

His mother noticed. "Sweetheart, you're not looking good. Should we call for the nurse?"

He nodded and pressed a call buzzer.

A friendly, middle-aged, matter-of-fact nurse arrived. She studied him.

"In pain, are you?" She studied his chart and said, "Almost time for your meds. Back in a minute." She returned, handed him a small medicine cup with the pills, and pointed to his water. "Lots of water with your pills, all right, hon?"

Hawksley nodded, swallowed the pills with the water. He relaxed his shoulders and sank back into the pillow.

"Maybe this is a good time to go," his mother said. "I'll come tomorrow, and see how things are."

He opened his eyes. "Yeah, sure, Mom."

*   *   *

Logan arrived mid-afternoon the next day, an hour after Nancy. He glanced from the patient to the patient's visitor. A toothy smile, a hand proffered, he said, "I think I've seen you before. You're Hawk's neighbor, right?"

He gave her no chance to reply. "I'm Logan, his better-looking brother."

She accepted the hand, returned his smile and said, "And modest too, I see."

"Once you get past my good looks, you can't help but notice my other fine qualities." He offered the claim with such playfulness, the other two couldn't help but laugh.

Logan asked Hawksley about his health, and listened with care.

Hawksley noticed his brother worked to draw Nancy into conversation. It came to Hawk, his younger brother's main focus had shifted to winning Nancy's good opinion. *He's flirting; he's got some finesse in his game. And look at her; she's digging it. Voice has gone up. Lots of eye contact.*

Visiting hours over, Nancy announced they'd have to leave. "I'll leave with you," Logan said. "I'm going to stay the night at Hawk's."

"You are?" a surprised Hawksley said. Before he could add more, Logan jumped in.

"Ah, all the stress you've been under. Forgot. I'll get your key before I leave."

"My key? Yeah, okay."

Logan turned to Nancy. "Would you mind if I talk to him for a few minutes? Personal stuff, you understand?"

"Oh, sure. I'll go wait by the elevators." Her eyes moved to Hawksley. "I'll see you tomorrow." A fast wave, and she disappeared.

They watched her walk away. Logan gave his attention back to his brother.

"You don't mind if I stay tonight, do you? I'll send the keys back with her."

"No."

"And you're not, you know, tight with her?"

"Not the way you mean tight. We're friends and she's seven years older than you."

"And it's a problem, why?"

Hawksley shrugged. "Don't know, but for starters, you live four-and-a-half hours from here."

"Dude, I'm not asking her to marry me. I like her, is all. Let's see what comes of it. And listen, before I get kicked out, this Kimball's behind this, right? Time to go talk to him."

Hawksley held up his hands. "Strange, coming from me, I know, but let it go. Look what it cost me getting payback. If nothing else happens, I'm done with all this."

"And if it does—happen again?"

Hawksley exhaled. "Dunno. Right now I'm avoiding any more occurrences. Besides, Dad said he was going to look into doing something."

"*Dad*?" Logan asked. "What can he do?"

"Said he knows Victor Mantachie. Even if he does, the guy's not going to stick his nose into this. What's in it for him?"

"So you want me to leave it alone?"

"Please. Hoping Kimball's got it out of his system."

"Hasn't been his pattern, has it?" a doubtful Logan said.

"No."

Okay, but if anything more happens, next time I'll finish it for good. You know what I told you about the Pardees?"

Logan threw a quick look over his shoulder before he turned back to his brother. "Take care."

"Will do, and you be nice to Nancy? You hurt her, and you got trouble with me."

"Be on my best behavior."

*   *   *

A nurse pushed Hawksley's wheelchair to the elevator the following morning. "This is stupid," he protested. "I'm not an invalid."

"Course, you're not," she agreed, "but hospital rules ... " She hit the elevator button. "So, you'll make an appointment with your family physician when you get home."

Hawksley held back from saying, *Yes, Nurse Ratched*, a comparison to the psychiatric nurse in *One Flew over the Cuckoo's Nest*. He couldn't blame this nurse for following protocol. Couldn't, but wanted to.

In the last few days he found himself becoming pricklier. His nature didn't lend itself to general irritability. Even-tempered, most would say. Yet now he saw a steady agitation within himself, far from placid or remote in manner. He didn't need a reason to fly off the handle.

He'd been warned about this—both in group and by his physician—his neurotoxins affected behavioral changes. They entered his body and took over, wreaked havoc on skin, joints, and the brain.

Recently Hawksley's father, the nutritionist, the nurses, all found themselves on the receiving end of his sharp tongue. An earlier Hawksley would have responded in a different manner.

He pulled out a memory of Dr. Meissner telling the group some sufferers never eradicated the toxins; others fought them to a draw, and still others managed to triumph over the invaders.

Hawksley hoped adjustment in his medications, his diet, lifestyle, would let him join the latter group. He also reminded himself to be extra vigilant, and not give in to outbursts. It didn't always work. Guilt and self-loathing piggybacked in the minute he finished expressing his annoyance.

*   *   *

Nancy's car sat at the curb. She saw him and pulled forward.

"Bye, Mr. Pardee," the nurse said.

Hawksley rose. The nurse spun away before he could answer. A minute later he sat in the passenger seat and buckled up. Nancy pulled away.

"Thanks for picking me up."

"Welcome."

He looked over his shoulder. "Bet they're glad to see the last of me."

"Rough on them, were you?"

He nodded. "And I hate it, Nance. Hate it, but I can't seem to stop it."

"Well, get to your group, talk to your doctor, and take it a day at a time."

They drove. Neither said anything for a few minutes. "So you had a little visit with Logan?"

"You're not going to yell at me, are you?" she teased.

He shook his head. "It's your lives—yours and his. Do what you gotta do."

"I like your brother, He's good-looking, but we'll see."

Hawksley snorted. "I guess. Doesn't do it for me."

Her eyes left the road. "I'd certainly hope not."

He stayed home and recuperated the following week. On the Friday afternoon his father phoned.

"Hey, son, how you feeling?"

"Better, Dad, thanks. What's up?"

"Wanted to call and say hi, and to tell you to check tomorrow's newspaper."

"Why, what's in it?"

"Check the articles carefully."

"All right, but why so mysterious? Going to tell me?"

"Nope. Check the paper."

"OK, Dad. Thanks for…whatever I guess."

*   *   *

Saturday morning Hawksley sat in *Has Beans*. He spotted the headline on the third page of *Southern Indiana Report*. Couldn't miss it. *Mysterious Car Blaze*.

The short article told readers of a Hyundai catching fire. It happened at a housing project on Erni Avenue in the middle of the night. Police were investigating. The car was registered to a Lourdy Pageotte, who shared an apartment with his common-law wife, Cami Abano, and her brother, Angel Abano. Neither Mr. Pageotte nor Mr. Abano could be located.

Hawksley's eyes flew up over the page of the paper. "I'll be damned," he said out loud.

Two women seated across from him stared. Embarrassed, he put his head down and stared at the newspaper. Was this the…? Had to be. But how, how could the old man bring this off?

Everyone whispered about the Mantachies—supposed to be connected to the underworld.

Victor Mantachie lived on a ranch on the outskirts of town. He drove an expensive car and kept a stable full of thoroughbred horses. In contrast, Daryl Pardee lived in a shabby apartment building. Two different universes, so what kind of pull did his father—by all accounts a pretty-near worthless person—have to bring this about?

Try as he might, the son of Daryl Pardee could not put those two things together. All he knew was the car didn't set itself on fire. And the sudden disappearance of two thugs? The whole thing smacked of something sinister. Organized sinister, and his father, Daryl Pardee, had something to do with it. Like something out of *The Godfather*. Incredible. In rural Indiana? Ab-so-lutely incredible.

There's a hellava of a story here, Hawksley told himself. Hellava story. *If the full facts ever got out.*

Whether his father would ever tell him, remained to be seen. One thing for sure; high and mighty or down and out, never take anyone for granted. 60

"You're right, Dad," he whispered. "I was surprised."

Chapter 15

Hawksley returned to work the following Monday, still sore and walking with a slight limp along the concrete floor.

"Hawksley Pardee to the office," the PA announced.

It took him two minutes before he made it to the front office. A minute later he sat in Shipley's office.

"You all right, Hawk?" the HR manager asked. "Can you handle the work? If you can't, we'll try to find some lighter duties for you."

"Thanks, Mr. Shipley. Appreciate your concern. I've known better days, but ready to go again. 'Sides, I don't do much of the heavy lifting anyway, or push hand trucks to the drier. I'm good."

"You're certain?"

The muscles in his forehead bunched up. He squinted at the HR director. *No, I'm telling you this to hear myself talk. I'm fine. Stop hassling me, and let me go to work.*

He fought to keep back the emotion. "Yeah, I'm good." Again, always on the edge of something dark; always ready to lose control. His stomach muscles tightened. Where the hell did those goddamn mood swings come from?

At his station, his co-workers fussed over him, and intervened whenever he lifted the end of a plywood sheet to inspect it for damage.

"Here, lemme get it, man."

"Wait, Hawk. Don't strain yourself. I'll do it."

"Wait up. I got it. Just relax."

Their caring came from a good place, he reminded himself. It shouldn't have agitated him, but it did.

His eyes found the clock. Less than an hour into the shift and he'd already come close to losing it with both Shipley and his co-workers. What kind of shape would he be in by the end of the day? The mere thought did nothing to improve his mental state. *This isn't me. Goddamn neurotoxins. Messing me up; turning me into a Jekyll and Hyde. I don't know from one minute to the next what'll come out of my mouth.*

It weighed on him, the disease taking over his mind. Could he, would he ever get back to his old self? He resolved he'd bring it up at group, and discuss it with Dr. Gurpal as well. Then again, he needed more than the group sessions. Maybe Meissner could help. Some of the group members saw her on an individual basis. He'd try; his benefit package covered it. She might be able to design some better coping strategies.

The idea cheered him. By noon he sensed a return to his old self. He laughed along with others at the table in the lunchroom when Maythorpe and Gainey traded light insults.

*   *   *

Dim street lights flickered in the industrial park when Hawksley brushed the light snow from his window and unlocked his car. He pulled out onto the empty street, and rotated his shoulders to release his pent-up tightness.

His stomach growled. Should he eat out? No, go for healthy—he had food at home. Besides, Torchy and Vesta wanted their dinner too.

More Christmas lights had festooned houses since the weekend. Hawksley pulled into his driveway and shot a fast toward Kimball. Did the man still bear a grudge? Nothing bad had happened since he returned from the hospital. But then, look how much time passed between the drive-by and the hit-and-run.

Hawksley couldn't escape the suspicion something would, again. *He's like a cat, toying with a mouse. And I'm the goddamn mouse.*

A counter-thought came to him: maybe there'd be no more payback. He recalled Nancy telling him about a police cruiser pulling into Kimball's driveway the day after the hit-and-run. "I heard about it. I asked Phil. He's pretty sure it had to do with what happened to you."

"Hope so. Whatever the reason, it gets Kimball the thing he doesn't want—attention from the law. Be nice if this whole thing has finally run its course."

"Be great," she said.

In the house Hawksley let Torchy out, and waited while she did her business. He scooped the offering, dropped it into the waste bin and called to her. "Come." Inside he flicked on the outside lights, and fed his pets. Chores done, he washed his hands and opened the fridge. He pulled out a stew he'd made the night before, ladled a generous helping into a bowl, and reached for the bread box when the phone rang.

"Lo."

"May I speak to Hawksley, please?"

Hawksley recognized the agile, rich voice at once. In an instant he found himself back at high school in the cafeteria. For a second he stopped breathing. His heart raced.

"Katie. Where you calling from?"

"Here. New Albany? You said I could give you a shout. Is this a bad time?"

"Uh, no, no," he stammered. "I thought you were back at Berkeley, or out west somewhere."

"Nope, not out west anywhere. Here. You rushed off so fast at the market, so I didn't get a chance to tell you. In fact I didn't get a chance to tell you anything. Uh, why I'm calling, my Mom told me about the hit-and-run thing today. How awful. Hope you're okay."

"Yeah, I'm good." He shifted the receiver to his other hand and wiped his sweaty palm on his pant leg. "So what's keeping you in New Albany? You didn't like Berkley? I thought it was supposed to be nice there."

"Nice? It's wonderful. I would have stayed if I could. I had a good job for three years until Sacramento went into economic free fall. First thing they did was cut back on transfer payments to the municipalities. Rippling effect. I lost my job. Not a big demand for laid-off urban planners. New Albany posted a job on their website. I applied, came for an interview, and here I am."

"Well, good, if it's what you want." He cupped the mouthpiece and exhaled. "To think you're here again. Living at your parents?"

"Only until a week Tuesday. Then I get my own apartment. When I get set up, would you like to come and see it?"

Does a pig like rolling in muck, he asked himself? In his best steady voice he said, "Be great, but listen, you're welcome to come here. I won't rush off this time, I promise."

"Um, sounds nice, but won't your girlfriend mind?"

"I don't have a girlfriend. I live alone. I was married, but you probably already heard."

A long pause, followed by a single word. "Yes."

Hawksley let out a half snort. "Small town. Word gets around."

"It does."

"Can't stop people talking, but back to the invitation, are you busy Friday night? I could cook us something."

"Friday night sounds good. What can I bring?"

"Yourself. You good with vegetarian fare?"

"Perfect. You're talking to a girl who spent six years in a place where vegetarian and vegan restaurants sit on every other block."

"All right, then. Come. We'll catch up. It'll be fun. And welcome back."

He hung up, delighted with the phone call. He scooped up Vesta and twirled her. "We're going to have company Friday night." Torchy, tail high, danced around his legs.

The excitement of the moment passed. He set Vesta down. *Ahead of yourself there, cowboy. What if she doesn't want what you want? What if she still thinks you're, you know, still buds, the two of you only getting together to yak about old times?* Not out of the realm of possibility, he allowed. No, best to play it cool, and take whatever the evening brought.

He clapped his hands. "Let's get dinner."

*   *   *

Katie leaned against the kitchen counter, sipped the wine she brought and watched Hawksley put finishing touches on the Rosti casserole with baked eggs.

"Say, you're quite the cook. Impressive."

"Thanks. You know what they say about necessity being the mother of invention? It's helped—eating healthy." He carried the dish to the dining room table. She followed him. "So, back to what you were telling me, he's behind everything?" She pointed toward Kimball's house.

Why had he told Katie about Kimball? The question nagged at Hawksley. He didn't have this kind of relationship with her, especially since she'd been gone all these years. Had he only blurted it out because of nervousness, to make conversation? If so, he'd better watch himself.

He pushed the thought away. "A hundred per cent sure."

"What I don't get is why he does this."

Hawksley returned to the kitchen for a spatula. *See what you started? Now she wants details.* "Asked myself the same question. Maybe he wants me to suffer in installments." He waved her toward the table. "Anyway, what say we change the subject and eat?"

Katie sat and pulled closer to the table. "Feel a bit guilty drinking when you can't."

Hawksley took his seat while an eager Torchy kept an eye on any possible offerings coming her way.

"No reason you can't drink. I tried for a while, but discovered booze and toxins in my body together—I pay for it." He examined the table with a critical eye, sat and handed her the lifter. "Dig in. I've got extra salad dressing if you want it."

Katie took a large slice of the grated potatoes. "No, I'm sure what's on the table is fine. Everything looks good and smells great."

While Katie transferred salad to her plate, Hawksley studied her oblong face with sunken-in cheeks, wheatish complexion, and emerald green eyes set against her reddish-brown hair. The same girl as in high school, yet different and…lovelier.

His breath caught for a moment. What changed, he asked himself? Why did he now see her in a different light?

Katie gave him no time to explore the question.

"I know we're not supposed to talk about this anymore, but would you mind? I've got questions."

Hawksley responded with a tight lip smile. "I guess. I can't add a lot more to what I've already said. I'm hoping everything's over and done with, but have to admit, a part of me is still waiting for the other shoe to drop."

Katie picked up her glass, sipped, set it down and said, "Been tough, what you've gone through."

"Some, but it could be worse. A lot." He steered the conversation back to her. "What I want to know, miss urban planner, what you're going to do about the increasing gridlock in our city core during rush hour?"

He hoped she heard the playfulness in his voice.

She did, tilted her head and grinned. "You mean the intense nine minute rush hour of New Albany?"

"The very same," Hawksley said and matched her grin. The humor set the tone for the rest of the evening: no lags in conversation, they shared laughter, talked about their families, old friends, touched on his ex-wife, and Katie's past relationships.

They stayed at the table for another hour before Hawksley suggested they move to the living area.

Katie tucked her legs under her on his couch. Vesta jumped up and nuzzled her neck. Katie stroked her. "Hi, kitty."

Hawksley approached the couch. "You like cats?"

"I do. Remember, my Mom and Dad had Shasta?"

"Shasta," Hawksley repeated. "I forgot about her." He sat next to Katie, careful to leave enough physical space to allow her to feel relaxed.

He'd wanted everything to be perfect, so earlier he'd asked Nancy how close he should sit next to Katie. "On the couch, you know. Don't want to spend the entire evening at the table."

"No, of course not," she said. "C'mon, Hawk, this isn't your first rodeo. You've dated women before. Have a little faith in yourself."

*   *   *

Hawksley turned his body toward Katie, one hand by his side, the other absently stroking Torchy's head. Katie smelled good, lilac or something, but not overpowering. He wanted to lean closer, inhale. *No*, his inner voice warned. *Don't. Too pervy. Stay where you are.*

"Would you like anything else," he asked? "More tea, wine?"

"Nope, fine, but I want to hear more about your Lyme. You mentioned you have it, and then changed the subject."

"Kind of boring."

"I doubt it. Spill."

He gave her a half-shrug, and explained how he contracted the disease, what worked, what hadn't worked, adjustments he'd made to his lifestyle.

"I'm hoping I'm one of the lucky ones who manage to get on top of this. It's my mood swings I worry about the most. I hate it."

Katie nodded.

Hawksley's eyes moved from Katie to the dog and back. She held his gaze. In those few seconds he blinked twice; she smiled, and something passed between them, something he couldn't put into words.

Her hand reached out and took his. The action caused his heart to race, his mouth to run dry. He barely noticed; he wanted to stay in this wonderful, exalted state forever.

Katie broke the spell. She placed a forefinger to her lips, kissed it and pressed it against his. "I better go," she said in a soft tone. "It's nice, being here with you, but freaky too thinking of you this way."

"Have to agree. We were always—well, not this. Does take a little getting used to."

She rose. "Thanks for a great evening, Hawk." She stepped closer. "You're okay we didn't—you know?"

He shook his head. "No. Lovely evening."

"So, you're not into tonsil hockey?"

He played along. "What's the cliché: always leave them wanting more. Don't you want me to want more?"

She licked her lips. "A seductive idea."

His palms sweated, and he experienced a mild prickling on the back of neck and base of spine.

Hawksley pretended amusement at her comment, and wagged a finger in mock disapproval. "Bad." He gestured toward the door. There he waited and held her coat open while she struggled into her boots, his mind full of sexual possibilities.

She pulled up on her collar. "Ready?" he asked.

"Ready."

They walked out to her car. She unlocked it, turned and kissed his cheek. "See you soon." She spun about and slid behind the wheel of her yellow VW Beetle. The engine started.

A euphoric Hawksley called Torchy to him, and watched her back out onto the street. She gave the horn a quick toot; he waved until he couldn't see her anymore, and returned to the house. "Well, Torchy, here's an evening I won't soon forget," He made for the kitchen. "Terrific, but God, exhausting."

*　　　*　　　*

Two days later Hawksley stood in the kitchen and prepared his dinner. He heard a car pull into his driveway, and peered out the window. Police. An older, heavyset uniformed cop, stepped out of the cruiser, slammed the door, and adjusted his cap. Hawksley met the man before he could knock.

"Hawksley Pardee?"

"Uh-huh."

The cop opened a notebook and consulted it. "Your father, Daryl Pardee, lives at 6855 Siegel Place?"

"Right." Hawksley's brain worked through likely permutations. Had his father fallen off the wagon again; had he been in an accident, or get into some scrap with the police?

"What's this all about?"

The hard lines softened in the other man's face.

"I'm sorry to tell you this, son, but your father's passed away. The neighbor below heard the crash, and called the super. The Medical Examiner's already come and gone. He ruled heart attack, and signed off on the death certificate."

The cop shut his notebook. "Buzz the super and he'll let you into the apartment. Your father's body is still there. Call any funeral home, and they'll help you with all the formalities. Sorry for your loss."

The message delivered, the cop left a stunned Hawksley to process what he heard.

He hadn't anticipated death like this. If he thought about it, he expected his father to die from lung cancer or chronic alcoholism in a hospice.

The old man used to joke and say, "Be a foot race to see what kills me first: cirrhosis or lung cancer."

Maybe one or both contributed to the heart attack.

Within the recesses of his mind, Hawksley pulled out a memory—his mother, returning from an Al-anon meeting, and leaving a pamphlet on the kitchen table. Hawksley had read it, and learned a new word, cardiomyopathy, a form of heart disease, common to alcoholics.

He called back about the word. *Booze, and cigarettes. I guess Dad's heart had enough.*

Ten minutes later Hawksley found himself on Siegel before he knew it. He buzzed the superintendent's apartment.

"Yes."

"Hawksley Pardee. I'm here for my father."

The door clicked. Hawksley entered the small lobby, and made for the superintendent's apartment. The slope-shouldered man with huge bags under his eyes met him at the door.

"Sorry, about your loss, Mr. Pardee," he whispered, shut the door and stepped into the hallway. Without another word he headed for the lobby. Hawksley followed. They walked up to the second floor. The man reached for his key reel, selected one and opened the door to Daryl Pardee's apartment.

"He's in here, the kitchen. I'll leave you to whatever you have to do. If you need me, knock on my door."

The matter of no further interest, the superintendent wheeled around and shut the door behind him. A strong, musty, pungent odor almost overpowered the lingering reek of cigarette smoke in the apartment. The former made Hawksley think of something between sewage and, what, fruity?

Despite the cold, he opened the windows wide. Done, he exhaled, drew air in through his mouth and entered the kitchen. Unsure of what to expect, or how he might react, he stared at his father's body, face down. Had the coroner moved him? It didn't matter; probably better he couldn't see the face, a face Hawksley assumed might look anguished.

Hawksley did his best to ignore the odor, crouched over his father and stroked the few wisps of his hair. Out of reverence, sentimentality, both—he didn't know—he bent and mussed the back of his father's head.

He straightened. "Aw, Dad, so sorry it ended this way for you. Nobody should die alone. You were far from perfect, but you were my father. Strange as it is to say, I miss you already."

His eyes transfixed on the body, Hawksley felt his throat tighten. He rose. Seconds later the first salty tears rolled down his cheeks. He did nothing to obstruct them; the tears continued; his vision blurred and deep sobs shook Hawksley's body. He cried for his father, his family, himself, for a relationship no longer possible.

When at last his body ceased convulsing, he swiped at his face with his palms, and searched for tissue or paper towel. On the counter he spied the latter, and stepped over the corpse. Several long, wet nose blows later he tossed the paper into a garbage next to the sink.

Hawksley allowed himself another quick look at the corpse and left the kitchen. A phone book sat under his father's telephone on an end table. Hawksley pulled it out, opened it and consulted the Yellow Pages for funeral homes. He picked up the phone and dialed. He finished the conversation with, "I'll be here. Buzz the apartment and I'll let you in."

The receiver back in the cradle, Hawksley crumpled onto the couch. His father, Daryl Pardee, always a force of nature, no longer walked this earth. His relationship with his family could best be described in one word—tempestuous. Even so, he had redeeming traits, but the older he got, the less they made appearances. Drinking, selfishness and impulsiveness drove them away.

Hawksley remembered his father taking them to see the *Reds* play, to the Indy 500, even to Disneyland. Even his final parental act—calling Victor Mantachie—demonstrated affection and caring.

He closed his eyes. Good or bad, it no longer mattered; the man who once inhabited the body in the kitchen slid into history. Gone, and nothing would bring him back.

One arm across his chest, the other resting on it, Hawksley used his fingertips to massage his forehead. A part of life, death, he told himself. You lose your parents, and with them you lose a piece of your history. Can't stop it. It's inevitable.

Eyes open again, Hawksley glanced around the room. Sparse since Sharon had walked out. Sparse and different; gone were the plants, nice furniture, the 32 inch flat screen TV, and the homey touch of a woman. In their place Daryl Pardee found mismatched furniture of pressboard, cigarette burns on some, a boxy television with an antenna, the feed connected to a converter, aluminum kitchen chairs with fake leather seats.

He shook his head. "Can only imagine what the bedroom looks like." He'd never visited his father after Sharon left.

"Up, up," he told himself and rose, determined to take a tour of the rest of the apartment. Careful not to look at the body in the kitchen, Hawksley made his way to the bedroom. There he found a banged-up dresser, a box spring mattress without its legs, the top sheets in disarray, and cardboard boxes against a far wall.

He opened the top drawer and rummaged through. Beneath socks and underwear his fingers touched flat plastic.

He tugged; it came out, wrapped around a manila envelope. With care, Hawksley pulled out the enveloped and retrieved a legal document—*Last Will and Testament of Daryl Farnsworth Pardee.*

Hawksley stared at it for a moment. He dropped down on the mattress and blinked in disbelief. A will? Daryl Pardee barely had a proverbial pot to piss in, yet here, in Hawksley's hand, a notarized will.

The will in his hand, Hawksley rose and returned to the living room. He stared at the corpse as if it might offer an answer about the will. It kept its precious secret. Hawksley had no further time to ponder the mystery. The apartment buzzer sounded. He moved to the intercom. Two men from the funeral parlor's transfer crew arrived.

Identification of the body confirmed, the three discussed an item of dress for Daryl Pardee. A quick search his belongings revealed he needed something more suitable than anything found. Hawksley promised he'd bring new clothes to the parlor next day.

Before Hawksley knew it, the two attendants wheeled the body out on a stretcher and into the hallway.

Back home he phoned his sister, brother, and mother. He held back on the news of the will. He didn't have the energy to discuss it with his siblings at the moment.

Chapter 16

The three Pardee children stood in the receiving line, along with their father's three surviving brothers and their families, during public visitation at the funeral home.

"Un-freaking-believable," Logan whispered and looked out to the foyer past Maddie and Daryl Pardee's two brothers. A couple signed the guest book.

"Dad, who always took the city bus, left us a hundred-and-eighty thou, and the rest of his pension." He paused. "I get the last part, but where'd he get the other money?"

Before either Maddie or Hawksley could comment, he moved on to the next item of interest. "And all these people. We sure we're burying the same man, our Dad?" His eyes took in the small room with an impressive number of mourners.

Hawksley followed his brother's inspection. He saw his mother and Alex in conversation with Mrs. Maines, Katie, her sister, Bailey, and Nancy.

He returned his attention to his siblings. "No kidding. Even Mom came. Big of her. I can only imagine what Dad would make of it."

"Well, I think it's nice," Maddie said. "She's come to support us. Besides, she was married to Dad for a long time. Strange, though, her not being in the receiving line."

"It wouldn't have been right," Logan said. He nudged Hawksley. "I see a certain someone came." He placed emphasis on the pronoun.

Hawksley groaned. "All *three Maines* came, all right. A sign of respect. Nothing more, so let's get onto something else." He scanned the room again. "I had no idea who would come, but this is impressive — all these people. Dad must have done something right."

His sister agreed. "Yes, he could be charming when he wanted to. And about the money, I guess we'll never know about it, or why he didn't use it. One for the ages." She gave her attention to Hawksley. "You got him dressed nicely. He looks good."

"Thanks."

"And you look good too, both of you," she said. "I can't remember the last time I saw you in a suit, Hawk."

"Been a while."

*   *   *

Tired and drained, the line waited for the last of the stragglers to arrive. The last, a large man in both height and girth, followed by two men. He moved forward, but they remained by the French doors.

He stuck out his hand to Logan. "Allow me to introduce myself. I'm Victor Mantachie." he said in a full-toned voice. His eyes moved from Logan to Maddie to Hawksley. "Sorry for your loss."

Logan accepted the hand. "Thank you."

"I knew your father," Mantachie said. "Fought his devils, he did, right to the end, but doesn't mean he wasn't a good man. He will be missed."

Mantachie released Logan's hand, shook Maddie's, and then Hawksley's, who caught a whiff of expensive cologne. He spotted the monogram on the white dress shirt, the flash of bling on the cufflink, and noted the precise tailoring of the pin stripe suit.

Somewhere between awe and trepidation, Hawksley managed a weak smile at the man likely responsible for the torching of the Hyundai and disappearance of its riders. It had to be him. Daryl Pardee could never have pulled it off.

"Thank you, sir. Our Dad spoke well of you."

"Kind of him. If I can be of assistance to any of you, I'm a phone call away. I owe your father an immeasurable debt."

His statement concluded, he spun about and headed back to the hallway. His two companions trailed behind.

Logan's eyes wide, he said, "Dude, *that* the Victor…?"

"The same. Damn curious to know what the 'immeasurable debt' was."

Logan nodded. "I feel like we were just in a scene from a *Godfather* movie."

"Yeah, me too, but Dad isn't here to say what the debt was. I doubt Mantachie will tell us. Guess we'll never know."

What are you two talking about?" Maddie demanded.

"Uh, Maddie—car catching fire, Hawk's neighbor."

She pointed to the foyer and whispered, "Him? He's behind the fire?"

"Hello, yes."

"Ohmigod. Wonder what Dad could have done for him?"

Logan shook his head. "Dad never said, and neither is he. Guess we'll never know."

Her brothers both nodded.

*   *   *

Nothing could have prepared Hawksley for a funeral service like the *Living Waters Revival Congregation* the next morning. Filled to capacity, the small church gave itself over to loud affirmations of *The Word*, followed by equal prayers for Brother Daryl, a damning of sin, and ended with the congregation dancing around the casket.

The staid funeral procession and brief ceremony at the crypt offered nothing equal to the manic church service.

A heaviness settled on Hawksley when he and five others lifted and guided the casket onto the gurney at the foot of a crypt. Disbelief and mild agitation competed with each other while the pastor read a few select passages from his bible. He bowed his head and finished with a prayer.

Cemetery employees stood nearby, ready to move the casket into the crypt. Without warning, Hawksley's eyes filled. He tried but failed to blink back the wetness. He reached into his pocket, pulled out a wad of tissue, and made a show of blowing his nose. He felt a palm rubbing his back. He turned to find his mother behind him.

Maddie too wiped at her nose.

The pastor offered up a final reading from his bible, and then closed it. The action signaled the end of the service. The mourners dispersed.

Hawksley tugged at the lapels of his overcoat, aware for the first time of the chill. He glanced up at the sky. The sun had played hide-and-seek all day. He doubted there'd ever be an ideal day for a funeral.

A female voice interrupted his musing. "Hi, Hawk."

Katie approached.

"Kate. Hi."

"I won't ask you how you are," she said. "Stupid question anyway. Wanted to tell you if you need anything, give me a call."

At another time the offer might have set his heart racing. This time he could only nod.

"Um, thanks. Good of you." Unable to add anything else, he stared over her shoulder.

"Okay, I'll let you go. Take care." She reached out a hand and squeezed his forearm. "Bye."

Hawksley watched her walk off in her long, blue, wool crepe coat, the hem covering the top of her boots. "Kill you to have extended yourself a bit more?" he whispered. "She was trying to reach out to you."

*   *   *

Maddie, ever the social enabler, had organized a small, formal lunch for some of the immediate family at *Brewed Awakening*, an English-style tavern.

The small party sat around a long rectangular table. The server passed out menus.

Maddie leaned forward from her end of the table, took the opportunity to clear her throat and announce, "Dad would have been pleased to know his wake is in a pub. Please, the tab's on him, so to speak."

The comment caused a ripple of polite laughter.

She continued. "Including anything from the menu."

Orders taken, the drinks set down.

Hawksley listened as his three uncles swapped amusing tales about Daryl Pardee. He noted his mother soon turned away and listened in on a different conversation.

Hawksley bit into his burger. His brother took a pull from a stein of dark beer, set it down and leaned across the table. "Strange, thinking Dad's gone."

Hawksley nodded. "S'right. Maybe he never qualified for father of the year, but say what you want, he did love us. In his way."

Maddie wiped at the corner of her mouth with a napkin.

"He did. Mr. Mantachie had it right—Dad fought his devils. Too bad they always won. Still, we do have some good memories of him."

"Not enough," Logan tossed in.

Something crossed Logan's face; Hawksley couldn't read it—disappointment, sadness? The moment passed, and Logan reached for his beer.

They settled into their private thoughts until Logan spoke again.

"Got plans what you're going to do with your share of the inheritance?"

Hawksley chased a lemon slice in his tea with a spoon. "A nice chunk of it on the house. I'll upgrade my furniture, maybe put up some new windows. How about you?"

"Bank it for now."

Maddie spoke up. "Us too." She turned to Hawksley. "You know, this might solve your problems with your unsafe neighbor. You could use the money to spruce up your house and sell it. From what I saw of the street, it looks like you've got more of those—what do they call them now, upwardly mobile?—types moving in. Might be a great time to sell."

Hawksley shook his head. "No, I'm staying put." The need to qualify his statement, he added, "It's not like I have an emotional attachment to the place because of Darlene. I lived there before I married her. Besides, real estate prices keep going up."

An hour-and-a-half later the party left the tavern, stood out on the sidewalk, shook hands, embraced, and separated.

Hawksley returned home. Vesta rubbed herself against him, but Torchy held back, showed agitation and barked. Hawksley studied her.

"What's up, Torch? Something's bothering you. What is it?"

The dog again barked.

What's she trying to tell me, Hawksley asked himself? He moved toward the door. "Have to go out?" She didn't move, and once more barked.

Hawksley caught her distress. He threw a quick glance around the room. Had something untoward happened?

His suspicion alerted, he gave himself over to inspecting the interior in search of what, he didn't know. A stubborn, middle box drawer on his antique night table drew his attention. As did highlight markers next to his text book.

The drawer caused him trouble from the moment he bought the table. At purchase he reasoned swelling and humidity caused it to change shape. He'd promised himself he'd take it to a woodworker. He hadn't, but instead pushed, wiggled, and used force to make it come even with the other two drawers. Thereafter he'd used only the top and bottom ones. Now the drawer sat slightly askew, and no longer flush with the other two.

His thick highlight markers—one light pink, the other yellow—to the right of his textbook, weren't where he left them—tucked against the book's spine. They now occupied space an eighth of an inch away from the book.

Hawksley's heart beat with violent energy at the discoveries. Someone had entered his house, looked through his things. Kimball. Had to be. He couldn't contend himself with vandalizing the house, torching it, or stealing belongings. No, he had to show off his special brand of perverted revenge.

Hawksley sat at the kitchen table. Psychological torture. Kimball intended to send a different message—Hawksley would never have peace of mind.

He clenched his jaw at the intrusion. Was this how women felt when they'd been violated? His mind raced through all kinds of other possibilities—had Kimball poisoned his food, or even the pet's food? Could be. He'd better toss out all perishables.

A new suspicion arrived—Kimball might have planted electronic bugs in his house. With care Hawksley checked his land phone, the lamps, under tables and chairs, his bed. Nothing. Finished, he stood in the bedroom, his body still full of agitation.

"Sonovabitch. The day, the very day I bury my father, you pull this. You couldn't wait. When is this going to stop?"

A distant memory returned to him. He'd read somewhere burglars studied obituaries, and zeroed in on homes when families were at funeral services. Some intruder had certainly entered this house, but left without taking a thing.

Hawksley inspected the front and back doors. No evidence of tampering. He next turned his attention to the windows. Locked. It meant the intruder came in through a door. The front held too great a risk of being seen; it had to be the back door. But how could the intruder know Nancy wasn't home, and might have seen him? Hawksley puzzled it out, but couldn't come up with an answer.

He next turned his attention to the lock. He'd watched enough crime shows, and scoffed at how easy thieves overcame a lock—a credit card most of the time. Fine, he supposed, if the locks were old-fashioned spring bolts. His weren't. Or in crime shows they used tumbler picks. A couple of seconds and badda boom, badda bing, they solved the obstacle. Pure Hollywood fantasy, but whatever the case, intruders, singular or plural, someone picked his back door lock.

Shallow breaths accompanied his clenched and unclenched hands. Now what? He couldn't go to the cops and tell them he discovered his middle drawer askew, and his markers not where he left them. They'd dismiss him as a nut bar.

Maybe he should move. But if he did, what's to say Kimball wouldn't continue his vendetta?

No real solution at hand, Hawksley made up his mind he'd stay—for now. With any luck other problems or troubles would divert Kimball's attention.

Hawksley studied the animals.

"Pity you two can't talk and tell me who came. I'm glad he didn't harm you. I gotta do a better job of protecting you. You, and what's mine."

*   *   *

Still filled with fury, Hawksley spent the next few hours scrubbing, vacuuming, and wiping any lingering spirit associated with this vile intrusion. Finished, he stepped into the bathroom for a Xanax.

Seated back at his kitchen table, he recalled telling Maddie and Logan he'd get new windows and furniture. For sure now, and he'd add door and window sensors as well as a motion-activated camera. Oh, and the garage—a new door with a keyless entry.

"An automatic garage door opener," he said out loud. "What would Darlene think if she knew?"

He rose and made for the computer. Time to go hunting for home renovations.

Chapter 17

Thursday night Mother Nature dumped four inches of powdery snow. In the morning Hawksley stayed home to watch technicians from *Eye Alert* install and secure entry points over the doors and windows.

Finished, a friendly and patient team leader went over the instructions with Hawksley a final time. He hiked his belt up over his protruding stomach. "You'll get used to this system fast enough. The manual's on your kitchen table. Now, be careful of who you give your password to."

"Will do. And my dog and cat—they won't set off the alarm?"

"No. Not at all, but somebody who shouldn't be here, he'll get all kinds of attention he won't like."

"Good."

"If you have any problems, call us."

"I doubt I will, and thanks."

The technicians gone, Hawksley sat and thumbed through the manual. He screwed up his face. All this for what? His mind took him back to the initial set-to with Kimball. His mouth twisted. *This whole summer. First Darlene, then Kimball, and then the Lyme. If only I had…* He frowned. Coulda, woulda, shoulda—didn't. A pointless exercise playing around with history. He couldn't change it, so why dwell on it?

He glanced at his watch. Still half a day left before his shift ended. Should he bother going to work? His phone rang and jarred him out of his thoughts.

"Hawk," a female voice said. "Saw the panel truck in the driveway. What's going on?"

"Oh, Nancy. Hi. I'm home for the morning while they installed a home alarm system."

"Ah. Probably a smart move, but you could have called me. I would have let them in."

"I know, but I didn't want to bother you."

"'Bother' me? You're not bothering me. You're my friend, remember. You don't call only when you want something. Anyway, can I ask—what spurred on this decision to get an alarm?"

He told her about the break-in. She listened without comment until he finished. "Oh, dear God. And Vesta and Torchy—he didn't harm them?"

"No, but I've tossed out everything not in a can in case of poison. Oh, and before I forget, I'll give you the password to get in. Got a pen?"

"Wait a sec." She came back and wrote the number down. "You know, maybe I better do the same—get an alarm system. This is scary, him picking a lock."

"Yeah, it is. Multi-talented, our neighborhood drug dealer. Unless he brought along a locksmith buddy. Anyway, yes, make your house safer. This guy's dangerous."

"No kidding. I'll do it. You think this happened when we were at your father's funeral?"

"Pretty sure everything was fine before I left. Torchy put me onto something being wrong."

"Why? What'd she do?"

"Got really agitated is what, and barked when I came home."

"Hmm. You know, I can't believe what I'm about to say next, especially since we've had some serious conversations about this. Maybe you should get a gun. Keep it with you all the time. Indiana isn't open carry, but I read you can get a permit to have one on you."

He snorted. "Ducky, Nance; I can see me carrying a gun on my hip at work. For sure I won't get talk-back from my team."

"Don't be a smarty."

"Sorry. I keep hoping things will blow over with him. In the meantime, if he sees I've put in an alarm system, he'll know I know he's been here."

He heard her soft breathing.

"Hawk, listen to what I'm saying. For a guy as bright as you, a guy whose studying chemistry, you can be really dumb or naïve, take your pick. I'll lay it out for you again. Torchy got poisoned. And you remember the drive-by, the hit-and-run, and now this? You're dealing with a dangerous lunatic. You think he's going to leave things here? If he's done all this, chances are good he's got a gun. Why give him all the advantages?"

"It's funny," he said, "us having this conversation."

"Not funny hah-hah."

"No, what you say makes sense, but I almost feel like you're a gun advocate."

Neither said anything for a moment.

Nancy cleared her throat. "Talk to you soon. In the meantime, be careful, but think about it some more." She fell quiet for a moment. "Um, before I let you go, I wanted to let you know Logan's coming down this weekend to stay with me. It's not going to trouble you, is it?"

"You're adults, Nance. You don't need my blessings. Do what makes you happy. I'm fine with your decision."

"You sure? You don't sound happy about it."

"I'm sure. Don't worry about it."

"Fine, then. We'll see how the weekend goes."

"Oh, all right, thanks. Listen, gotta get back to work. Talk to you later."

"Are you all right, Hawk?"

"Yeah, why?"

"I don't know, you sounded…sad."

"I'm not. You're reading too much into my voice."

No sooner were his words out than his brain pulled out a memory. He'd listened to an NPR program where a psychologist said deceptions were easier to catch over the phone; people didn't have visual cues, and so tuned in to tone, the rate of words, and so on.

Nancy sounded unconvinced. "All right then. I'll let you get back to work. If you need anything, give me a call. Love you."

"Love you too, Nance. Oh, before you hang up. Don't say anything about this to Logan. I don't want to get him riled up."

* * *

By the end of his shift Hawksley had for the most part returned to his old self, careful to not over-react to things. Grateful for the busy demands of work, he had no time for brooding.

At home after dinner he finished reviewing the instructions in the manual. Done, he rose, slipped on his pea jacket and reached for Torchy's leash. The phone rang.

"'Lo."

"Hi, Hawk," Katie said.

In an instant Hawksley's mind flitted about in manic fashion at hearing her voice. As well, his palms sweated, his heart raced. Regret too piggybacked in over his last meeting with her.

"Katie, hi," he croaked. "I was thinking about you earlier today."

"Good things, I hope."

"Course. Um, I, I wanted to say how sorry I am about my end of the conversation at the cemetery."

Her voice, a balm to his nervous admission, set him at ease.

"Don't worry about it, Hawk. I understand. Believe me. You've had a lot on your mind, so put down your whip. All is forgotten."

He let out a rush of air and said, "Thanks. So, what's up?"

"I called for two reasons. To give you my new address, and to see if you could stand another visit."

He hadn't heard from Katie since his father's funeral. He called several times; well, almost called. She'd sought him out, offered her sincere expression of sympathy. He responded with indifference.

Hawksley well knew he could have shown more class. Each time he'd picked up the phone to call and explain himself, he'd placed it back in its cradle. He had no clear plan on how to start. Maybe he should text her? He ruled it out; too impersonal, too cowardly.

Ever since his first crush in middle school, Hawksley never made the first move with girls. He relied on a time-tested method—better to be safe than sorry. He put out signals, but never came right out with his feelings. He would rather have crawled through glass than face embarrassment, or worse, rejection. Here Katie Maines, his best friend in high school, and now possible target of romantic feelings, did what he wouldn't.

"Sure. I was getting ready to take Torchy for a walk."

"Everything all right?"

"What do you mean?"

"You sound—I don't know—sad."

"Really? You're the second woman today."

"Second woman what?

"Who told me I sound sad."

"There must be a reason."

"Whatever. So like I said, Torchy and I are off to get some air."

"You're still walking?"

"Yep. A lot more careful when I'm out. I'm not going to be a prisoner in my house. "

"Do you want some company on your walk?"

Did he? Of course he did, but kept his voice under control. "Yeah, of course. Happy to have it. We'll wait for you."

"Great. See you in about ten minutes."

Hawksley's heart beat faster when Katie's Beetle pulled into the driveway. He dried his sweaty palms on his pants and warned himself to stay cool. "Deep breath," he murmured.

He grabbed the leash from the wall. "Ready for your walk, Torch?" Torchy barked excitedly. They moved out into the driveway.

"Picked a lovely evening," Katie shouted as she stepped out of the yellow vehicle. "I like your Christmas lights."

"Gotta keep in the spirit." Hawksley approached. Both flashed nervous smiles, and offered each other a quick, light kiss. The awkwardness and excitement of the moment done, Katie slammed the car door and zipped up her down coat.

"Ready?"

"Ready."

Without thinking, Hawksley took Katie's hand, delighted she accepted it. The unexpected action stunned him. What had come over him? Had some alien taken over his mind? He, Mr. slow-and-steady-wins-the-race, behaved like Logan Pardee instead of Hawksley Pardee.

His glove, Katie's woollen mitt, separated naked touch of skin, yet Hawksley believed the warmth of her hand reached him.

He marveled at this change in their relationship. In high school Katie had a boyfriend whom she dumped in their senior year. Hawksley dated several girls, none for any length of time. When Maddie, Logan and others teased him about his friendship with Katie, he'd say they had over-active imaginations. "Friends, is all. F-r-i-e-n-d-s. Nothing more, nothing less. We like a lot of the same things, and each other, but not in the way you mean."

Yet here, long after graduation, the unexpected happened—Hawksley found himself at love's door.

*   *   *

They left the driveway and turned left onto Delaney, away from Kimball's. Both shot a fast look at his house.

Katie picked up on Hawksley's general sense of disquiet. Every time they heard or saw a car approach, they stepped onto someone's lawn and waited for it to pass.

Katie spoke. "I feel so bad for you, about all this you're going through."

"Thanks. Been a bit of a nightmare."

"Has something else happened?"

Hands in front, palms open, he said, "Somebody broke into my house. Well, kind of... They picked the lock, and came in."

"No. How do you know?"

"When I got home from my Dad's funeral, Torchy was agitated, and then I noticed a few things out of place."

Katie stopped and faced him. "Anything taken?"

"No. Somebody came, looked around and left. I think they wanted me to know they'd be in the house."

"In-credible," she said. "So I assume it's this Kimball neighbor. Have you gone to the police?"

"No point. I have no proof, but I know it's my neighbor. Nancy, told me I should get a gun to protect myself."

"And will you?"

"No. I don't want to be around those things. Still have the faint hope this'll die out."

"But you don't sound convinced."

He shook his head. "No. I'll have to find some other way to fix this. What, I don't know, but I'll keep at it until I come up with something."

Her response caught him off guard. She slipped her arm through his, squeezed it and said, "And you won't be alone."

Chapter 18

He couldn't have imagined better if he tried; a simple walk with Katie on a winter's night turned into much more. It allowed him to put all worries about Kimball aside. The nearness of Katie, the anticipation of something more made his heart flip. *Poor ticker*, he told himself. *If it's not dealing with one kind of stress, it's dealing with another. All in all, though, I prefer this kind of stress.*

Cheeks red, noses dripping, the two made their way back to his house. Hawksley busied himself in the kitchen while Katie sat in the living room and played with Vesta. The dutiful host returned with hot chocolate, cookies, tea with lemon, almond butter and apple slices. He set the tray on the coffee table.

"Nice," Katie said and pointed, "but is all this for both of us?"

"I can't eat the cookies," Hawksley said, "and refined sugar's bad for me." He plunked himself next to Katie. "Sorry I have to go through all this rigmarole."

"No need to be sorry. I understand. Take care of yourself." Katie reached for a ginger snap. "Love these."

Torchy, eager for some or all of the cookie, placed her head in Katie's lap. "Can she have some?" Katie asked.

"Yeah, sure, why not? She's not supposed to mooch, but does anyway." He watched while Katie sipped her chocolate. "Ask you something?"

"Yes, sure."

"How come we never hooked up in high school?"

"High school's long gone," she scoffed, "and now you ask? I was waiting for *you*."

He whipped his head toward her. "What. *Me*? You went out with Mr. Homecoming King, um, um..." He snapped his fingers to help pull up the name.

She supplied the name. "Todd Pawel."

"Yeah, right...Pawel, Student Council president, and president of Young Republicans. We all figured you two would get married. And then you dumped him in senior year."

Katie corrected him. "I did not '*dump* him. I outgrew him, and we decided to call it quits. We left on good terms, so there."

Hawksley's ears burned at the rebuke. He shouldn't have been so blunt. Would she think less of him? She'd only offered a counter-opinion. Facts, not judgment. He reminded himself he wasn't made of porcelain; he wouldn't shatter, yet...

On one level Hawksley recognized a simple truth for all three Pardee children—they bore the emotional scars of their troubled childhood. Security, trust and love, the essential triad of character-building of childhood, never arrived in equal measure and predictability in the Pardee household. Yvonne Pardee did her best to give her children what they needed, but always fell short. In the end, no longer able to cope with the runaway train of a husband, she left.

Hawksley worked hard to not internalize Katie's comments as rejection. He reached for an apple slice and dipped it into the jar of spread.

"Sorry. Got it wrong. About you and me back then, you know, I always wanted to ask you, but never had the nerve."

She answered with a shrug.

"So what happened to Todd?" Hawksley asked. "Where'd he get to?"

"Connecticut. Working for Aetna, selling corporate insurance plans. But back to your first question, you had your girlfriends, remember, and your chance in senior year?"

In reply, he stared at her, mouth open.

She giggled. "Hawk, if ever there's an example of someone's face showing dumbfoundness, if there's such a word, it's yours." She reached out a hand and stroked his face.

Hawksley offered up a light smile. "Men, huh?"

Katie nodded. "Men. High school is ancient history. We're here together now."

"You good with it?"

She tilted her head and smiled. "What do you think?"

Hawksley moved closer. The scent of her, the closeness of her, wonderful—nothing else mattered. Their lips touched. He hungered for her, but forced himself to go slow. Her soft and warm lips matched his tempo, slow, and perfect. The open palm of his free hand stroked her hip.

Katie at last broke away. "Wow, Hawk, what a kisser." She fanned her face. "Gotta come up for some air. I need a cold drink now, not hot chocolate." She followed the comment with a broad, nothing-held-back seductive smile.

*   *   *

Katie spent the night. A glorious night. Hawksley hadn't been with a woman since Darlene.

Torchy and Vesta banished to the hallway, the new lovers indulged themselves with abandon. Later, entwined, they spoke in soft voices—Katie shared about her time in Berkeley, Hawksley about his marriage to Darlene, his work, the disease, and his friendship with Nancy. He withheld the mention of her affair with Darlene: all in the past.

Sleep at last claimed them.

Hawksley woke in the night to use the bathroom. He almost tripped over Torchy. In turn she jumped up onto the bed.

He returned a few minutes later, glad he hadn't awoke Katie. He fought for his piece of the bed with Torchy and Vesta. His last thought before he returned to sleep—*I have the woman I want.*

*   *   *

An insistent feline, impervious to any of her owner's lingering post-coital bliss, rubbed her face against his, the purr machine on high volume. Up, up, the cat demanded. *Up and feed me*. Hawksley awoke and massaged her head, and stared past her to Katie—beautiful, enchanting Katie. She opened her eyes rich green and smiled at him. She leaned forward, pecked him, and rubbed Vesta's head.

"Good morning, lover. You don't object to the word, do you?"

He shook her head. "Not a bit. I like it coming from you." So different from temperamental Darlene, he told himself.

Katie slid out of bed and stood at the edge. She invited him to shower with her.

Hawksley needed no coaxing. Together they washed each other; then aroused, did more than wash.

Katie stepped out of the shower first. He admired her body, especially her long, runway model legs. Wearing his housecoat, she volunteered to make them breakfast.

They sat at the kitchen table. "Don't know why, but I'm always ravenous after sex." She winked at him. "Mr. Stud Muffin."

He felt himself redden, not used to this kind of unfiltered language. It might take a bit of getting used to. Once more he found himself comparing Darlene to his new lover.

Katie waved a hand in front of him. "Hello, Hawk. Where are you, and what're you thinking?"

He answered with a shake of his head. "You. You're such a free spirit, so comfortable with your sexuality, with everything."

"Only way to be."

"You got me on board."

Hawksley washed the dishes while Katie dried. Both found themselves lost in separate thoughts for a few minutes. She spoke.

"Got plans for Christmas?"

"Christmas?"

"Yes, you know, the once-a-year thing where we re-enact pagan rituals of decorating evergreens, have Yule logs, and pass out gifts; the 'Jesus is the reason for the Season' thing."

He laughed. "Still got it, Katie."

She stepped closer and poked his chest with a finger. "Never lost it." She followed the comment with a confident, half-smile, pulled him to her, tilted her head and waited for him to kiss her. He obliged, tasted her soft lips and felt the tip of her tongue in his mouth. In turn he slipped his hand into the housecoat.

She jumped back. "Uh-uh. Not now. I showered."

"Tease. It's a kiss, is all."

"And a kiss leads to other things. Anyway, 'lover,' care to say if you have plans for Christmas?"

"My brother and his girlfriend have invited me to spend Christmas with them, otherwise I don't have any plans. Why? What's on your mind?"

"I want to show off my new boyfriend, is what's on my mind."

She couldn't have said anything more golden.

His eyebrows rose. "Well, thank you kindly, Miss Kitty."

"Huh?"

"*Gunsmoke* reruns on cable. Guess I do a bad imitation of Marshal Dillon."

She waited for him to finish. "This will work out perfectly if you come for Christmas dinner. Mom likes to drag us all to church in the mornings, and then go crazy getting the turkey and everything ready. It's kind of funny watching her." She placed the tea towel on the rack. "Back to what I was saying. They all know you, and like you." She stopped. "You do like my family, right?"

He didn't hesitate.

"I do, and your Mom and Bailey were kind enough to come to my Dad's funeral. Yeah, sure—if they don't mind the company."

"Course not. It's why I'm asking." She held up her hands. "Kidding. We'll set an extra plate for you, and I'll google anything you shouldn't eat."

"Not necessary."

"Not listening to you."

"Fine. What should I bring?"

"Yourself."

"Ri-i-ight. Like I'd show up empty-handed."

"Then come with whatever." She crouched in front of Torchy and stroked the dog. "Guess what, Torchy. Hawk and I will have Christmas together. I'd invite you, but Mom and

Dad have a cat. Our kitty's not like Vesta. She doesn't like dogs."

If Torchy objected, the happy swoosh her tail gave belied the claim.

*   *   *

Determined to bring something to the Maines family, Hawksley agonized for two days on what to buy. After consultation with some of his female co-workers, who delighted in speculating about his new romance, he selected an expensive gourmet chocolate gift basket for Katie's parents and sister. Everybody feasted on chocolate of one kind or another at Christmas, but few sampled gourmet.

Katie: buying for her would be tricky this early in the relationship. Nothing too intimate, the women told him. Best not to rush or send her the wrong message. Nothing impersonal either.

In the end he bought a long blue-violet cashmere scarf. He showed it to his co-workers in the lunchroom, and received a consensus of approval.

Hawksley spent Christmas Eve with Katie at her apartment in a new four-story building. Everything sparkled new, even the brushed steel elevator doors. He stepped into the elevator and pushed four.

Katie met him at the door of her apartment. He sniffed and stepped in. "Smells great in here. Somebody's been cooking."

Katie hung up his coat. "She has, and hopes everything will agree with your taste buds."

Hawksley inspected the apartment: bright bold colors mixed with soothing pastels everywhere, the walls painted a reddish-brown; scented candles of various sizes in abundance. He couldn't help but be impressed. "Wow," he said when she gave him a tour, "so different from my place. I like it"

"Yes, but I like your place, too. This is me, my personality, and it took me a while to put it all together. I'm happy to say most of my things arrived from California in one piece."

"Well, this all suits you." Hawksley let his eyes take in the furniture and decoration in her living room—Ethan Allen, Pottery Barn or something equivalent, he guessed—large lustrous pillows and throws, solid, ceramic and other pieces or art on tables or on the floor. The walls held high-priced copies of Monet, Van Gogh, and modern ones Hawksley couldn't identify.

He faced Katie. "Very, very nice. You have talent. I wish I had your decorating sense."

She stepped closer and threw her arms around him. "Lucky you, then; you have me. Now, let's eat. I've made turmeric fries and baked chicken with artichokes. It's all food you can eat."

The Bajofondo Tango Club album played as background while they ate. Contentment washed over Hawksley. This is how it should be. Lost in thought he watched Katie as she pushed a strand of fine chestnut hair behind an ear and continued with her story. He couldn't claim they'd been high school sweethearts, he'd never pursued her. But the girl he loved since adolescence now belonged to him.

He studied her pale and baby soft skin, a feature of all the Maines women. In a room full of beautiful women, Katie Maines might not have been the first to catch a man's eye. She didn't have the outward raw sexuality of Darlene, or the runway model looks of her sister. Hawksley didn't care. No sonnet, no love poem would ever find the perfect words for her.

"…at the end of the hall."

Katie set her fork down, tilted her head and stared at Hawksley. "Something tells me you didn't hear a word I said. Did you?" She held up a hand. "No, wait; I remember this look. I saw it on you in high school sometimes."

A smile filled with meaning formed. "Did you, now? The things you remember. I'm happy to be here, with you."

"Aw, and I'm glad. The feeling's mutual."

*   *   *

Hawksley phoned his sister Christmas morning. After a quick discussion, he asked if she'd put his mother on the line.

"Merry Christmas, Hawk."

"You too, Mom, and to Alex. Hope Santa's been or about to be good to you."

"He has, and you?"

They spent a few minutes in pleasant conversation. She asked about his health, and his plans for the rest of the day.

"I'm going to see Logan next door in a few minutes."

"Oh, right. I heard. He phoned. Have a great day, darling, say hello for us, and keep well."

"Okay, Mom. Bye."

Presents in hand, Hawksley knocked on Nancy's door. An unshaven Logan answered the door in a housecoat. "Merry Christmas, bro'."

"Good morning, and same to you. Looking very *Vogue* this Christmas day. Trying out the new casual chic, are we?"

Logan opened his mouth to speak when Nancy entered the room in an attractive red sweater and skirt set, and full makeup. She pulled Hawksley into the house and kissed his cheek. "I asked him to get dressed earlier." Her gaze shifted to Logan. "It's Christmas. Please get into the spirit by getting shaved, washed and dressed."

Christmas music played while Nancy fussed in the kitchen. Hawksley kept her company.

They sat at her dining room table. Nancy made crepes for all three, and served coffee and tea.

Hawksley warmed to the idea of his neighbor and brother together. From what he could tell, they got on quite well. After breakfast, the three adjourned to Nancy's living room and exchanged presents.

Hawksley gave Nancy a pen and stationery set, and a new biography on Thomas Jefferson. For Logan, he bought a fitness tracker. In turn, he received a silk tie and a gift card from

Logan, and small, portable wireless home speakers from Nancy.

Later, tea and coffee cups re-filled, the three indulged themselves in idle conversation.

"Anything more since the break-in?" Nancy said. The words no sooner out than both she and Hawksley froze.

Logan's eyes flitted from one to the other. "What break-in? What are you two talking about?"

"Not worth mentioning," Hawksley said, eager to get Logan off the subject. "Something in the neighborhood."

Logan would have none of it. "It's me, remember, bro'? I know when you're lying. The right side of your mouth gets the little twitchy. C'mon, give. What happened?"

Hawksley had not envisioned this. He cast a fast look at Nancy, and hoped she'd telepathically pick up on the look. *Damn. You let the cat out of the bag. I told you not to say anything to Logan.*

She closed her eyes and gave a small shake of her head.

Hawksley exhaled and trained his sight on his brother. "Somebody picked the lock on my house before I got the alarm system. Pretty sure, no, positive, it was Kimball. They didn't take a thing; all the more reason why it had to be Kimball."

"You call the cops?"

"What for? No proof. Nothing."

"So he's at it again?"

Hawksley sought to soften the effect. "Uh, yeah, but then again, no. Not like before. Nothing was taken."

"But he breaks into your house. This has to end. Like I said before, nobody fucks with a Pardee." Logan turned to Nancy. "Sorry for the language."

Hawksley jumped in. "Let it be, Logan? I've changed the locks, I've got a state of the art alarm system now, and all I want to do is have this whole thing over and done with."

Logan's eyes narrowed.

"You listenin' to me, Hawk? This guy is never going to leave you alone. Never. He's got a hard-on for you, and the only way this is going to end is when he gets satisfaction. You've got his full attention, but somebody needs to get his complete attention."

And so it went. Neither Nancy nor Hawksley managed to shift Logan's point of view. The heated discussion wound down a bit when Logan mollified the other two with, "All right, it's Christmas, so let's drop the whole thing. This isn't doing anybody any good."

In spite of the somewhat conciliatory statement, Hawksley found little comfort in it. It worried him Logan might do something.

By the time he said his goodbyes, he hurt all over.

*   *   *

The comfort and warmth of Katie and her family did much to alleviate Hawksley's stress. Had he been able to pick a family to grow up in, the Maines would have been first and only choice.

Mr. Maines clapped him on the back, welcomed him, and asked him if he wanted a drink. His wife pulled Hawksley to her.

"How are you holding up, you dear boy? You look a little pale."

"I'm fine, Mrs. Maines. Thanks for asking, and for inviting me." He handed her the designer shopping bag of presents. "For under the tree."

Bailey too hugged him. "Good to see you, Hawk. It's going to be so much fun having you here."

"Thanks, Bailey."

Katie at last got to him. She gave him a territorial peck on his cheek.

"Let me take your coat."

He handed it to her while the rest of the family moved into other rooms. She moved closer and peered at him. "What's the matter?" she whispered.

Hawksley matched his voice to hers.

"A little stressed," he said while she hung up his coat. "Logan." Another pause, a quick intake of air, and he recapped the conversation with Logan.

Her eyes never left his face. "Maybe it'll be all right. You know Logan has always worn his heart on his sleeve. I'm sure he meant well, and it sounds like you and Nancy talked some sense into him." She took his hand and squeezed. "Come join Dad. He's watching *It's A Wonderful Life*. We've made some yummy snacks you can eat. Soon you'll be your old self again."

Hawksley nodded. "Yeah, you're probably right," he said, not comforted by the balm of her words.

She studied him. "Okay, knock it off, buster. It's Christmas. You're over-analyzing this. Nothing's going to come of this. Even if it did, well, you'll deal with it then — *if* anything happens. Worrying isn't going to do anything to change the situation."

He held up his hands in surrender. "Agreed. I'll try to put it out of my mind. Thanks for your help, but by the way, you can be bossy."

She dismissed the claim with a wave of her hand, and pulled him into the living room. "Have to be with someone who's hard-headed."

Chapter 19

Christmas at the Maines turned into something special, with plenty of refreshments, good conversation, and lots of laughter. An hour after he arrived, Hawksley had almost forgotten his body aches.

By mid-afternoon, Bailey's boyfriend, Patrice, arrived, as did Mrs. Maines parents. The crowded dining table buzzed.

Hawksley fell into conversation with Patrice, who studied business at Louisville. He liked the amiable exchange student from Belgium with his easy-going smile. Both he and Bailey could well have modeled for the cover of a fashion magazine.

Hawksley complimented him on his English.

"Thank you. I think it is not so good, but… in Europe, we all learn languages, and we all watch American movies and television."

"But you didn't go home for Christmas? Aren't you homesick?"

"I miss my family, but will see them at the end of May. It is too expensive to fly home twice a year. We have an International Students Club on campus. They hold Christmas events." He pointed to Katie's sister. "Bailey, she made up her mind I must come and have Christmas at her house."

Hawksley chuckled. "Yeah, they're pushy, those Maines women. Well, I'm glad she forced you to come. Is she taking business too?"

"No. English major. She likes the Romantic poets. We met at the environmental club on campus."

"And do you model too?" The Belgian laughed and shook his head. "Me? No. Why?"

"You look like you could."

Bit by bit the conversation wandered into politics. Hawksley found it fascinating to hear a European's view on world events. Neither man took much notice of others rising from the table.

Bailey arrived and threw her arms around Patrice. "Is he boring you with politics, Hawk?"

"Not at all. We're having a good time."

"Carry on, I guess. We're all scattered around the house. Dad's putting in *Home Alone* if you're interested."

"Okay." Hawksley turned back to the Belgian. "Good talking to you, Patrice. Maybe we can continue this at another time."

"Yes. It would be nice."

Hawksley helped clear the table. "This is really nice," he said and kept his voice low.

Katie smiled and matched his voice. "Are you happy?"

"You bet. Thanks for inviting me. And I really liked your sister's boyfriend." Feeling emotionally safe, he took a risk and revealed something of his inner self. "A while back I watched *Love Affair*, you know, the Warren Beatty-Annette Bening remake."

"Yes. Great movie."

"Anyway, it made me sad, and started me thinking of you. I remember wishing I had what they had."

She turned her head and pecked him on the cheek. "And now you do. As we're sharing, I have a confession — when I heard you split up with Darlene, I made up my mind I'd come after you."

"You did?"

"Yep. Couldn't wait any longer for you to get your act together."

Hawksley threw his arms around her and squeezed. "You are the best, Katie Maines. The very best."

"Glad you think so. Not so bad yourself."

A flutter of electricity ran through him at the words. He squeezed tighter. She giggled. "Careful, you'll break my bones."

They joined the others and sat on the carpet in the crowded living room. Katie snuggled into him.

Close to seven, Hawksley said he had to return home and feed his pets. Several minutes of goodbyes, thank-yous, he kissed Katie and headed out to his car. All proved right with the world on a starry Christmas night.

Arriving home, Hawksley let Torchy out to do her business. He paid scant attention to the cold. One magical moment after another played over in his mind as he reviewed his time at the Maines home. "I can't imagine it ever getting better than this," he whispered to the night.

*   *   *

By luck Hawksley saw a notice on the company bulletin board of someone selling two pair of hard-to-get tickets to the New Year's Eve ball at the *Sheraton* in Louisville. He called: they were still available. A flurry of phone calls to Katie, Nancy, and Logan resulted in a buy. All three offered to split the cost with him. He refused all three.

"Does it feel strange double-dating with your brother and potential sister-in-law?" Katie asked while she played with her earrings in front of his mirror. "It looks like those two are getting serious about each other."

"It does. You know, it still amazes me they got together. I never made Nancy to be Logan's type. You remember the kinds of girls he went after in school."

Katie nodded. Both remembered Logan's reputation as a skirt chaser. Deserved or not, the girls who dated him were either pitied, or found themselves on the receiving end of snippy comments.

"People change," she said, "and I bet your brother and Nancy think the same thing about us."

"Maybe not. Something Logan once said makes me think otherwise."

"Why, what did he say?"

"About it being well known I had a crush on you."

Katie turned away from the mirror, smiled and approached him. Her fingertips ran over the lapels of his tuxedo. "You look elegant."

"And you look sexy. His palm followed the contour of the hips of her black, backless dress with crisscross straps. "Short cocktail dress and heels. Any full-bloodied man's dreams. Grrr."

Katie gave him a winsome smile. "Why thank you, gallant sir."

His phone rang. He answered and listened. "Good. See you outside." He hung up. "We're going in Logan's Audi," he said. "Not the greatest room in the back seat, but it's a nice ride."

The four made small talk as the car crossed over into Louisville. Hawksley recalled an earlier conversation with Katie about double-dating. He'd never done anything like this with his brother. In high school they moved in different circles, had different interests.

"Let's get a couple of pictures of the two of us in our tuxes," he said to Logan. "For Mom and Maddie. They'd like it."

"We'll get more than a few," Nancy added.

Logan pulled up by the front doors of the hotel to let the women escape into the lobby. "See you in a few minutes," he called out. Hawksley stayed with him. "So," Hawksley asked when they walked across the parking lot back to the hotel, "you rent or buy your tux?"

"I own it. You?"

"Me? Nah. Still part of the proletarian. Work in a factory, remember?"

Logan snorted. "'Proletarian'? Where do you get this crap from—*Commies Today*?"

Hawksley gave him a sideway look. "It's not crap. It's part of history, and the English language. I read. You should try it too—opening a book." He gave his brother a playful push. "Anyhow, Katie scored this for me for the evening. I cannot believe her. First, I didn't think I'd get a tux this late; second, If I did, I thought it would probably be something out-of-date with shiny pants, and not the right size or shape. This one's new or almost new, and fits me like a glove. And get this, Katie knows how to tie a real tuxedo bow tie—not one of those cheap clip-ons."

"She's a jewel," Logan said. "Good thing she finally ignored you being a dumbass, and went after you." He followed the comment with how own playful push. "You do look good in it. Glad you invited me and Nancy."

Their dates waited for them in the hotel lobby. The four checked their coats. Hawksley commented on Nancy's long-sleeved deep red knit dress. "Your dress looks stunning."

She looked down at herself. "You like?"

"I do. Nice. Really shows off your figure."

"Thank you."

They surrendered their tickets at the ballroom door and entered the decorated dance hall. A DJ at the front offered up dance-like electronica choices.

Hawksley took a quick look around; a third of the room's tables were already claimed, most by people his or close to his age, in quality dresses, tuxedos or high-priced suits.

The four wandered about in search of their assigned table, under an extensive ceiling net which covered much of the room and held a ponderous display of purple and red balloons. Navy and white tablecloths covered each of the round tables. Fancy place settings included champagne flute glasses with the hotel's name engraved on them. Purple serpentine streamers and hi-hats sat next to cutlery. Noise makers sat atop soup bowls.

They found their seats near the dance floor. Soon three other couples arrived. Introductions were made while servers flitted about with baskets of bread, butter, and poured sparkling wine.

"How're you liking the evening so far?" Hawksley asked Katie.

"It's lovely, really lovely. It feels special. Our first formal date, Very romantic."

Dinner out of the way, revelers moved to the dance floor. The catchy group dance song, "The Macarena" came on.

"Come on," Katie said and pulled Hawksley to the floor. "This is fun. Let's do it." A powerless Hawksley turned to his brother for assistance.

"Don't look at me," Logan said. "You're on your own."

"No, he's not," Nancy said and rose. She pulled Logan to his feet. "You're coming too."

Several songs later Hawksley made for the washroom. At the sink he unloosened his tie and turned on a tap to wash his hands. The outside door opened. Hawksley looked up into the mirror and met the surprised gaze of Brian Kimball.

His neighbor's hair had the just-cut look, the sides shaved close. If Hawksley's opinion hadn't been tainted, he might have thought Kimball's lean frame fit his evening wear. But for the tattoos on his hand, he could have been in a style magazine. He chose a black, open, hip-length three-button dinner jacket with a mandarin collar. An ivory white shirt underneath with pearl buttons made a sharp contrast. Patent leather shoes finished off his ensemble.

Caught unawares, the two adversaries stood frozen in place for a brief moment. Hawksley blinked once, and gave himself over to the task of washing his hands. His muscles seized. He found it difficult to draw sufficient air into his lungs. His mouth ran dry.

Kimball, moved past and stood at one of the urinals. Long seconds later, he zipped up his fly, turned around and made for one of the other sinks.

Hawksley stared after him.

Hands shaking, Hawksley placed them under the dryer and rubbed in a fast manner. Here—Kimball, here, of all places. The whole damn world, and he had to attend the same New Year's party. Still, this could be an opportunity to fix things. He drew in a deep lungful of air, ready to speak when the door opened again. Logan.

"Gotta make my bladder gladder," he said into the mirror and caught Hawksley's gaze. "S'matter? You look like you saw a ghost."

Hawksley slowly shook his head. Leave it alone. If Logan understood, he didn't let on. His eyes moved from Hawksley to Kimball in the mirror. The drug dealer kept his light brown eyes locked in on him while he washed his hands. In reply Logan's jaw jutted forward. "Help you?" His voice dropped an octave and gave out the warning.

Kimball behaved as if he hadn't heard. He shook excess water from his hands, spun about and reached for a paper towel. At last he faced Logan. The corners of his mouth turned up and produced the smug look of amusement Hawksley knew only too well.

With Logan, the look resulted in challenge. "Something funny?"

Kimball's gaze moved from Logan to Hawksley. "Better tell your friend here to chill."

"'Friend,'" Logan repeated and turned to his brother. "You know this guy?"

Hawksley moved to the door. "C'mon, let's go. You can take a leak somewhere else. This is my neighbor."

"Your neigh..." Logan's head moved from Hawksley to Kimball and back. Once more he pointed to Kimball. "Him? This is the asshole who's caused you all the trouble? Doesn't look like much."

Hawksley tugged on his brother's sleeve. "Logan. Time to go." He pulled open the door, stepped out into the large ballroom and stomped over to their table. Katie and Nancy at once ceased their talk.

"What's the matter?" Katie asked and leaned forward.

"Yeah, and where's Logan?" Nancy tossed in.

The latter question caught Hawksley off guard. He assumed Logan had followed him. He whipped his head around. No Logan.

His face tight, Hawksley hurried back to the washroom. Inside a few men stood and watched a drama unfold—Logan with his forearm against Kimball's windpipe.

"You stay away from Hawksley," he hissed through clenched teeth. "If anything more happens, I come for you." He released the drug dealer, who indulged in a spasm of coughing. His eyes wide, his brows raised, his lips tight, Kimball pointed to the small audience and managed to say, "I have witnesses."

"You think so?" Logan challenged. He turned to the other men. "Any of you see anything going on here?"

Fast shakes of heads and quick denials assured him they hadn't. "There you have it, buttercup," a self-satisfied Logan said. "Nobody saw a thing. Now, fun's over with my brother. First and last warning. Oh, and Happy New Year."

His face reddened, his eyes wide open, the mouth narrow and thin, Kimball scanned the faces around him. He tugged at his jacket with force and left the washroom. The small audience returned to other activities.

Logan faced his brother. Eyes narrowed to near slits, he waited until the room emptied.

"What have you done?" Hawksley asked in a hushed tone. He stepped closer to his brother. "What the fuck have you done?"

Whether Logan had an answer or chose to answer, Hawksley didn't care, and pushed on. "I'll tell you what you've done. You've made things worse, so much worse. I kept hoping this whole thing would blow over with Kimball. Maybe it would have. I even got myself ready to talk to him."

He chopped the air. "Now, as sure as God makes little green apples, Kimball will stew and plot more revenge. Thanks for nothing. Shit." He pounded the sink counter. "This isn't Afghanistan, and you're not out scaring the shit out of some goatherd or whatever."

"Okay, calm down," Logan said. "Told you before — nobody fucks with a Pardee. I didn't expect a marching parade, but didn't guess you'd go all ape shit on me either. Like now. Well, fuck you."

Something about the statement unnerved Hawksley. Fists bunched, he stepped closer.

"Fuck *me*? No. Fuck you." His right arm shot out, hit the tight skin on Logan's cheek and split it. In an instant Logan reeled back, ran his palm to his face, saw the blood and retaliated with an open hand jujitsu strike. It made contact with Hawksley's nose, and sent him backward.

Two strangers entered to find two others bleeding and glaring at one another. The new arrivals sized up the situation and left.

Hawksley spit blood into the sink. Head tilted back, he managed to get tissues to his nose, balled several pieces, and used them to plug up his nostrils.

"Ape shit?" he said, his voice wet. "Was I the one here trying to crush someone's windpipe earlier? Your answer for everything—brute force. All the way through high school, who spent more time in the vice-principal's office for fighting? You don't back down from anyone. I get it, maybe this kind of thing works for the war machine and the private military thing employing you. Newsflash, asshole. It doesn't." He broke off, turned his head for a moment, and returned his attention to his brother. "I'm done with you."

Face red, lips thin, Logan's chest heaved. He refused to hold his brother's gaze, and stared at something over Hawksley's shoulder.

Nothing else to do, the two brothers left in silence. Mouths open, their dates gawked when their escorts returned to the table, one with his head tilted up to the ceiling, the other with a paper tissue to a cut on his cheek.

By coincidence and in unison, six hundred or so other New Year's Eve revelers called out a cadence—"Six, five, four, three, two, one. Happy New Year!"

Purple and red balloons floated down from the ceiling while excited couples kissed, shook hands or slapped backs.

Neither of the Pardee brothers would answer questions about what happened in the washroom.

Hawksley managed to staunch his bleeding, but found it awkward to breathe through his nose. His shoulders, neck and jaw hurt. His stomach roiled, and a headache behind his eyes manifested itself. He squinted and wished he could be in bed and pull the covers over his head, block out the world.

Kimball still on his mind, Hawksley searched the room for him. He at last spotted him at a large table with his girlfriend, her hair piled, silver hoop earrings dangling above a strapless silver micro mini dress. Both glared in his direction.

The look only managed to increase Hawksley's inner tension.

Katie stepped closer and placed her mouth next to his ear. "Your body's hurting isn't it?"

The hint of a frown gave her the answer.

"Will you tell me what happened in the washroom?"

Hawksley placed an elbow on the table, leaned closer and gave her a quick account.

Katie blew out her lips. "Want to go home?"

"Please."

"It's midnight. Not much point staying anymore." She pulled away, spoke to Nancy, who heard her out, and bobbed her head up and down.

*　　　*　　　*

A cumbersome silence filled the interior of the Audi. No one cared or dared to say anything.

Logan at last steered the car into the shared driveway. "Night," he muttered while Katie and Hawksley extracted themselves from the back.

"Night," an unenthused Hawksley replied, and made for the back door.

"Good night, Nancy, Logan," Katie said through the open driver's window. "Terrific evening." Her eyebrows knitted together. "Well, most of it. Anyway, new day, new year, so let's keep both in mind."

Logan offered up a fast nod. "Night, Katie."

"Yes, good night," Nancy added. "Enjoyed your company a lot. Take care." Logan powered up the window while Katie stepped aside for an eager Torchy, happy to be outside.

"You wanna talk some more about it?" Katie asked as she massaged Hawksley's shoulders.

Hawksley shook his head. "I'm going to take something for the headache and go to bed. Assuming I can manage it."

"Maybe you should talk a little more about what happened tonight," Katie advised. "Rather than lie awake stewing. Or taking it into your sleep."

Hawksley held her gaze. "I might have been able to fix this, with Kimball. Had my chance. Now I'll never know. What I do know is I'm on edge, like I was a while back. Every nerve in my body wants to scream."

He stared down at his shaking hands, and then up at Katie.

"This damn feud or whatever it is, stays alive because Logan thinks he can solve anything with a punch up." He moved to the edge of his bed and sat. His head fell to his chest.

"All I wanted was for this to be over. Now look. It'll never be. Maybe I should sell the house."

She sat beside him and held his hand.

"It's the middle of the night, Hawk, so nothing to be done about anything. Try to sleep. We can talk about it some more in the morning if you want."

He exhaled. "Yeah, I suppose. Thanks for being there for me."

*   *   *

The evening's stress messed with a good night's sleep. Hawksley's body stayed hyperactive; it twitched and thrashed around the bed. What sleep he succeeded in getting, had more to do with exhaustion than anything else.

He opened his eyes in the morning to find Katie's side of the bed empty. Faint noises and the smell of coffee from the kitchen drew him to her location. He glanced on the floor beside his bed; Torchy too had abandoned him. No Vesta, either. Katie, had somehow bribed the two to come with her to the kitchen.   "Well, good morning," the bright and cheery Katie said. "Welcome to the first full day of the new year. Feel like breakfast? I can make you some oatmeal, and put on some tea."

An achy Hawksley stepped closer and put his arms around her.

"Good morning. So glad you're here. I have to tell you something, warn you of something. My mental state isn't good.

Not good at all. I don't trust myself, and I don't think you should trust me either."

"Really hard on you, last night, wasn't it?"

"Yes," he whispered into her neck.

Over his second cup of tea she asked him if he still intended to sell the house. He raised a shoulder. "I don't know. It's a big deal what Logan did. Like it or not, it's on me as far as Kimball is concerned. As far as I can tell my only choices are to move or get a gun."

"You're not serious about the gun, are you?"

Hawksley threw up his hands. "I'm serious about surviving. If you look at Kimball's pattern, he takes his time to mete out punishment, and each time it gets worse. All I can do now is wait for the inevitable, thanks to my moronic brother. And I'm really pissed at him for what he did."

"Do you think maybe you're being too hard on him?"

"Katie, we're not talking about some tactless act here. He's put my life at greater risk."

Chapter 20

Nancy sat with Hawksley and Katie at his kitchen table. "Logan loves you, you know?"

Hawksley's hand trembled when he set down his mug. It caused a bit of the tea to slosh onto the table. Why couldn't she stay out of it? Both of the women, as a matter of fact. He had enough on his mind without going through this intervention about Logan.

He forced himself to keep his voice calm. "Maybe, but I'm the one who's bound to pay for his recklessness."

"He's sorry, Hawk. You two not talking to each other — what's the point? I get it, but two grown men, brothers, working hard to pretend the other isn't there. Is it worth it? Come on, Hawk; we all make mistakes. Haven't you?"

Hawksley fought hard to keep an edge out of his voice. "This comes down on me with Kimball. Me." His eyes moved from Nancy to Katie. "Why don't you two get it?"

Katie spoke. "We do, but he's your family. It should count for something."

Self-restraint, something Hawksley possessed in good supply under normal circumstances, almost failed him in the moment. Twice in the past few weeks he'd had meltdowns with Katie, both his own doing. Over nothing, and he and Katie were supposed to be in the first bloom of love. Similar blow-ups happened at work. He knew his team walked on eggs around him, yet he couldn't control his emotions. He had seen 'd seen the hurt on Katie's face, and confusion and annoyance in his staff.

Whenever he lost control, guilt and shame piggybacked in afterwards. He'd apologize, promise not to do it again, and beat up on himself. Here in his kitchen he again wanted to unload and demand they not preach to him.

Keep it together. Katie'll walk if you give in to your emotions.

Hawksley couldn't see the free-roaming neurotoxins wreaking havoc inside him. Couldn't see, yet felt the results. Logan's singular cowboy act set everything into motion again. Until then Hawksley almost felt like his old self. His medication, diet, attending group, yoga, all lulled him into a false sense of security. The disease now again controlled his mental state.

He let out a whoosh of air, and fought hard not to thump the table. Instead he said, "Let's review. Me, Hawksley Pardee, am solely on the receiving end of Brian Kimball's criminal vendetta. He's poisoned my dog, stalked me, tried to run me over and broke into my house. See a pattern here? We're not talking about somebody gossiping about me. And there, a few weeks ago, I maybe had a chance to square things. Who comes in and makes it worse? Logan. And when I call him on it, he tells me to go fuck myself."

"It's not quite what he said," Nancy replied.

"No, not word for word, but anyway, who cares?"

Katie spoke again. "He told Nancy he admits he made a mistake."

Hawksley flexed and un-flexed his fingers.

"Oh, he did, did he? How nice of him." A derisive snort followed. Hawksley shook his head and stared at the floor. "Told Nancy," he whispered.

He raised his eyes and met their gaze. "I'll say it again— this is not about simple bad judgment; this is about endangering my life."

"I didn't mean to…"

Hawksley's earlier resolve failed him. "No." He rose, not wanting to hear more. "Done with this conversation, with Logan, and his apologists."

"Hawk." an excited Katie almost shouted. "Stop it. Think of what you're saying."

He wheeled on her. "You want to defend Nancy," he shouted, "then you go with her." Her eyes narrowed. He saw the muscles in her jaw clench and unclench. "You kick me out, I'm gone for good."

He shook his head at the challenge. "Do what you gotta do."

The two women rose, glanced at each other, and without a word walked to the back door. He heard it shut with little noise.

Alone, a defiant yet frightened Hawksley, sat at the kitchen table and stared off into space. What had he done? What in God's name had he done? So sudden; everything happened in a flash. He couldn't stop it and now…

A deep sadness settled on him—a sadness connected to loss and the inability to be master of his fate, captain of his soul. He hadn't experienced the likes of this since his split-up with Darlene. No, what he went through then couldn't come close to what he felt now.

His eyes teared up.

Torchy approached and placed her head in his lap. He stroked her. Things had been going so well for him until New Year's. Now he'd spun out of control. He'd fallen out with his brother, disowned both his girlfriend and best friend, alienated his staff, and returned to his old Jekyll and Hyde personality. And to top it all, Kimball loomed larger.

Hawksley wilted in his chair, stuck out a hand and petted his dog. "You get to see firsthand, Torchy, how things unravel. At least for me."

The telephone rang. He failed to hear it, caught in the grip of his acute misery.

His chest tightened; what air he drew in arrived in short, shallow pulls. Along with his physical misery came a solid conviction nothing good would ever come his way again.

The first tear broke free and made its way down his cheek to his jawline. Others followed in quick succession. He made no effort to impede their progress. His jaw wet, he stared out the kitchen window and petted Torchy in a mechanical manner. *I am a godawful person.*

For the first time in his young life, Hawksley Pardee toyed with the idea of killing himself. It would all be over. No more misery, suffering. But how would he do it? Then too, what if he tried and failed?

The brief flirtation with self-annihilation couldn't compete with the powerful urge to live. He abandoned the idea when a poem from Miss Laughton's English class returned to him. Who wrote it? He squeezed his eyes shut as if to help him pull it out of his memory. Yes, Dorothy Parker; pretty sure it belonged to her.

> *Razors pain you;*
> *Rivers are damp;*
> *Acids stain you;*
> *And drugs cause cramp.*
> *Guns aren't lawful;*
> *Nooses give;*
> *Gas smells awful;*
> *You might as well live.*

Yeah, the whole thing would be messy. There had to be other solutions to his problems.

Long minutes passed before Hawksley moved. In spite of his slide into self-loathing, he recognized he had value. Enough with the negativity. He'd made mistakes, whoppers, but people make mistakes all the time; it's why pencils had erasers.

Hawksley adjusted himself in his chair. All right, time to size things up. He'd burned his bridges with Katie and Nancy. He'd carry the shame and loss for a long time; nothing more to be done, but suck it up and move on.

He repeated the phrase to himself. Suck it up and move on. Bumper sticker. Maybe, his inner voice replied, but how—how would he move on? Where would he start?

His eyes moved upward, as if the answers might trickle down to him. The muscles in his forehead relaxed. It came to him—Meissner. He'd get counseling from her. His EAP would cover it. All right, he'd call for an appointment. And he'd return to the basics—diet, exercise and meditation.

*   *   *

Over the next few weeks Hawksley regained much of his emotional equilibrium. He credited Dr. Meissner for his recovery. She strengthened him through better coping skills, and challenged much of his negative self-talk. Keep things in perspective long before you get to blow-ups, she advised.

She also encouraged him to return to his doctor and review his medications. "What about approaching your friends and your co-workers?" she asked in one of their sessions. "See if you can maybe make amends?"

"I can at work, but it's too late with my girlfriend and my neighbor."

"May I ask why?"

"It is, is all. I know you think it's wrong, but I can't do anything about it."

The middle-aged therapist shifted in her chair, and in her soft, soothing voice said, "It's not for me to judge. You have power over your life. Only *you*, and *you alone* get to choose. In time it may change your position, and find other courses of action more appealing."

*   *   *

Hawksley took a small measure of pride at his recovery. He brought his team together for another of his public mea culpa.

"I'm sorry," he said. "I know I've said this before, and gone back to being an asshole. I only have myself to blame. Yes, it has to do with my disease. For what it's worth, I'm getting help and doing other things. I ask for your forgiveness, and hope I can earn your respect back."

Ellen Maythorpe later heard about the speech.

"They do care about you, Hawk," she said. "Lot of people do." She lowered her voice and craned her neck toward him. "We're friends, right?"

"Yep. For sure."

"And you told me about what happened at your place."

"I did."

"So can I ask you a question?"

"Shoot."

"Thing I don't get is you take the risk and tell your team you're an asshole, but you don't do it with your girlfriend and your neighbor. Why not?"

Hawksley shrugged. "My therapist asked me the same thing. I don't know, and I do. I can't explain it, but it's different. Not so it matters, but they wouldn't talk to me anyway."

"How do you know?"

"Water under the bridge, Ellen. The one I burned."

She peered into his face. "Men. You and your stupid egos. But it's still eating away at you. I can tell."

"Yeah, how?"

"I got your number, that's how. You look better than you did before. Not great, but better. Getting enough sleep?"

"Improving. Slowly."

"There's your answer." She tapped his arm with the back of her hand. "Take better care of yourself. Gotta go."

He watched her walk away. She did have his number. A good night's sleep might be five hours, not the eight he needed. The rest he'd use up thinking, wondering, worrying about Katie.

Several times he picked up the phone and punched in most of the seven digits to her phone. Panic seized him before he got to the sixth. He hung up.

At home the anxiety of running into his brother or Nancy caused him to check and re-check before he stepped out into the shared driveway. He'd press the fob for the garage door opener, hurry into his car, and back out.

He hadn't run into either Nancy or Logan—so far. The day would come. What would he say; what would he do?

Once, Hawksley happened by the kitchen window and saw a yellow Beetle outside Nancy's house. In panic mode, he jumped back, terrified the owner might see him. His heart raced, his hands shook. Calm down, he told himself; this is what Dr. Meissner told you about perspective. Calm down, think things through. Katie's now Nancy's friend, so why wouldn't she visit? It's about those two, not you.

He did calm himself, yet played the scene over and over in his mind for the next hour.

*   *   *

A light frosting covered Hawksley's car window when he finished his usual shift. One of the last out of the plant, Hawksley cleared his window and hurried back into the car. Lights on, he headed home. No longer on his usual high alert, Hawksley failed to take in the big-nosed, clunky Chrysler opposite his driveway.

He stopped next to his mailbox and got out. The sound of a car door slamming caused him to turn and look toward the street. A man in a black-on-black football jacket raced across the street. He held something in his right hand.

"Hey, buddy, c'mere. Wanna talk to you." Before Hawksley had time to puzzle out the stranger's intent, the man raised his arm and fired his pistol.

Hawksley heard a loud, firecracker-like sound. Propelled by its kinetic energy, the bullet tore through his upper arm and exited.

Struck dumb in both astonishment and surprise, Hawksley stared at his arm. His brain hadn't yet comprehended what happened.

The stranger raced back to his car. Hawksley's eyes saw but didn't register someone else inside. Pain made itself know;

blood poured out of his arm. Hawksley heard tires squeal, and saw the car tear away. He lurched toward the street, lost his balance, and fell. A passing motorist rushed out of his car and to help.

Sirens blaring, the ambulance rushed a shocked Hawksley to Floyd Memorial.

"You'll be all right, sir," the female EMT said. "It looks like the bullet went through. Good thing. Much better than it staying in you."

She frowned down at him. "Wait a minute. I know you. Yes, you're the man who got hit by a car some time back."

Shocked and frightened, a pale Hawksley, an oxygen mask covering much of his face, could only stare at the ceiling.

"GST," he heard someone shout while EMT responders wheeled him through the emergency doors. "Penetrating trauma."

Hospital staff rushed to the stretcher, and transferred Hawksley to a gurney. "Triage," a male voice said. Moments later hands removed Hawksley's coat, sweater and the oxygen mask. A calming male voice said, "Everything's going to be all right, sir."

They elevated Hawksley's arm and inserted an intravenous line into him. Next, a trauma nurse covered him with a pre-warmed blanket, while a different one assessed his injury and asked questions. She left and returned with an ER doctor.

"Hi, I'm Doctor Saffrey," he said while he inspected the wound. "We've met before. I've got your chart. "

"Yeah, the last time I came in somebody tried to run me over."

The Resident asked more questions—how did Hawksley feel, could he move his arm, did he experience nausea?

"We'll send you up to x-ray," Saffrey said. He tried for a joke. "You keep coming in here; maybe it's a sign you have to leave the state, or get the guy who's trying to kill you."

Hawksley replied with a dramatic close of his eyes.

"All right," the Resident said. "You're on tomorrow morning's surgery list. There'll be some soreness for quite a while afterwards, but other than scar tissue, you won't even notice."

"Before you go," Hawksley said, "I've got nobody to look after my pets. Can someone call my friend?"

"Sure. I'll send a nurse in here. You can give her the information."

When the nurse arrived, Hawksley asked her to phone Maythorpe.

"Can you do it fast, please? She has a key to my place. My dog and cat have been alone for a long time."

"What's the number?"

*   *   *

By noon the next day Hawksley lay in the hospital ward recovering from the surgery. They'd keep him for a couple of days, they told him. "For observation."

He watched hospital staff walk past, everyone in a hurry. *And here I am again because of Kimball.*

It struck him how calm he took the incident, given its severity. He'd expected his inner dogs of hell, the neurotoxins, to kick in, yet they hadn't. What could account for it? He couldn't offer an acceptable answer, so credited his response to Dr. Meissner.

Eyewitness News came on in the patient lounge. A coiffed blonde female news reader led with his story. Doing her best to look horrified, she read the teleprompter.   "This sleepy town in southern Indiana woke up to find one of its citizens gunned down under cover of darkness."

Hawksley gaped at the screen. Gunned down? Could they be any more dramatic? Who came up with this crap? No wonder he didn't watch local news.

An on-the-scene male reporter faced the camera and brought viewers up-to-date on last night's incident. Film footage showed the street, filled with police cars, a crime scene investigation unit, and neighbors aplenty gawking at the drama.

The reporter speculated the shooting might be related to organized crime. Hawksley silently spoke to him. *Crime all right, but I'm not sure how organized.*

The reporter spoke to several of the residents on the street, two Hawksley didn't recognize. "It's a small community," one of them, a woman, said. "This is the kind of thing you hear about in Los Angeles, Chicago, but not here.

New Albany is a small, great town. I can't believe this has happened, here, on our street."

                    *   *   *

    Maythorpe and two plainclothes detectives arrived at the same time.

    She deferred to them. "I'll go get a coffee, Hawk, and come back later. Want anything?"

    "No thanks."

    The detectives peppered him with questions. Could he speculate why this happened? Of course: his neighbor, Brian Kimball, was behind this. Who else? They should check their records about the hit-and-run?

    They wrote his words down in their notebooks. Did he have any proof?

    No, he said, but look at the evidence. It all leads back to the man.

    They promised to interview Kimball. Hawksley knew nothing would come of it. They left.

    Maythorpe returned and glanced at the curtains around him before she spoke. "How're you feeling, Hawk?"

    "All right, I guess. They'll release me tomorrow. Can you get me some clean clothes?"

    "Sure, and I'll come and pick you up. Whaddaya need?"

    "Anything. I don't care, and thanks for all you've done."

"Welcome. You hear from your family?"

He shook his head. "Not talking to my brother. Not sure if my sister knows, and my mother's in Arizona for the winter. One of my sibs will probably call her, but who knows?"

Maythorpe let her eyes wander around the room before they settled on his bandaged arm. "You're on TV. Man-oh-man, Hawk, this is bad. What are you going to do?"

"No idea, but I better do something."

"No kidding. It's not paranoia when somebody tries to kill you."

*   *   *

He returned home. An insanely happy Torchy bounced, twirled, and tried to jump on him.

Vesta rubbed herself against his leg. He gave them both treats. Next he called HR to request a few extra days off. "To rest my arm," he told Karen, Gordon Shipley's assistant.

"No problem, Mr. Pardee. Mr. Shipley was expecting you anyway. We're all really sorry to hear about what happened. How horrible. We're pulling for you."

He next addressed the blinking light on his voice mail. Sixteen messages. Time to answer them.

A part of him felt a small bit of dread, mixed with hope, he might find a message from Nancy, Logan or Katie. But if he did, what would he do, how would he respond? He needn't have concerned himself: most of the messages came from co-workers; some from concerned neighbors, and two from his family. He erased all but his mother and sister's messages. They knew.

He answered his mother's call first. A wash of relief shot through him when her answering machine kicked in. She'd been checking out flights to Indianapolis. He'd have to head her off. She'd mean well, but he wasn't in the mood for any kind of overreaction.

He left a message and assured her he'd returned home, and had everything under control.

"I don't know what happened here, Mom, probably mistaken identity. It's still a good neighborhood, so don't worry. Love you, Hawk. Talk to you soon"

He hung up, expelled his breath and said, "Onto the next one."

Maddie picked up on the second ring. He identified himself.

"Hawk!" she said when he identified himself. "We only heard about it yesterday. Sorry I didn't come. I couldn't get away so fast."

"S'ok, sis. Don't worry about it."

"I do, and you can't stop me. We're all worried about you, even Logan."

Logan. The mere mention of his brother's name caused a shot of anger in Hawksley. He remained silent, sure she'd wait him out. One steamboat, two steamboat, three...

At six she spoke again. "He's your brother, Logan."

He felt a tension rise in him. He didn't want to get into a fight with Maddie about this.

"Maddie, not in the mood for this."

Once more the line fell silent. Once more she charged in. "So it wasn't the best thing to do, but it's Logan; it's the way he is."

"And I'm the way I am. He put me in greater harm's way, even when he knew what was at stake. The least he could have done was apologize."

"But he's family."

"People keep saying that. Because of him, I'll either have to move or buy a gun. I'm living next door to a dangerous psychopath."

She tried again. "You don't know for sure this wouldn't have happened if Logan didn't do what he did."

"No, and neither do you. I'm going on probability. My psycho neighbor keeps raising the stakes."

She started to say something, but he cut her off.

"Getting worked up, Maddie, so let's get off this. I can't afford to bring on any unnecessary stress. Gonna go now. Say hi to Ken and those great kids. I left Mom a message. Bye for now."

Mid-day Sunday found Hawksley in *Has Beans* trying to read the *New York Times*. His mind still full of images of guns, he found it hard to concentrate on the paper.

Last night he'd spent hours on the internet reading about hand guns. He accepted it might be the only way to protect himself against Kimball. Still, so many choices, both domestic and foreign. God help any invader: he knew the U.S. owned the singular distinction of being the most heavily armed country in the world. One in three Americans owned a firearm. He'd soon be a statistical one of those three, but he'd be damned if he joined the ranks of those dangerous crackpots of the NRA.

An exhaustive two hours later, Hawksley narrowed his selection to a *Heckler and Koch*.

He next filled-out an online gun application with the Indiana State Police. As soon as he cleared, he'd go over to Louisville and make his purchase. Something else: he'd better check out gun-training courses in the area. Those too were easy enough to find; he wrote down costs, times and places.

Here in the café, he set down the paper and took a last spoonful of his crisp, and reached for his cup of tea. He failed to notice the two new arrivals who stopped next to his lounge chair, neither speaking.

Some unnatural sense at last awakened Hawksley to their presence. His head shot up to find Bailey Maines and her mother smiling down at him.

He recovered, tossed the newspaper on the table in front of him and rose.

"Mrs. Maines, Bailey. Sorry, didn't see or hear you there."

His mind worked through the possible protocols of a sticky situation: what do you tell the family of a loved one you rejected? Should you smile, and how much? Unsure, Hawksley offered up a tight-lips-over-teeth smile, and held out an arm to the settee opposite the coffee table. "Please, join me."

Awkward, awkward, he told himself, and wished they would go. Anywhere.

"Hello, Hawk," Mrs. Maines said and leaned forward to brush his cheek with a kiss. Bailey followed suit.

The elder woman and took a comfortable chair; Bailey another. She wore jeans tucked into boots, and a gray long jacket with a red scarf. Her mother favored a caramel cashmere wrap coat with a red bucket hat.

A nervous Hawksley waited. "Can I get you something to drink?" he asked.

Both declined. Mrs. Maines pointed outside.

"Bailey was sure the Honda belonged to you. We thought we'd come in and visit. Do you mind?"

Visit? On what planet would two women, mother and sister of the woman he threw out of his house, want to visit? So yes, he minded; he minded a lot. He'd never doubted Katie told them about his meltdown. Why wouldn't she?

His mind flashed back to the infamous day. Yes, Katie and Nancy refused to see his position, but no matter, his response could still be described as shameful. And yet here in front of him, two women he liked, would, one way or another, touch on the subject he so wanted to forget.

He waited for them to start.

Mrs. Maines opened up the conversation. "It's none of our business. We love Katie, of course, and we're fond of you. We were horrified to read in the paper what happened. And today, as I said, Bailey saw your car."

She paused and pointed to his arm. "How is it?"

"Getting better, thank you, Mrs. Maine."

A fast, weak smile and the woman continued. "She misses you terribly, and she's lost weight."

Bailey did her best to add some levity to the comment. "And you know Katie. She can't afford to lose weight."

Hawksley fought the urge to give in to his first instinct, to say, *you're right, it is none of your business*, but remembered Dr. Meissner.

"I miss her too, but there's nothing I can do about what happened. Whether either of you believes this or not, I never set out to hurt her. Sometimes people get caught in the moment and find themselves somewhere they didn't intend to be."

His gaze dipped and returned to the two. "I know it all sounds vague and touchy-feely, but there it is. She has her pride, and I have mine."

"So pride's the only thing standing in the way of you getting back together?" Mrs. Maines said. "Pride for both of you?"

Hawksley rubbed his hand over.

"I can't speak for Katie, but I have a right to this pride. My idiot brother put me in grave danger. It might have ended there, but when I called him on it he told me to go fuck myself. Pardon my French."

"I've heard worse," Mrs. Maines said.

"Me too," Bailey added. "Much worse."

Hawksley drew in a breath of air.

"But it isn't only what he said, it's Katie and Nancy dismissing my feelings about it—oh, it's nothing. I shouldn't feel the way I feel about it. I did, and do. Look, I don't want to get into all this anymore. I keep having to do it, keep explaining my position."

He stopped, and in almost a whisper added, "On top of it all, I have toxins in my body from Lyme disease. They screw me up bad, screw up my thoughts. It's not an excuse, but it played a big part."

Bailey moved forward on the small sofa. Her voice slow, calm, and measured, she said, "I think it took a lot of courage for you to share this. I hope we didn't stress you out."

Hawksley screwed up his face.

"Here's me who said he doesn't want to talk about it anymore, and what am I doing? I won't lie and say this has been an easy conversation. When I think back what's happened with Katie and my friend, Nancy, a whole lot of self-incriminating feelings rush in. If I could turn back the clock…" He threw his hands in the air.

Katie's mother rose, Hawksley and Bailey with her.

"We better go now, Hawk," Mrs. Maines said, "but remember, our door is always open to you."

"Thank you. It's good to see you, and I mean it. Take care of yourselves."

"You as well," the elder Maines woman said. She held out her hand, took his and squeezed.

Hawksley released it.

Bailey moved forward and into him. She pulled him to her and whispered into his ear, "We'll pray for you."

The sentiment touched him and brought a lump to his throat. Bailey strengthened. Hawksley heard his voice crack.

"Bye, Mrs. Maines, Bailey."

They spun away and left. He watched them; an overwhelming sense of isolation came over him.

Hawksley couldn't tell whether his neighbors viewed him as something of a local hero, a freak, or both. Cars he recognized would slow; windows would roll down, and the occupants would gape at his house. No one approached or said anything.

Nancy still kept her distance.

His co-workers didn't suffer the same restraint as his neighbors. They asked lots of questions and offered a great number of opinions.

He asked to speak to Shipley. The HR manager pointed to Hawksley's sling. "How's the arm?"

"Fine, I guess. Still aches, but getting better. The specialist said I'd probably have some nerve damage, and I need physiotherapy. Could have been worse, much worse."

Shipley nodded. "The understatement of the year." He followed the statement with a nod. "So, what can I do for you?"

"My life's in danger, Mr. Shipley, because of a psycho neighbor. I'm now going to carry a gun. I wanted to let you know."

Shipley stroked his chin.

All right—as long as you keep it in your locker. Don't flash it around coming or leaving our property. Let's hope and pray you never have to use it anywhere."

Friday after shift Hawksley drove down Delaney and spotted Katie's yellow Beetle in front of Nancy's house. At once he felt the adrenaline rush. His heart beat faster. His muscles tightened.

Without delay he made himself think of Dr. Meissner's advice. *Emotional response, is all. My body's going into fight-or-flight reaction. I have to expect this, especially since Nancy's next door. Amazing. I'm more worried about running into them than meeting a possible killer.*

Eyes straight ahead, Hawksley pulled into the driveway and pushed the fob button for the garage door. He turned off the engine and checked his rear view mirror for any sign of trouble, or worse, a possible bump into Katie or Nancy.

Satisfied he wouldn't encounter anyone in the driveway, Hawksley left the garage and opened the back door to let Torchy out. Deep breaths in, out, he ordered himself, while he waited for her to finish her business.

Inside his home, Hawksley filled Torchy and Vesta's bowls, washed his hands, and prepared his dinner. He cut up vegetables and forced himself to stay away from the window. None of his business who visited Nancy, he reminded himself, or whether he knew them or not. Still, it took all of his resolve not to gawk at Nancy's house. *Think of something else, anything.*

What came to mind? All right, what about the cops: would they ever find the guy who shot him? Or connect him to

Kimball? He doubted it. They said they'd bring Kimball in for questioning; if they did, Hawksley would never know.

He hadn't heard anything more about the shooting. And if they ever found the shooter, Hawksley couldn't identify him. It all happened too fast. A guy rushed up under cover of darkness, shot him, and took off. Not much for the cops to go on. In fact, next to nothing.

From what Hawksley heard, the police canvassed the whole street. According to Lofton, no one came forward as a credible witness. A few people vaguely remembered seeing a big Chrysler, brownish-red maybe, but nothing else.

"Nothing suspicious," Lofton added. "You know how it is here, teenage boyfriends park on the street or in driveways, waiting for their dates."

*   *   *

Hawksley brought his dinner to the kitchen table. Of late he'd disciplined himself not to eat his meals in front of the TV. He'd read an article about the dangers of eating while watching the boob tube. Far better to sit at the table, the article advised, and get into a Zen of eating, not wolfing down your food.

He picked up a fork in one hand and *A Brief History of Time* in the other, and opened the book to page 173. Yet his mind gave him no rest. The words meant nothing. Again and again his mind wandered back to Nancy and her guest, Katie. Odd, both Darlene and Katie hung out at Nancy's. He rebuked himself for the thought. Katie didn't hang out there. He'd seen her car a few times; not exactly hanging out.

A third of the way through his meal a distraction saved Hawksley from further self-torment. He heard a car pull into the driveway. A moment later someone knocked on his front door, a determined, authoritative kind of knock.

Torchy barked.

Hawksley rose, glanced out his front window to see a police vehicle. He opened the door.

"Hawksley Pardee?"

"Uh-huh."

"We've arrested the man who shot you. Could you come down tomorrow morning to the station for an identification?"

His eyebrows shot up at the news.

"Arrested? What. No. Yeah, sure, I'll come but like I told the detectives before, I didn't really see the guy. Everything happened in a blur. I don't know how good I'll be to you."

"Well, maybe if you come down anyway you might think of something you forgot or overlooked."

"Yeah, I suppose."

"Ask for Detective Gorson at the front desk. He'll walk you through this thing."

"Fine, then. Hope I can be of some help."

"You might surprise yourself. I'll let them know you'll be there."

He shut the door. They'd found the shooter. All manner of possibilities flashed through Hawksley's mind. Maybe, just maybe, the guy would finger Kimball. Wonderful! He'd be gone—gone for good, or for a long time.

Comforted by this new possibility, Hawksley allowed himself to believe he'd at last be free of the drug dealer.

Chapter 21

Hawksley arrived at the police station and asked for Gorson. The gap-toothed, stocky, mid-adulthood man with deep wrinkles on his cheeks and forehead, didn't fit Hawksley's image of a detective. Had he met Gorson elsewhere, he might have imagined him as some low-level bureaucrat lurking outside the back door of the City Hall.

Gorson approached, offered a generous smile and held out his hand. "Hello. I'm Detective Gorson. Thanks for coming in." He pumped Hawksley's hand twice and let go. "Follow me." He led the way through a room scattered with particle board desks. A few men looked up from their monitors or paper work, or called out to him.

Once in an interview room the detective invited Hawksley to sit at a rectangular table. "Sorry to hear what happened to you, Mr. Pardee."

Hawksley rewarded the comment with a nod. "Thanks. You can call me Hawksley if you like."

"Okay…" Gorson pulled up a chair next to Hawksley. "Interesting name you have."

"Yeah. Long story."

Gorson patted a thick mug book on the table. "All right, now, why you're here – we're holding the man we think shot you. I'm going to show you some pictures in one of our mug books. Take your time and look through it. See if you can identify him."

Hawksley shook his head. "Like I said before, it was dark, and everything happened in a flash. I'm pretty sure I won't be able to help you there."

"I understand, but try anyway?"

Hawksley obliged. He opened the book and looked through the pages. He came across a photograph of Kimball, but nothing else. His gaze left the mug book. "No, nobody. Sorry. Can I ask how you caught him?"

"We got lucky," Gorson said. He flipped through the pages, and stopped close to the middle. With his index finger he tapped a mug shot of a man Hawksley's age. A long face, sunken-in cheeks, wispy strands of blond hair, and tattoos up to his chin, stared with defiance at the camera. The downturned corners of his mouth suggested malevolence. The eyes, small, almost reptilian, caught Hawksley's attention.

"He's your guy," Gorson said. "Marion Foley. Goes by the nickname of Casper."

"Casper? Yeah. Fits. Kind of looks like he could use a lot more sun."

"Not where he's going. An officer pulled him and his pal over for running a stop sign. They both got nervous, so the officer ran their names through the computer. Both felons.

"Foley's out on parole. We asked for permission to search the car. He refused, but because he's on parole we didn't need a search warrant. And we found a gun. Ballistics matched it to the bullet we found from your driveway. Lucky it wasn't smashed-up. Your shooter's looking at going away forever. He's got this attempted murder rap on top of a three strikes law. So he's trying to get himself the best deal."

"And did he name my neighbor, Brian Kimball?"

Gorson did a slow shake of his head. "I can't comment beyond this. It's still an ongoing investigation."

Hawksley stayed another few minutes before the detective thanked him for coming in. They rose.

"You'll be asked to testify at the trial," Gorson said, and led Hawksley out into a hallway.

"Thought as much," Hawksley said. He shook Gorson's hand again and left. In his car, he imagined Foley ratting out Kimball. Why wouldn't he, to cut himself the best deal?

The idea of his drug dealing neighbor behind bars again excited Hawksley. What charge would they stick on him? Didn't it have something to do with planning a murder? It didn't much matter. If the cops linked Kimball to this, he'd go away for a long time.

Pleased at the mess Kimball would soon find himself in, Hawksley started the engine. He'd go to *Has Beans*, get a big mug of tea, maybe a dessert, work through the Saturday papers, and revel in what might happen to Kimball.

On second thought, maybe not the best idea. What if he got waylaid by Bailey and her mother again? He doubted his mental state could survive another bout of shame. Then again, he reminded himself, they didn't cause his shame. He'd managed to do it all by himself. No, he would go to *Has Beans*, his favorite place.

*   *   *

Two hours later Hawksley stepped out of the café and walked to his car. He passed the alleyway where he found Torchy.

The image of the puppy brought on a warmth of nostalgia, and in turn introduced a tumble of other memories. One concerned Nancy. He reminded himself he'd phoned *her* the night he took sick. Nancy, not his family, Maythorpe, or any of his other friends. Hadn't she deserved better than what he'd dished out after the New Year's Eve party?

Well, yeah, of course, he admitted, but in fairness he'd been stressed out after the incident. Stressed out and suffering the effects of a full Lyme attack episode.

He snorted. The Lyme attack: would it become his go-to defense whenever things didn't go his way? No, of course not, but the toxins damn well took over his body and mind. How could he reason things out when he found himself going buggy through no fault of his own?

The argument within him still raged while he pulled out of the parking lot *of Has Beans*. He barely recalled the trip to his house. By the time he pushed the garage door opener he vowed he'd apologize to Nancy. Maybe she'd refuse the apology, but at least he'd offer it.

He hadn't settled on how he'd approach her, but it did cause him to think of his brother. If he apologized to Nancy, shouldn't he bury the hatchet with Logan? He dismissed the idea as soon as it came to him. No. Let it be.

And Katie, he asked himself: what about her? He had no acceptable solution. He'd lost her. His own doing. He missed her; he doubted an hour passed when he didn't think about her. It didn't help.

A quote from something came to him; he struggled to remember who said it—some ancient Greek maybe? You cannot
step into the same river twice. *There you have it*, he consoled himself. *The waters move along, and so does life and everything with it.*

*   *   *

Torchy's bark stirred him from his nap in front of the TV. She ran to the back door. Hawksley stared after her and rose. Who'd be knocking? Should he arm himself first? He approached the door with caution. He flicked on the outside overhead light and peeked through the blinds. Katie. Katie in her wool coat, fat snowflakes settling on her head.

Hawksley's heart beat fast and loud. His hand trembling, he unlocked the door and held it open. Torchy charged past him and danced around their unexpected visitor, her tail offering broad, excited wags. Katie bent her knees to pet Torchy, but kept her full gaze on Hawksley. She presented him with a fleeting smile and said, "Hi, Hawk."

"Katie."

In an almost whisper, she said, "So, is it all right if I talk to you?"

He wet his dry lips. "Um, yeah," He opened the door wider. "Come on in. Please."

"You sure?"

"I am, yes, and it's snowing outside to boot."

She entered.

Afraid to say anything, Hawksley waited—for what he didn't know.

Katie pressed her lips together, exhaled and said, "I'm sorry, Hawk." Speaking in a quiet tone, her eyes blurred with tears she continued. "I feel bad about so many things. I feel bad we fought. I feel bad I dismissed your feelings about New Year's Eve. It wasn't my place." She pointed to his arm. "And mostly, I'm really sorry all this happened to you."

He opened his mouth to say something, but she cut him off.

"I did want to talk to you for so long, but couldn't build up the nerve to phone or knock. Tonight I made up my mind to just come. If you don't want to talk to me, I understand, but…"

She exhaled.

Something about her message, her vulnerability, drove away all his anxiety, and made him want to enfold her in his arms. How could he ever have been mad at her?

A different thought chased this one away: today of all days, when he made up his mind to apologize to Nancy, who should come knocking on his door? Serendipitous?

Whatever you do, he warned himself, do not let this opportunity slip through your fingers.

He gestured to the living room, and worked to keep his voice calm. "We can sit and talk better."

She considered the offer, nodded, and took off her boots.

"Get you something to drink?"

"No, but thanks."

He helped her with her coat.

Both sat on his couch, but at a respectable distance. Hawksley started. "Thanks for sharing, but since we're trading confidences…" He told her about his earlier commitment to reach out to Nancy. "Didn't have much of a plan on how I was going to do it. And here, on the same day, you knock."

He chewed his bottom lip. "First, I wish I'd found your courage, and did what you're doing. A day hasn't gone by when I haven't thought about you, us, and what a moron I've been. Second, I'm the one who owes you an apology. I can't excuse it all because of my health. I still had choices."

He saw her face relax while he explained himself. "And you're better now?" she asked when he finished.

"Other than the shame I've carried, yes. I've been going to a therapist, and really working harder at stress management. It's not always easy, but I think I'm moving in the right direction."

He licked his lips. "Is there any chance we can put this behind us? I know it will take time to feel better, but I want to try—if you'll let me."

She answered by reaching out her hand, taking his, and squeezing.

*   *   *

Good to his word, Hawksley swallowed his pride and knocked on Nancy's door Sunday evening. He'd waited until Logan's car pulled away, certain he'd be on his way back to work.

He braced himself for the worst; perhaps she'd reject him.

Nancy proved every bit as bighearted as Katie. She had lots of questions and more than enough comments. "We've been through too much together to let our friendship die, Hawk," she said when they at last embraced.

He left, satisfied she understood his position about his brother. "I don't want to be caught in the middle between you two," she told him. "Maybe you'll fix it; maybe you won't. Logan does owe you an apology, and knows it. Someday, when he gets over his own wounded pride, he may approach you. I hope you'll give him a chance."

*   *   *

News of Brian Kimball's arrest swept up and down Delaney long before Hawksley returned from his shift. Many neighbors pumped Phil Lofton, the 9-1-1 dispatcher, for information. His wife, Arlene, turned them all away. "He's a dispatcher, and he's sleeping. Even if he knew something, he's not allowed to say. Bye now."

Hawksley heard the news from Nancy.

"Yeah, I got home from shopping," she said, "and saw squad cars in his driveway and on the street. People milling about; you'd have thought we caught some fugitive from a prison break. Pretty exciting stuff, especially here, on Delaney."

Hawksley phoned Gorson. It took four tries before the detective returned his call. "Sorry, Mr. Pardee. Been caught up in a lot of things. You're calling about the arrest, I bet?"

"Yeah, what's going on?"

"What's going on is we've arrested your neighbor, Brian Kimball, for conspiracy to commit murder. He's been booked and will be held overnight. With his record, I doubt he'll get bail, but who knows? Stranger things happen all the time."

Hawksley furrowed his forehead. "You think there's a chance? You sound like a pessimist."

Gorson shrugged off the comment. "I've been a cop too long. Seen too many things. You know what they say—a pessimist is an optimist with experience."

The detective pulled him out of his daydream. "You'll be called as a witness to the case. This is going to hit the news soon. My advice if anyone calls you or knocks on your door, the less you say, the better."

Hawksley answered with a fast nod. "I'll take your advice. Thanks for the warning."

They spoke for another minute before Gorson hung up. Hawksley couldn't resist doing a jig. "It's over; it has finally come to an end." Torchy, excited by Hawksley's antics, pranced around him. Vesta stared at them with a casual lack of concern. Hawksley scooped her up. "C'mon, Vesta, get into the spirit. Kimball's about to go up the river, and I get to have my life back again."

*   *   *

As Gorson predicted, the media did cover the arrest. Local talk shows called Hawksley for comments. So too did the newspaper and television station. The local newspaper made it the front story, and posted mug shots of both Foley and Kimball. At work, Hawksley again became the focus of attention and comments. It'll die down, he told himself. Let it run its course.

The arrest ran its course faster than anyone imagined. Two days after being taken into custody, a freed Kimball stood alongside noted Kansas City criminal attorney, Carmi Reis. The canny lawyer had his publicist announce a news conference on the steps of the county jail.

Aware of cameras on him, Reis flashed the cufflinks on his white Marcella dress shirt, ran a palm over his mane of hair and said, "Welcome, ladies and gentlemen. I have an important announcement to make." He stiffened his arm and held it out to Kimball. "As you all know, my client, Brian Kimball, was arrested and charged with conspiracy to commit murder. In the simplest terms, he was railroaded by the overzealous New Albany Police Department. The circumstantial case against him rests on the disreputable word of one petty criminal, Marion Foley, someone Mr. Kimball never knew."

He paused as if to let the weight of his pronouncement sink in to his audience.

"This travesty was by every legal measure a wrongful arrest. My client's good name has been tarnished, a name he cannot win back easily. As such, we have no recourse but to proceed with a civil action against the New Albany Police Department, and the District Attorney's Office."

Again he stopped. "Now we will take questions…"

The questions came in a waterfall. Why was Kimball arrested in the first place? How did the lawyer get the charges dropped? Kimball had a criminal record: did it play a role in the laying of the charges?

A casual passer-by might have noted how much Reis basked in the glow of the attention. He took question after question, batted away any insinuation, and used every opportunity to bemoan the injustice done to his client.

For his part, Kimball, his hands clasped over his crotch, stood alongside Reis. He stared off at some far-away distance while his attorney Reis handled all questions directed at him. The look on Kimball's face suggested a man a thousand miles away.

The loquacious Reis failed or didn't bother to announce a significant detail—Marion Foley lay on an autopsy table in the coroner's basement. Blood red eyes, and a red welt around his neck gave evidence of strangulation.

Prison officials at the county jail found Foley in the morning. Detectives from the Sheriff's Department were called in to investigate. They questioned every correctional officer on shift, and every prisoner on the ward. No one saw or heard anything to help them in their investigation.

Kimball's release, followed by news of Foley's death, had tongues wagging even more. This couldn't be a coincidence, people said. It had to be Kimball who arranged the killing. What else would explain it?

One rumor followed another.

The guards had to be in on it. How much did they get to look the other way? The cops bungled the investigation; bungled it, or were in on the cover-up.

How come everyone's playing, see no evil, hear no evil?

The *Indiana Report's* editorial called for a formal state-sponsored investigation. The paper laid out its argument.

While Mr. Foley might not have been characterized as anyone's idea of a model citizen, let us remember he was only charged, but not convicted of a crime. Guilty or not, he deserved the full protection and care of the Floyd County Jail. As such, we hold The Sheriff's Office to a higher accountability. Jails must provide safe and secure settings, not only for their inmate populations, but for staff, those who have business within jails, and the population at large. To do less is morally irresponsible.

None of this helped Hawksley. It took all his willpower, two sessions with Dr. Meissner, and the assurance of both Katie and Nancy to calm him.

"I'm back to carrying my gun again," he told Katie over hot drinks. "And here, only a little while ago, I thought buying the gun was a stupid idea. Now I'm not so sure. I have this bad feeling this is not going to end well. For me."

Katie reached out a hand to stroke his arm. "Maybe you should consider putting this house up for sale."

"I know. Except thanks to the media, everyone knows where I live—next to a dangerous psycho. I'm not sure I'd get any takers." He squeezed his eyes shut, opened them and said, "The guy skates on everything. I'm sorry you got caught in all this. I bet you regret running into me at the market."

She shook her head. "I don't, so stop it. Nobody comes with a guarantee. We'll find some way to sort this out."

*   *   *

Kimball's release did result in one favorable thing: Hawksley made up with his brother.

He heard a knock on the back door. Torchy jumped, barked and rushed to the door. Hawksley followed, removed his pistol from a holster on the wall, and checked the blinds. Logan. He opened the door and faced his younger brother.

"Can I talk to you?" Logan said.

In response Hawksley jerked his head to the interior.

Logan stepped in. He pointed to the pistol. "Come to that?"

"It has, yeah. Finally got my arm out of the sling, but it's a constant reminder of what I'm up against." Hawksley locked the door, returned the weapon to its holster, and walked into the kitchen.

"Listen, Hawk, if anyone knows, you'd know I'm not good at apologies. I screwed up. I could have handled everything better. What happened to you has really bothered me. Nancy pushed me to come talk to you." He licked his lips. "I would have on my own, but you know me; it takes me longer."

Any antagonism Hawksley carried toward Logan melted away at the confession. Logan had it right about apologies. If Hawksley had to guess, he might be able to count on one or two fingers the times Logan apologized for anything. It wasn't his way. If he fought with you, he'd make peace later through small acts of kindness.

"Forget it. I could have handled things better too."

"So we're good?"

"Yeah, we're good."

The brothers stepped closer together, embraced each other with several thumps on backs, and pulled apart. Feeling somewhat awkward about the intimacy, Hawksley said, "Want some coffee?"

"Yeah, coffee's fine."

"All right then; coffee for you, tea for me."

They sat, talked, and settled back into their more familiar, relaxed style. Topics flitted from one thing to the next.

"The gun," Logan said. "Know how to use it?"

"I do. Took lessons and I go to the firing range."

"Huh."

Both fell silent for a moment.

"So, things looking serious for you and Nancy?" Logan set down his mug.

"Yeah. Guess it's obvious, my car's here every week. We're talking about me moving in."

"Wow. What about your company in Chicago? The distance, I mean."

"What about it? Not hard as long as I make all my meetings and assignments at Skipstone. All they care about is I show up on time and deliver."

"Well, good for you then—and Nancy. The world's a funny place. I would never have imagined you living next door to me. But then again I wouldn't have imagined having a murderer on the other side either."

"Anything new happening with him?"

"No. Maybe something, finally, will happen to get the asshole out of my life."

"What about Mr. Mantachie? Remember what he told us if we needed anything…?"

"Funny you mention him. It crossed my mind, but I'm not sure how I'd approach him. What would I say?"

Logan shook his head. "My offer's still good, you know."

"I know, but it's not as simple as laying a beating on him. He's upped the stakes by hiring someone to gun me down."

"It's bad. You gotta do something."

"Tell me about it. I'm still hoping the whole thing will go away."

"How?"

"Yeah, how? I read somewhere there are conflict evaders and conflict embracers. You, you're the embracers. You charge ahead and take things head on. Me, I'm a wimp. I don't like conflict, and deal with it by not dealing with it." He stopped and forked fingers through his hair. "I suppose I have to get more desperate to do something. If this was the Wild West, I'd go over and shoot him and be done with it."

"You think you would?"

"I don't know. Probably empty talk."

Logan pointed to the gun. "Your piece sends a message. Not too wimpy."

Hawksley made a face. "I'll say this—I've no intention of making it easy for him to take me out."

Chapter 22

Out on his front yard, a few days later, Hawksley set his multi-position ladder up against the front of the house, climbed it, and took down his Christmas lights. Back on the ground, while looping the string of lights between his elbow and hand, movement from his peripheral vision caught his attention. He turned his head to see Brian Kimball walk to the edge of his own property.

Without thinking, Hawksley dropped the lights and pulled up the bottom of his hoodie to reveal the pistol.

Kimball's eyes moved to the pistol. Legs straight, shoulders back, his hands by his side, his eyes found Hawksley's. "Society today, huh?" he called from his property. "Sad, law-abiding citizens have to look after their own protection."

His words came out low and measured, accompanied by a look of self-satisfaction.

A rush of adrenaline ran through Hawksley. *Don't respond, he told himself. He's a mental case. A dangerous one, and he's goading you. Leave.* He returned to his task and folded the ladder.

Kimball stared at him for another few seconds before he disappeared between the two houses. Seconds later he reappeared. "You have yourself a good day, there, neighbor," he said over his shoulder. "Good you're staying alert. Never know what life throws at you, right? Well, gotta get on with my day."

With a swagger he disappeared around the front of his house.

Shaken, Hawksley fought the urge to shout, *Doing what—making sure the kids on school property see your drug pushers hanging around?*

Hawksley returned to the house pumped full of rising blood sugar levels, excessive hormones, and aches.

He sat at his kitchen table. He remembered a poster he once saw of a kitten hanging in the air, its claws in a knot of rope, and a cutesy phrase underneath: *when you reach the end of your rope, hang on.* Easier said than done. He'd been hanging on for a long time—way, way too long. How much more could he take? At this young age, if his heart didn't give out, something else would take him. If only Kimball would disappear.

He let himself fantasize about killing the man.

A conversation with Logan came back to him. Victor Mantachie. Hawksley closed his eyes and fought to pull back Mantachie's exact words. At last he had them: "If I can be of assistance to any of you, I'm a phone call away."

He opened his eyes. Maybe he should talk to the man. But how—how would he start the conversation? He imagined some latter-day Godfather scene, where he, cap in hand, knelt in front of Mantachie. *Godfather, there's a drug dealer living next to me and making my life miserable. Can you take care of him?*

Then again, if he asked for a favor, would Mantachie oblige? Maybe "assistance" meant something entirely different than what he imagined. Wouldn't he be a fool and ask Kimball to be rubbed out, only to find Mantachie meant something else?

In the end Hawksley realized if any killing happened, he'd have to do it. He'd had his chance, right there in the front yard. How much better could it get? He'd go to prison, sure, but then maybe not. A good lawyer might make the case he acted as a result of fear—his dog poisoned, men running him over, Foley hired to kill him. Worst case, he might get off with a light sentence. Or better, probation.

Just a fantasy, he told himself. Leave it be and get better, focus on his health. Yes, good plan. Even so, he had trouble bringing himself back under control over the following hours. He ached in every muscle.

What had he done to deserve all this? He didn't ask for Kimball to move in next door, didn't ask to be bitten by a small bug, and didn't ask to have free-ranging bacteria to wreak havoc.

His throat tightened, and his eyes glistened with moisture. Wretched, Hawksley folded his arms on the table, put his head down and wept.

Torchy approached and slid her nose into his lap. He freed a hand and in an absentminded-manner ran his palm over her head.

*   *   *

"Ohmigod, Hawk," a dismayed Katie said when he opened the door late in the afternoon. She gently nudged him back into the kitchen and shut the door behind her. "What's happened? You're gray, and your eyes are squinting. Come on. Sit down and tell me. Something's happened? What?"

He offered a weak smile.

"So tell me, what's going on?"

While she prepared tea he told her about his encounter with Kimball. "Should have seen him, Katie. So, so...uh, arrogant prick."

"But you got upset because he's cocky?"

Hawksley stiffened at the judgment.

"No, I got upset because I really miss his company." He stopped and reminded himself not to over-react. His voice more modulated, he continued. "Sorry. Look, how my body responds is how my body responds. This is the guy who put a hit out on me, walked, and now delivers another veiled threat. So, yes, what you see in front of you is my body's reaction."

Katie took his hand. "I take it back. I guess I meant...never mind. You did well not to get into anything with him. You should be proud. Now, what can I do to make you feel better?"

Do, he wanted to say? She couldn't do anything about improving his well-being. The responsibility for feeling better lay with him, not her; his choice about how he reacted to Kimball.

Hawksley gave her his best warm smile. "Being here is enough, Katie. I've still got to work on a lot of things, what Dr. Meissner calls better communication skills. It takes time, is all."

"More than time. You're living next to a scary criminal, and I should keep it in mind. You can't go on like this. Do you think it's time to reconsider putting your house up for sale?"

"People keep asking me the same thing. I think it's time. I can't go on like this anymore."

Two days later a *For Sale* sign appeared on Hawksley's lawn. He harbored misgivings about advertising the sale: it meant Kimball won. And would the low life destroy the sign or vandalize the house for spite? *You can't worry about it*, Hawksley told himself. *Stay focused: what happens, happens.*

Selling the house caused a few tongues to wag on the street. The talk didn't last long.

"I'm going to miss you as a neighbor," Nancy said over tea. "You're going from the street, but not from my life. We'll still have lots of contact. You know, it's probably best, you leaving."

Hawksley twirled his mug. "I guess. Only hope the psycho doesn't follow me to my next house."

A few families and couples toured the house over the next few months. One couple made a bid well below his asking price. He dismissed the offer, yet worried he might not sell the house. Did his proximity to Kimball influence prospective buyers, the time of year when sales were slow, both, or something else? Whatever the case, he might as well leave the sign up until the contract expired. Maybe something good would happen to change his fortune. He'd remain positive.

Katie now spent most nights at his house; he cleared out a drawer in the bathroom for her toiletries. They grew more comfortable with each other, and ventured into new territory—talking about their future.

"So, what do you think is next for us?" she asked one night while they sat on the couch. "I mean, after all, I think we've long passed the adrenalin rush of first dates, and stopped being self-conscious being naked around each other. It must mean something."

"It means a lot. And I'd rather be home with you then out doing the guy thing."

She grinned. "You'd better say that, buster."

He raised his hand in a mock swearing-on-the-bible gesture. "Honest, and the longer I'm around you, the more I know we want the same things, and are perfect for each other."

*   *   *

Hawksley continued to see Dr. Meissner. It helped. In addition to his sessions, diet, and meditation, he kept Katie up on his mental and physical state when under stress. With good humor, they adapted a 60s song as his mantra—*I just dropped in to see what condition my condition was in.*

Something new pushed problems with his neighbor aside—the potential of a looming strike.

Labor negotiations between Houghton management and local 416 of BPPW had begun in earnest a month-and-a-half ago. Word had it the other plywood and veneer factories intended to use Houghton as a precedent. True or not, both management and the union executive were on edge. Both were sworn to secrecy during negotiations, but news of the lack of progress still managed to leak out.

"Getting worried about a possible strike," Hawksley said in bed with Katie.

"How come?"

"Uh, I don't want it, for starters. Nobody wants it, but the scuttlebutt is we might be out for a long time if one came. For sure I can't afford to sit out a long strike."

"Fill me in—is money the issue?"

He stared over her shoulder for a second.

"Money's almost always the issue. Management wants to go to a two-tier compensation system like the Detroit auto industry negotiated. You know what I'm talking about?"

"Uh-huh. New workers come in at lower pay; old workers keep their pay. It can get divisive."

Her mouth curved into a smile. "You didn't think I knew anything about labor issues? I do read and pay attention to the world around me, you know."

"Okay, you showed me. I apologize. Anyway, it's exactly what you said, but it also affects benefits. Both sides are playing hardball. If talks break down and the union votes to strike, good chance we're out for a long time. It's bad news for me."

"What's Plan B in your playbook?"

"Plan B? I don't have a Plan B. Why? What're you getting at?"

"Maybe this is the universe's way of telling you it's time to move on. What if you quit?"

"What? No. No can do. It's a good-paying job. I have a house to pay off, remember? And what would I do?"

"Uh, go to school full time at Indiana. There's a satellite campus here, as you well know. You still got some of your dad's inheritance, right?"

"Some. What I didn't spend on the house, but for sure not enough to get me through three years of school."

"And you have savings?"

"I do."

"If you applied your savings, and I could help you…"

"Wow. You do dream big. We're not exactly strangers, but you're taking an awfully big bite so early in the game."

She stroked his cheek. "I like to think of it as an investment with bigger dividends down the line. Think about it, Hawk. Follow your bliss. You said yourself there's not a whole lot of mental stimulation at Houghton. And we both know you put in killer hours."

He snickered. "'Follow my bliss?' Did you see that on some coffee mug or bumper sticker?"

"Can we have an intelligent conversation about this, or do you want to behave like a jackass?"

He laughed. "If those are my only two choices, then this conversation." He reached for her. "You know, you turn me on when you get all serious."

She slapped his hand away. "Come on. Focus, and think about what I said about following your bliss."

"All right, all right." He pretended to pout. "Party pooper. I will think about what you said, but I guess you've got more faith in me than I do."

"So it seems. Anyway, nothing tangible yet. We're only talking, right? But when you sell the house, let's talk some more."

*   *   *

Close to two months passed and the house still hadn't sold; worse, at work, the bargaining process with Houghton broke down.

On a Thursday morning, a crowded union hall waited to hear from the Executive Council. Stan Dykstra, the amicable president, who often played Santa Claus at the Christmas parties, cleared his throat, held up his hands and asked for quiet from the membership.

"We've got nowhere, folks. It's clear the other side has no intention of bargaining in good faith. This is about more than money or principle. The world's watching, and we have to show we have steel in our spines." He stopped as a gentle murmur flitted around the hall. Another breath of air, and he said, "With reluctance, your Executive Council recommends strike."

Tempers and voices high, speeches, accusations and counter-accusations flew around the union hall. Go back, some members yelled. It's too early to call a strike. Others shouted out different messages. Screw them; they're screwing us.

Hawksley listened and couldn't help thinking of the saying, *when all is said and done, there's a lot more said, than done.*

In the end a fired-up membership voted in favor of a strike. Done, the executive called for volunteers to put together a strike committee and staff a strike center. Lists would be made and handed out at who worked the picket lines at the plant.

A dispirited, Hawksley drove home. "Time to tighten the belt," he murmured. Two hundred meager bucks a week; the union paid its members two hundred dollars in strike pay. But for how long? Hawksley could only hope no new money problems arose while on strike.

Dr. Meissner's advice came back to him. *Day at a time, and remember about negative thinking: mind affects body, so stay strong to be strong. Things could be a lot worse. You could be out of work altogether.*

He pulled into the garage. Yes, things could be much worse, but knowing it didn't stop the stress. Kimball was bad enough, but now he had this added stress. He'd have to be careful, real careful; small things, any small things could easily be blown out of proportion because of stress. Already he felt an unwelcome tension in his body.

"Deep breaths. Take deep breaths."

Four deep, luxurious breaths later he stepped out of the car. He'd do his relaxation exercises when he got into the house. And Torchy and Vesta: wouldn't they be pleased to have him home all day? Yes, a good, happy thought there.

A different one came to him while he unlocked the door—Katie's suggestion about going to school. Time to give it another look—if he sold the house. In the meantime, maybe he should put more effort into sprucing up the interior? Anything to improve his chances for a sale. His luck could change: someone could come along and put in a serious offer.

Nancy knocked on his door an hour later. "Saw you pull in," she said when she stepped into the kitchen. "Funny to see you home, but sorry at the same time. I hope it's a short strike."

"Me too."

"So when are we picketing?"

"*We*?'"

"Yes. Katie, Logan, and me. We talked about it, and decided we could lend support."

Hawksley pulled her to him and embraced her. "You're the best friend. It's nice of you. All of you. I'm touched."

"Thanks."

He broke away. "All right, then. I'll let you know when I know the details. Happy for the company and support."

"How're you holding up?"

"Not bad, for the most part. Trying to keep my worry under control. Big stressor, this strike."

"I don't doubt it. Don't let the stress manage you."

"I won't," he promised, although he sensed corrosive worries already seeping in. Experience told him he'd have to work extra hard to keep them in check. He'd make a quick appointment with Dr. Meissner. She'd told him she'd waive her fees as long as the strike continued.

*   *   *

Hawksley signed up for the 6-9 A.M. picketing shift. He saw the two police cruisers in front of the main building when he drew closer.

Filled with the rightness of their cause, three dozen early picketers *of Local 416* and sympathizers from other unions, hovered around the main gate waving signs and shouting slogans. Others walked up and down the sidewalk facing the front office.

Tobias Simonsen, one of the shop stewards, approached as Hawksley drew close. "Welcome, Brother Pardee," the older man said and clapped a palm on Hawksley's shoulder. "We'll get you a sign, but…" His eyes moved to Hawksley's hip, and the holstered pistol. "You can't be seen with this. You've either got to cover it or leave it at home. The cops won't think too kindly if they see it."

Hawksley stared down at the pistol.

"Oh, right, right." He pulled his bomber jacket over the weapon.

At first Hawksley thought the picketing experience novel, even somewhat entertaining. It had a kind of carnival-like feel to it. Spirits ran high, and members buoyed each other with slogans and chants. Some volunteers handed out Styrofoam cups of coffee as well as donuts; two oil barrels gave off much-welcomed heat for those wanting to warm their hands.

Waving his sign, Hawksley strolled back and forth on the sidewalk with Maythorpe. Some of the strikers taunted cars and trucks entering Houghton property. A few of the more boisterous strikers slapped car and truck windows and shouted profanities.

Every so often Hawksley heard Simonsen's voice rise above the others.

"Easy, Brothers and Sisters. We can't hinder anyone's right to enter or leave private property. Let's stay within the confines of the law, and not jeopardize our cause."

*   *   *

The general exuberance of the strikers fell by the second week. The weather had a lot to do with it. Volunteers continued to hand out cups of coffee, but winds bit at noses, ears and fingertips. Men and women marched the sidewalks in mostly silence.

The weather changed over the next few days. A cold front moved out, replaced by a warm air mass. With it came rain. Disposable rain ponchos were passed out, but they didn't stop the bottom of pants getting wet, or shoes or boots.

"I'm all for unions, bro'," Logan said while he walked with Hawksley on the sodden sidewalk, "but goddamn this fucking weather ... " He sniffled. "It's supposed to be winter."

He caught himself and turned to the woman behind him. "Sorry, ma'am."

She gave him a close-mouthed smile. "Heard worse, and yeah, ditto on what you said."

Logan turned his head and lowered his voice. "The old man was a true blue union man, but this crap, I don't know…"

Hawksley nodded. "Good of you to come. You don't have to stay."

"I'm staying," Logan insisted. "My older brother got shot on my account, so the least I can do is walk with him."

"Gotta let it go, Logan. No one's blaming you."

"I am. All right, let's move on. How're things with you and Katie?"

"Great. I hear the same for you with Nancy."

Logan nodded. "Can't ask better. So back to you and Katie—you're happy?"

"No question. If this strike wasn't on, and I could sell the house, everything would be perfect." He paused. "Well, perfect except for Mr. Psycho."

"Haven't heard you mention him in a while," Logan said.

Hawksley wiped at his nose. "It does worry me a bit. Every time I let my guard down, he attacks."

Logan mock-punched Hawksley's arm. "Rough man. Don't let it get you sick."

"Trying not to. Thanks for the concern. I get the same spiel from Nancy and Katie."

"And there's a reason." Logan gestured with his hand. "You look stiff. You all right?"

"The disease. It is what it is, and I'm what I am. There's only so much I can do about it."

Chapter 23

If letters to the editors were anything to go by, the strike stirred up a fair bit of community passion. The town's largest newspaper printed letters for both sides of the issue. Some letter writers went so far as to suggest unions be outlawed. One even insisted the country *"send all those lefties back to Stalinist Russia. Us Americans would be better off without them."*

The letter found received particular attention on the picket line.

"Moron," Gabe Haswick, the senior forklift operator at the plant, said when he read it. "Grammar's a real challenge for this nitwit." He slowly shook his head. "There's a perfect argument for why public education doesn't work. If he had another brain, it'd still be lonely."

One letter came from a professor at Indiana University.

"Anyone paying attention will know there is a pervasive assault on the labor movement in this country," he wrote. *"Leading the charge against unions has been a well-funded lobby, claiming unions are unneeded in this modern economy. True or not, labor is on the run. In four decades union membership has tumbled from thirty-five percent to an all-time historic low of eleven. Please remember, if we lose unions, we lose a significant counterweight against predatory capitalism.*

I strongly encourage all to support The Brotherhood of Progressive Pulp and Paper Workers in any way possible."

Some of the town's citizenry did little to hide their anti-union antipathy. Several downtown businesses had their storefront windows defaced with "Fuck Unions." From time to time passing cars drove by the plant, their owners honking horns, powering down windows and giving picketers the finger.

On one occasion an aggressive female driver challenged the picket line, and came perilously close to inciting a riot. Doors locked, the worker made no effort to slow down in entering the parking lot.

Hawksley and two others barely had time to get out of the way. Enraged, they tore after her and pummeled her car with signs and fists when she parked.

Two on-duty cops rushed over and intervened. It took a while for things to simmer down. Men and women cheered when the cops at last handcuffed and led the woman away.

Others in the community supported and spoke out for the strike and its aims. Different motorists honked their horns and waved. Strangers stopped and brought coffee and sandwiches for the picketers.

Rumors flew among the membership: the company refused to negotiate further. Management intended to hire non-unionized scab laborers. Houghton had engaged a big New York union-busting consulting firm. The firm intended to drive fear and loathing into the workers, thus dividing and conquering. Houghton planned to dangle a cash payment out for anyone returning to work. The company's war chest had enough to wait out the strike until the contract expired. When it did, the union would be on its knees, and management would demand big concessions.

Whether any of the rumors had substance, no one knew. The membership did learn the Council and management agreed to an arbitration hearing. Unlike earlier negotiations, nothing leaked as to success or failure. The rank and file were left to guess and feed off rumors.

"Who starts these stupid rumors?" an annoyed Maythorpe asked while she walked alongside Hawksley.

Hawksley sniffled and shook his head. The weather once again changed. Temperatures dripped.

He tugged at his scarf. "More important, who spreads them? Then again, rumors are like a lifeline for us now. We've got nothing of real substance. I really want this thing to be over. I don't know if I can hold out a whole lot longer. I've had to dip into the remains of my Dad's inheritance. If something doesn't break soon, I'm in serious doo-doo." He stopped. "Sorry. Feeling sorry for myself. Like it's a picnic for you and everybody else here."

""S'okay. I understand. What's all this doing to, you know, your health?"

"Not helping. I've worked hard at not worrying…"

"Almost contradictory, isn't it—working at not worrying?"

"Yeah, I suppose. Anyway, it's an uphill battle. Katie's been a great support. I still go to my meetings, still see my psychologist."

Hawksley finished his shift and headed home. He allowed himself a fast, longing look at *Has Beans*. No, he couldn't go anymore. He'd trimmed back on all non-essentials. As much as he missed it, *Has Beans*, it became a non-essential.

The specter of going broke loomed larger every week. He played with ideas for earning income, like driving a truck, but that required training for a Class A license. He didn't have the money. Trucks, he'd probably enjoy driving. He'd checked out the cost of driver training for a Commercial Driver's License. Too expensive. What about real estate? He imagined his personality would lend itself to selling. He checked into the cost of getting a real estate license. Still pricy. How about general sales? He could learn, but he had no experience. Who'd hire him without some kind of track record?

*   *   *

As the strike wore on, Hawksley did his best to put on a brave face for Katie, to show he hadn't succumbed to worry. In every practical sense she now lived with him.

"This strike is really stressing you out, isn't it?" she said while she washed dishes. "Not so it wouldn't stress anyone."

He dried a plate, careful not to make eye contact. "No."

"Liar. You'll never make a good poker player. You give yourself away."

"Yeah? What do I do?"

"I'm not telling. If I do, you'll hide it—or try to."

"No, tell me. What am I doing to give myself away?"

"Easy. You've been itching and scratching a lot. And your eyes get squinty, and your pupils dilate, get wider."

"I know what dilate means."

She stared at him. "You wanted me to tell you, so I'm telling you. Don't get mad at me."

"I'm trying to stay up, positive, but it's hard."

"I know, I know," Katie said. "If things get to the desperation stage, there are things we can do. I could move in here and help with costs."

"I guess, but it's my problem, not yours."

Katie shook water off her hands and faced him. Her tone soft, she said, "So, we're big into the go-it-alone-thing, are we?"

"C'mon, Katie, be fair."

She shook her head. "Sorry, no, *you* be fair. The odds are against you managing all this on your own with your Lyme disease, and succeeding. We lend each other strength and love, you and me—or at least we're supposed to. I'd hope you'd do the same for me if the shoe was on the other foot."

"Yeah, but…"

She held up a hand. "No yeah-buts, Mister. If things get worse, I'm going to help."

He held her gaze for a moment, stepped forward and pulled her to him. "I love you, Katie Maines," he whispered.

In reply she squeezed him, kissed his cheek, and said, "Good. Get it together, and keep it together." She stepped away. "What say we go sit in the living room and watch TV?"

"You don't mind watching it on the antenna? Not as many stations since I stopped cable, but I do have a digital box."

"So? We had rabbit ears on our TV most of my growing up."

He chuckled. "The antenna's high tech compared to rabbit ears."

"I suppose." Her eyes moved to the kitchen table and settled on the pistol. She pointed. "Hawk, I don't want to complain, but this always makes me nervous. Can you at least keep it in the bedroom?"

"It's not much good to me in the bedroom during the day. It's there for a reason. I go in and out with it. Someone tried to murder me, remember?"

"Yes. Hard to forget. All right, can you at least put it in a drawer or something?"

"Yeah, no problem."

*   *   *

They sat side by side, staring at the television screen. Hawksley turned to her. "Ask you a question?"

"Ask away."

"Why do you stay with me?"

Katie turned her head, and considered him. "Where is that coming from?"

Hawksley waited for a moment. "Well, look at me—I'm an unemployed blue collar worker, sick with Lyme disease. My girlfriend is a professional, going places, the world at her feet…"

Her eyes misted. She reached out a hand and took his. "You are feeling more stressed, aren't you?" She gave him no chance to reply. "Tell me about it."

Embarrassed at being caught out, he reddened. She'd seen into his soul. "It's nothing," he said and kept his eyes downward.

"No, it's everything. Tell me."

"It's, it's… I don't deserve you. You can do better, much better than me. How did they say it in those old English novels? My prospects aren't good. Aren't good at all."

She reached out and raised his chin. "You don't think much of yourself, do you?"

"No, I just think you can do better."

Forehead puckered, she said, "Listen, dumbass, I stay because I want to and because I love you. You are *not* a wrong partner, but neither are you perfect. Same for me. This is *not* a wrong relationship. Your disease brings challenges, I'll admit, but I'm not in a relationship with a disease; I'm in a relationship with a man who has a disease. It's not stopping me from loving you. As long as we love, respect and care for each other, we'll come out fine. But I can't do this alone, without you. Your disease is not a life sentence—unless you make it one."

Feels like it."

"Feeling and being are two different things. I accept you as you are. If you love me, you'll return the compliment, including my wanting to be with you."

His shoulders caved. "I don't deserve you."

"Stop it! I need you to believe in yourself and us. You're doing all the right things as far as lifestyle goes, but talk to me, Dr. Meissner, whoever, about maintaining faith in yourself."

He nodded his agreement. "Feels like a little school kid being scolded by the teacher."

She smiled, pulled his hand forward, and kissed it. "Class is now out. Tell me what's going on inside you."

He rolled his eyes. "Stress," he whispered. "What else? I try, try hard, Katie, honest, but the worries creep in."

"So what are you feeling now?"

About what you'd expect from me. Not sure I'm handling life well. Tired. Depressed. I sleep in and, and don't always return phone calls. I got into a stupid argument with Ellen."

He gave a slow, disapproving shake of his head. "Ellen. You can't get any better a friend than Ellen, and look who picks a fight with her? I apologized, but still… And then there's the nut bar who barreled through the picket line; it's a wonder the cops didn't arrest me as well. I also have trouble remembering things. All of this on top of the usual body crap you hear me complain about."

"And your main strategy is the stiff upper lip and carrying on?"

"Yeah, I suppose."

"How's it working out for you?"

"You know the answer."

"So, if crazy is doing the same thing over and over again and expecting different results, you're a prime example. Your stiff upper lip thing isn't working."

He shook his head.

"We need to change your strategy."

"Right."

"And you need to be more up-front with Dr. Meissner, and go see your G.P. again."

The talk helped some. He prodded himself to share more freely to Dr. Meissner and with those in his inner circle. On Katie's suggestion, he even allowed himself an every-other-Saturday morning visit to *Has Beans*, grateful for the free newspapers on the racks.

Engrossed in an article about bats in the science section of the newspaper, he reached for his tea on the small table. In doing so, his eyes moved up to find a woman with an ash-blonde pixie haircut staring at him.

Of late, hostile pathogens in Hawksley's body made it difficult to pull up memories when he needed them. In this case, synapses made a connection, and recognition came. Darlene.

He gawked at her when she left the counter and walked toward him. In all the years he'd known her, she had never come into the café. Yet here she stood in front of him.

"Hi, Hawk."

He did his best to compose his face into something akin to a welcoming smile. "Darlene. Didn't recognize you with the haircut. In my defense, I've also been a little out-of-it lately." He paused and searched for something else to say. "What's the etiquette in meeting up with your ex?"

"Beats me," she said. "Haven't boned up on it, but I decided to come over and say hi. Anyway, how are you?"

"Good. I'm good, yeah. Self?"

"Also good." She gestured to the empty chair opposite the table. "Okay if I sit for a moment? Won't be long."

He nodded. "Yeah, sure, please."

She tugged at the bottom of her fur-trimmed parka, and sat, back straight, knees together, hands folded in her lap.

Hawksley moved about in his chair. *Now what do we talk about?* he asked himself as he matched his fixed smile with her own. *We haven't exactly got the highest comfort level.*

She spoke. "Haven't seen you around in a while?"

"Yeah, small-enough town, so you'd think we'd run into each other more."

"True. I heard about the strike."

He tossed a shoulder. "Well, what can you do? Shit happens."

"I've been thinking of you."

Please, don't, he silently said. *You thinking of me is the kiss of death.* The thought no sooner out, than he chided himself. *Come on. She gave you an unintended gift. Maybe she's changed.*

"Thanks. Not easy. These things never are. So what have you been up to?"

"All sorts of stuff. I'm working at a different place now, and getting married next year. A nice guy—like you."

The sentiment touched him, and he responded with a genuine smile. "Glad to hear it, and congrats."

"Thanks, and after the wedding we're moving to Boise. My fiancée's an engineer."

"An engineer. Wow."

"And you, Hawk. Got anybody?"

Something about this new Darlene, maybe her demeanor, caused Hawksley to feel less secretive, less determined to withhold any information.

"I'm with Katie Maines now. I'm sure you heard me mention her. It's going very well."

"I'm glad, Hawk, and believe it or not, I'm sorry for the pain I brought you. You deserved better, but you got a lot less. I don't know if you'll agree, but I don't think we had enough gas to go the distance."

He answered with a fast nod, and followed with, "You're right. It was all for the best, I guess. Let's chalk it up to being young. I wish you well in Boise or wherever you go. Thanks for coming over to talk to me. Took a lot of guts."

"Kind of you to say, and I hope the strike ends real soon, for you and everybody else at Houghton. I'll pray for you. Now, I better get my coffee and run. Bye, Hawk."

"Bye, Dar."

What surprised him more came next surprised him. "Can I give you a hug?"

"Yeah, sure." Before he managed to get up, she hovered over him, bent and pressed into him. He had no aversion to physical affection; in fact, liked hugs from Katie, but this felt awkward, almost put-upon.

Tough it out, he ordered himself. *This is meeting some need in her. She'll pull away soon enough.*

She did, unbent, gave him another smile, waved, and made for the counter. A surprised Hawksley stared after the woman in red parka and tight jeans. *Will wonders never cease*?

Chapter 24

The strike made news almost daily. In its third month, it showed no signs of letting up. While the quarreling parties remained at the arbitration table, neither shifted from its respective position. Union reps accused management of exacerbating tensions by hiring scab drivers to bring in goods and materials.

The Teamsters Union joined the picket lines.

Slumped shoulders, a dispirited Hawksley sat in Nancy's living room earlier in the week.

"I can only give it two more months, tops. If nothing's happened by then, I have to do something. What, though, I have no idea."

"Hold on a bit longer," Logan said. "I can always float you some of the money Dad left."

Hawksley shook his head. "I can't take your money. Dad left it for you, not me."

Exasperation in her voice, Nancy said, "Listen to him, Hawk. Your brother's offering to help. This is no time for you to be proud."

Hawksley turned to Katie for an answer. She gave a slow shake of her head. "Love you, babe, but I have to agree with them. Wait a bit more, please. Easier said than done, I know, but don't panic yet."

"Hey listen, bro'," Logan said. "Not to upset you more, but what's happening with your scumbag neighbor? Things settled down?"

Hawksley shrugged. "I haven't forgotten about him. It's why I have a gun. Don't trust him, but my mind's mostly been on other things. It crosses my mind if he's waiting for me to let my guard down, like the other times."

*   *   *

Logan took a morning off to walk the picket line with his brother on the picket line. A spring thaw had earlier arrived, cancelled out by a fast-moving Alberta Clipper from the Canadian Rockies. It put an end to temperate weather, and delivered packed snow, cold temps and high winds. Now, hands deep in pockets, heads down, shoulders hunched in a turtle-like position, the brothers marched along the sidewalk and through the snow with the other picketers. Every so often they'd stop by the oil drums to warm their hands.

"You know, bro'," Logan said, "if you gotta leave this job, in the next one, get a cushy one without a union."

Hawksley threw a quick look over his shoulder. "Not so loud. Let's remember where we are. As for your advice, got any good leads?"

"No." Logan stamped his feet. "Fuck, its cold. So cold I saw a gangsta pull up his pants."

Hawksley gave up a soft laugh. "Good one. Where'd you steal it?"

Logan shrugged. "Not sure. Probably read it somewhere. So, ready to march again on behalf of workers' rights?"

"Sarcasm aside, yes, let's go." Signs slung over their shoulders, the brothers walked along the narrow sidewalk.

Two Class-2 cargo vans caught everyone's attention. The van slowed and signaled to turn toward the main gate of the plant. A host of picketers in front of the driveway parted with reluctance, but not before they thumped the hood and sides of the cab with their fists. Cries of "Scab," "Fucking low life," "You're stealing our pay," "Where's your decency?" filled the air.

In the early stages of the strike, a heavy police presence made itself known. Now, windows up, heater on, a sole cop sat in his cruiser and talked on his cell phone. He ignored the commotion.

In spite of the picketers' objections, the driver inched onto the Houghton property and made for the main gate. Security guards let him pass.

Perhaps emboldened by their show of defiance, picketers bunched up in front of the driveway to provoke the second van.

Hawksley took in the confrontation. "Oh-oh, I better go help." He hurried as fast as he could along the slippery sidewalk, Logan behind him. They joined the others, and nudged their way to the front of the human barricade.

Inside the cab of the van, Hawksley saw two, dour, burly men. The passenger shot the picketers a middle finger. The driver rolled down his window. "Outta my way!"

"Fuck you, asshole!" someone shouted back. "This is a picket line, and you're a scab." He slammed his sign against the truck.

The challenge resulted in the driver putting the truck into neutral and revving the engine. Picketers slowly gave way, but not without taunts. "Can't find first gear?" someone shouted. "Want us to show you?" a different voice called out.

A hard snowball hurled through the air. It hit the van's windshield. Whether in response, the driver shifted into first and gunned the vehicle. It lurched forward. He slid into second gear and then jammed the brake pedal. The icy conditions caused the brakes to lock. The driver lost control of the vehicle. The van skidded sideways,

Men and women yelled, screamed, and rushed to get out of the way of five thousand pounds of metal veering toward them. All but five got clear.

Logan took the brunt of the hit. Standing next to Hawksley, he body-slammed his brother away, but couldn't save himself. His feet gave out under him. The van crushed his right leg below the knee and stopped. His scream pierced the air.

A horrified Hawksley climbed to his feet in the bitter, cold air, his mind unable to fully comprehend the agony and terror of his brother pinned under the van. People rushed over as fast as they could, and crowded around a moaning Logan.

Everyone stood stock still. Until the driver made to climb out of his cab.

"Him!" someone shouted. "He caused this."

In a second, compassion for Logan turned to anger against the driver. Infuriated, picketers turned into a sudden, vengeful mob. They hurried toward the driver and pulled him to the snow-covered ground. His partner tore out of the passenger side to lend him assistance. Boots and fists rained down on the driver while the second man fought off his own attackers.

Three non-union Houghton employees and security guards hurried out of the main gate and joined the fray. What had moments ago been a peaceful protest, became a melee.

At the increasing noise, the cop's head whipped around to see men brawl in front and to the side of the truck. He dropped his cell phone and radioed in a *Code 1, Hot Response Riot. Send back-up and EMTs.*

Hawksley bent a knee and stared into the ashen face of his brother. "We'll get this truck off you. Logan. Help's gonna come. Help's coming. I'd move the truck, but I don't know if I'll make things worse. Hold on, please." He gripped his brother's hand.

If Logan heard, he didn't respond. He stared up past Hawksley; his face a ghostly color. He took sharp, fast breaths.

Two ambulances arrived and pulled up behind a different police cruiser. More sirens blared. First responders rushed over, spotted Logan and hurried over.

The brawl ended as fast as it started with the arrival of more cops. The crowd now gave its full attention to Logan.

More people arrived—gawkers from the neighborhood.

A cameraman and news reporter from a local station jumped out of their van and rushed to the scene.

The police worked to return calm to the situation. "Back up, back up," a sergeant ordered onlookers while two paramedics attended to Logan.

"I'm his brother," Hawksley said.

"Fine. You stay, but don't get in anybody's way."

"Easy, easy, son," a male paramedic said to an ashen Logan. "We'll get you free, but we need to stabilize you first. I'm going to give you something." He turned and reached into his medical kit. A moment later he plunged a hypodermic needle into Logan's upper leg. He retracted the needle and looked up at the police sergeant. "Get the damn wheel off him. Then we've got to apply a C-A-T."

"Got it," the cop said and moved to the cab. "Anybody know how to drive this rig?" he shouted out.

"Yeah, me." The voice came from the roughed-up passenger of the van.

The cop pointed. "Get going."

The other man placed himself behind the wheel, and rolled down the window. With yells of "slow," "stop," "forward now," the van moved off Logan's leg.

Hawksley watched while a paramedic used scissors to cut the cloth away from Logan's leg. He examined the deformed leg and lifted his eyes to his partner. A fast nod. The two men applied a plastic C-A-T, Combat Application Tourniquet, above the knee. Less than a minute later, four EMTs managed to get Logan onto a gurney and into the back of an ambulance.

"I wanna come," Hawksley said. "I'm his brother."

"Get in," a paramedic said. "Time's a-wasting."

Hawksley sat next to his brother and held his hand. Like a mantra, he kept repeating, "It's going to be all right, Logan. It's going to be all right." Yet he himself didn't believe it.

They rushed Logan into the trauma unit of the closest hospital.

Hawksley sat in the waiting room on a fake leather couch. Stiff, his muscles ached; he couldn't make himself calm.

He'd better call his mother and sister, he told himself, but couldn't bring himself to do it yet. How would he explain this, what would he say? He imagined his delivery. *Logan was walking the picket line with me, at a place he didn't work. A truck ploughed into a bunch of us. I got away because of him. Because of me, he didn't.*

A heaviness settled on his chest. He let out a deep, exasperated sigh. "I'm the terrible person who brought this onto Logan," he whispered.

His mind raced, and gave him no rest. When it didn't occupy itself with self-blame, it played the hideous accident over and over again.

A male voice broke into his thoughts. "Excuse me. Are you a relative of Mr. Pardee?"

Hawksley raised his head to see a dark-skinned, balding man with oversized eye glasses in front of him.

He rose. "Yes. I'm his brother."

"I'm Dr. Syed, Mr. Pardee. Chief Surgeon here." The surgeon extended his hand. Hawksley took it.

"I've come to talk to you about your brother, Mr. Pardee."

Hawksley released the hand.

"Is he married, your brother?"

"No. Not yet. I have to call his, um, fiancé. I haven't be able to do anything yet."

"I see. And you are his next of kin?"

"One of them, yes."

Syed considered the answer for a moment. "It goes very bad for your brother, Mr. Pardee. He has both tibia and fibula — the two important bones in the leg — crushed. They cannot be mended. To preserve his life, we must amputate, and must do it now."

"And you've told him?"

"Yes. He did not at first agree, but we explained about sepsis, toxins in the blood, which will kill him. In order for him to survive, we must remove the leg. Waiting is life-threatening. He has consented."

At the news, Hawksley stared open-mouthed. "When can I see him?"

"Not now and he needs to be prepped for surgery. It may be some time before you can see him. Later, when he wakes up."

"All right, then. Thanks for coming out and telling me."

The surgeon nodded, spun around and left.

"Poor Logan," Hawksley whispered to the man's back. "Oh, God, poor, poor Logan."

*   *   *

Heels clicking furiously on the linoleum floor, Nancy marched down the hospital corridor to find Hawksley, elbows on his knees, his head and body bent.

"Hawk."

His head shot up at the sound of his name. He made to get up.

"No, stay put," Nancy said, folded her skirt under her and dropped beside him. "I heard it on the radio. Something told me either you or Logan were involved. I called here, and they told me Logan was a patient." She blinked several times. "What happened?"

Hawksley explained. Nancy heard the catch in his voice. "They're about to cut off his right leg. It's the only choice they have."

Dumbfounded, she nodded and whispered, "Oh God." Her eyes grew wet. She pointed to the surgery doors. "In there?"

"Yeah. It's going to be long hours before anyone can see him."

I cannot believe this," she said. "I saw you two leave this morning, and now...now..."

Silence filled the long seconds before she said, "You're not holding up well, are you? She gave him a closer inspection. "Is it the Lyme disease?"

"Uh-uh." He held back for a moment, and then spoke.

"The truck hit five of us. Logan caught the worst of it. The rest of us are going to be black-and-blue in various stages. Nothing more. Anyway, I don't want to turn this on me, so I'll say I'm fine and leave it there."

Nancy tilted her head and studied him.

"Oh, no you don't. I'm your friend, remember? Before Logan stepped into my life." She pointed to the surgery doors. "Logan'll be in there for some time. There's nothing anyone can do for him at the moment, except pray. I want to know about you, so tell me."

Hawksley studied her face for a moment, composed his answer, and said,

"Incredible, I keep playing it over and over in my head. What disturbs me more is I feel responsible for what happened to Logan. If he hadn't been there…if he hadn't been there, good chance I could have been under the truck."

Nancy reached out a hand. "You don't know for sure."

"Some part of me agrees; the rest doesn't."

Nancy leaned closer.

"You're not going to like what I have to say." She gave out an exasperated sigh. "It must be tough trying to be saint-like, always holding yourself to high, unachievable standards—the same standards you don't always hold others to. I cheated with your wife on you, you know, broke one of the

Ten Commandments. A moral failing, if ever there was one. Yet you forgave me. Here, through no fault of yours, a runaway truck crushes Logan's leg, and what you do—you blame yourself? No one else but you will see this as a moral failing? Stop being so hard on yourself, assuming moral responsibilities not yours."

She continued in a fast, whispered monologue, sibilants hovering in the air, full of passion. She finished by reminding him of past insightful conversations, and quoted Dr. Meissner back to him.

"No fair," Hawksley said, "repeating Meissner back to me."

She batted away his argument. "It *is* fair, especially since Logan's down, and you need to be up—up and strong. No more time for useless self-accusations. Logan deserves better, and so do you. "Capisce?"

"Capisce," a chastened Hawksley said.

"And you're better?"

"I'll get there again. Man, I'm glad I've got you and Katie to keep me on the straight and narrow."

Chapter 25

Hawksley and Nancy sat through four torturous hours waiting to hear the outcome of Logan's surgery. Throughout much of it Hawksley's legs bounced up and down in nervousness. Nancy gave him a wearied long, sigh.

"Make a suggestion?"

"Yeah, sure."

"You won't get all squirrely on me?"

"Nothing to get squirrely about."

She reached out a hand and took his. "I love you, hon, but those nervous legs of yours bobbing up and down all the time, is wearing on me. Be grateful you have both, and think of your brother. Now, why don't you go walk around, get some coffee. I'll be here. Maybe you should call your Mom and sister."

"Yeah, you're right. I should have done it long before anyway. I don't have much to tell them right now. They'll have lots of questions."

"Tell them what you know, and take it from there."

He rose. "Good idea. You want me to bring you back some coffee."

"Yes. No. Make it tea. I can imagine what the coffee tastes like this hour of the day."

*   *   *

Four-and-a-half-hours later, they saw an OR nurse wheel Logan out of surgery. They jumped to their feet and watched Logan and the nurse disappear through heavy swinging doors. Another two hours passed before a Recovery Room nurse approached them.

"He's doing as fine as he can be. You'll only have a short visit. No more than twenty minutes, please."

Nancy and Hawksley entered the Recovery Room. Ashen, unfocused, and groggy, Logan tried his best to communicate. His speech slurred, he had trouble keeping up with simple conversation.

Nancy's lips trembled at the sight of Logan. With slow deliberation she leaned over and kissed his brow. "Logan. Great to see you. We'll get you better. Do you need anything?"

"Water," he rasped.

"Coming," she said, her voice brittle. She reached for a carafe beside his bed, poured water into a glass, and inserted a flexible straw. He lifted his head and put the straw in his mouth.

A slack-faced Hawksley willed himself to say something, anything to his brother. The best he could manage was, "Hi, Logan. You comfortable? Can I get you anything?"

The words no sooner out than he felt himself redden and cursed himself. *Is he comfortable? No, moron; he's not comfortable. He's had his leg sawn off. Would you be comfortable? Can you be any dumber?*

He took a deep breath, stepped to the other side of Logan's bed. Never had he seen Logan so, so…frail. All the way through school and beyond, Logan oozed a measure of confidence Hawksley admired and envied. Now with a drip line running into him, this Logan no longer resembled the brother of Hawksley's youth.

He let his gaze drift to the outline under the blankets. One, not two legs. Logan now only had one good leg. Unthinkable, his brother, the mighty Logan, would now make his way through life with one good leg.

Long, quiet minutes passed, broken up by a nurse who entered and checked Logan's blood pressure.

*   *   *

A small army waited to see and hear about Logan the next morning during visiting hours.

Word of the previous night's incident spread. A young ambulance chaser tried to enter Logan's room. Hawksley stopped him.

The chinless lawyer with wire-rimmed glasses introduced himself as Ian Garret, and held out his card. "From what I can gather, Mr. Pardee," he said to Hawksley, "your brother has an excellent lawsuit here against those who perpetrated this outrage on him."

"Maybe so, but it won't bring back his leg, will it?"

The lawyer agreed.

"It won't, but let's make them pay where it hurts—their pocket books, and give your brother a solid source of income for life." He handed over the business card. "Are you sure I can't talk to him for a few minutes?"

"No, but I'll give him your card, and pass along your message."

"All right, then. Please consider talking to your brother about what I said. Our firm is well established. You can review summaries of settlements on our website."

"Thanks. I'll pass the information along."

"You should think about going home," Katie said. "I'll stay here."

"Thanks, but I'm all right. My Mom and sister will be here soon."

They arrived two hours later, husbands in tow. "My poor boys," Yvonne Hildebrandt said softly while the family stood around Logan's bed. "One with Lyme disease, and the other loses a leg."

Logan answered. "Yeah, you wonder what god we offended."

*   *   *

The incident at Houghton drew considerable attention. News outlets from as far away as Chicago and St. Louis arrived.

The Governor, up for re-election and behind in the polls, seized on an opportunity for free publicity. He called a news conference and announced he ordered the State Police to investigate and lay any and all necessary criminal charges.

"We cannot allow Big Labor to bring in professional thugs and run roughshod over the day-to-day workings of industry. Our state, our country will not allow it."

Both union and management accused each other of inciting the violence; conflicting accounts stymied investigators. In spite of a general popularity of camera phones, not a single picture or video of the noisy, riotous fight emerged. In the end only the truck driver found himself in the court docket, facing attempted vehicular homicide causing bodily harm, criminal negligence, and resisting arrest.

Funny, people later said; both sides whaling away at each other, and the cops could only find one guy to charge? Something didn't add up.

The strike produced one good thing—a contract. Within days, a combined union-management press conference announced they agreed to a tentative settlement. The Union Council quickly urged its members to vote in favor of the contract.

"It wasn't worth Logan losing a leg," Hawksley said one evening when he fed Vesta. Wasn't worth it, but at least we get to go back to work, and I, we, get to keep this house."

Katie dried her hands at the sink. "The house still hasn't sold. What's the plan now? Are we going to let the contract with the agent expire, remove the sign, or try another agent?"

"What do you think?"

Kate propped a hand on her hip.

"I vote we sell the house, and start out somewhere new. Let's get a new realtor. Spring's here now, and it's supposed to be a good time to sell."

Hawksley agreed. "You're right. I'll be happy to see the last of Kimball."

*   *   *

Logan sued both the truck company and Houghton. He found a St. Louis firm, and through them asked for 40 million dollars in damages.

"My lawyer says it's a waste of time to get the company to admit to any kind of fault," he said one night over drinks.

"You mean like an apology?" Hawksley asked.

"Exactly. No apology, but they will have to settle. Probably in the low twenties. Even after I pay the lawyers off, I'll still be in good shape financially."

Katie gestured to the absent leg. "You're taking all this very well."

Logan hadn't yet been fitted with a prosthetic. He still required considerable physiotherapy. He screwed up his face. "No point staring into the rearview mirror. Hawk'll tell you. I'm not the kind of guy who lives in the past."

"It's true," Hawksley added. He turned his gaze back to Logan, who pointed to the empty space once occupied by his leg. "Not a goddamn thing I can do to get my leg back. So getting pissed off does nothing for me. All's I can do is pay attention to what's in front of me." He stretched for his coffee. "You know what's really ironic?"

"What?" Katie asked.

"All the time I was in Iraq, there wasn't a day when I didn't wonder if an IED would find me. We all did. A couple of my buddies lost legs and other things." He waved a hand over his body. "I survive Iraq, come home and lose a leg because of some idiot behind a wheel."

"I'd give anything to wish it hadn't happened," Hawksley said.

"Makes two of us, but the idiot's going to jail, and I'll wind up with a lot of money because of him. So I'll get a titanium state-of-the art leg. They say they're almost as good as a real one."

Nancy interjected. "Nothing's as good as a real one."

"Fine, I'll concede, but at least I won't have to use crutches for the rest of my life." He mock-punched Hawksley's arm. "Brother or not, no more picket lines for me."

Hawksley glanced at the floor. "Wish I could be more like you. I do look in the rearview mirror. What happened to you is going to bother me for a long time." He slowly shook his head in dismay.

Logan let out a sigh of exasperation. "Final time. I...am...not...blaming...you."

"I know, I know." Hawksley said. "I'll drop the subject." He searched for something else to say. "I'm not really sure now to ask this, or if I should, but how's your pain level these days?"

"Manageable some days; not so much on others. You know how you hear about people having phantom pains after they lose a limb?"

"Uh-huh."

"It's true. There are times I almost swear my leg is still attached. Heard about this kind of thing in Afghanistan. Our guys would step on an IED the Ali Babas buried, and lose a leg. You'd talk to them later on Skype, and they'd tell about this thing called phantom limb symptom." He pointed to his stump. "I swear it's like nerves in what's left of my leg are trying to tell my brain the whole thing's still there."

He stopped and considered what he said. "Weird."

Chapter 26

Balmy weather at last replaced the remains of winter away. Snows melted; roads and sidewalks held small pools of icy water.

Katie and Hawksley spent the better part of the day visiting with Nancy and Logan. As Hawksley expected, Logan did exactly as he promised—put all matters related to the truck incident behind him.

"Done," he said, a hint of a sharp tone in his voice, when Hawksley steered the subject back to the incident. "Do me a favor, Hawk. Stop talking about it. Geez, you and Maddie; the two of you should open up some kind of warm fuzzies therapy group. I've only got one leg, and I'm gonna be a rich man. There's no more to say. No, wait, one more thing. Not ready-to-wear shorts for me this summer. I may have a state of the art new leg, but I'm too self-conscious to show it off yet."

Hawksley pulled into his driveway when the last of the rays skimmed the rooftops. Katie let both pets out while Hawksley put the car into the garage. He waited for both. Torchy returned, but not Vesta.

"Probably out making her rounds," he murmured to himself, and entered the house. He'd check on her in a few minutes.

Five minutes later he opened the back door.

"Vesta."

No cat, or soft tinkle of a little bell against the cat tag of her collar.

"C'mon, kitty, where are you? Vesta. Vesta. Vesta."

Still no answer. Where'd she get to? She always came when he called. Unwilling to wait any longer, he shut the door and re-entered his house.

He re-filled Torchy's water bowl. The sound of a car pulling into the driveway caught his attention. Had to be Katie. She said she'd be a little late. Sure enough, seconds later Katie unlocked the door and entered.

Hawksley approached and kissed her. "Vesta with you?"

"No. I didn't see her. Why? Did you lose her?"

"Sort of. It's not like her to not come when I call. She usually checks out her turf, looks to see if there's any birds she can pounce on, and then comes back. Remember the time she brought us a dead mouse as a gift?"

Katie chuckled. "I do. I'll go out and call her?"

After a few minutes, Katie returned and offered an empty-handed gesture. "Don't know. Look, let's eat, and if she's not back by then, let's go search for her."

*   *   *

Flashlights in hand, the couple searched the small backyard, and peered over adjacent fences. No sign of Vesta.

Both called out her name to no avail. Next, they patrolled the neighborhood.

"You think she's been hit by a car or something?" Hawksley asked when they made their way back to the house.

"It's a possibility," Katie said, "but I doubt it. We didn't see anything on the road. I doubt she'd have run away."

"Then what explains her disappearing? The longest she's ever been out is, what, maybe five, ten minutes."

A thought came to Hawksley, one he'd been reluctant to entertain. "You don't think…?"

Katie responded with a puzzled look, and then said. "Nooo. You're getting ahead of yourself. Probably some simple explanation, and she's waiting for us at the back door."

She wasn't.

Unable to relax, Hawksley opened the back door every few minutes.

"Something's happened to her," he insisted. "I don't know what, but I'm getting a bad vibe about this."

Katie held up a hand. "I get it you suspect Kimball, but what say we give it a little more time before we hang this on him? There could be a simple explanation—something not involving Kimball."

Easy, Hawksley warned himself. *Remember what Dr. Meissner told you. Tell Katie how you feel, and stay rational.*

"Fair enough, but I've got a bad feeling something's wrong. I miss her, and so does Torchy."

Katie squeezed his arm. "I understand, but it's too early yet to draw any conclusions."

*   *   *

Vesta still hadn't appeared when they readied for bed. Flashlight in hand, Hawksley stepped out into the night a final time and called her name. Once more, nothing.

Dejected, he locked the door and joined Katie in the bedroom. Sleep wouldn't come much of the night; he lay and stared up at the ceiling, alert for any mewing or cat-like noise outside. Exhaustion at last claimed him in the later hours of the night.

Hawksley readied for work in the morning, but not before he patrolled the neighborhood. He came up empty, and didn't know how he'd managed through the day, his thoughts never far from Vesta. Memories of her teasing Torchy, romping after a piece of paper he tied to the end of a string and dangled in front of her, how she nestled into the space between his ear and shoulder when he slept and she came to him. She and Torchy—he credited both for rescuing him when his marriage collapsed.

A block from home he visualized Vesta in the driveway, waiting for him. Disappointed, he entered the house, certain he'd never see her again.

He couldn't shake the idea Kimball had something to do with her disappearance. No point talking to Katie about it again. She'd likely say he was overreacting. Not to his mind. Cause and effect: Kimball brought cause; he himself suffered the effect.

"I'm going over to the mall to get copies run off for a picture of Vesta," he said during dinner. He pushed his food around the plate.

"What's the matter?" Katie asked.

He hadn't fooled her. "Worried, is all. She's been gone for over twenty-four hours. I'll tape them everywhere I can."

"Want me to come with you?"

"Sure, if you like."

"Maybe some kid picked her up, took off her collar and convinced his parents she was homeless," Katie said in the car.

Hawksley kept his gaze on the road. "Doubt it. Anybody could see she was too well-fed to be homeless."

"Just trying to look on the bright side."

With Torchy tagging along, the couple taped posters of Vesta to lampposts. *"Have you seen our cat? Reward."* A picture of Vesta stared out at the reader. Below, Hawksley had information about her, and his phone number. They also drove and stuck them on cork boards of supermarkets, donut shops, and coffee houses.

Days passed with no sign or information of Vesta. Hawksley grew heartsick; so too did Torchy. She refused food, and barely drank water from her bowl. Vigorous and animated at most times, she grew listless, lay on the kitchen floor, her head between her paws.

*   *   *

How's Hawk holding up?" Bailey asked her sister over coffee.

Katie shook her head. "Wish I could say fine. I encouraged him to take some more sessions with his psychologist. She's been helping him with the Lyme thing. At the moment living with him is like walking in a mine field. It's hard on him, what's happened, but in a different way, it's harder on me."

"Can you talk to him some more about this?" Bailey asked.

"Yes. I can talk, but it doesn't mean he'll listen. He's trying really hard, bless him, and I see him keeping himself in check. It's like someone else is inhabiting his body."

"It is, in a manner of speaking," Bailey said. "Lyme disease."

"Well … maybe, but there's more to it. The cat disappearing right after the strike was the last of it for Hawk. Torchy poisoned, him getting run over, shot at, Logan losing his leg, and now this. He's carrying a lot of stuff."

She drank her coffee and set it down.

"Hawk feels things, maybe more than most, but it's one of the things I love about him. He's not a 'whatever' kind of guy. And it's not only his love of animals, but his commitment to everything he cares about. I see it, see his vulnerability in not finding Vesta. He feels like he's somehow let her down. Anyway, I'm not giving up, and neither is he. If only we knew what happened to Vesta."

* * *

Nine days later the U.S, Postal Service left a notice in Hawksley's mailbox. A parcel was held for him at the post office. He tilted his head. Who would send him a parcel? He couldn't think of anyone.

Katie picked up the notice when she returned home. "It's too late now, Hawk, but do you want me to pick this up on my lunch break?"

"Would you?"

"Yes, of course. How are you feeling?"

"A bit better, I think," he lied. "And Torchy's returning to a bit of her old self again. She really misses Vesta. Thanks for hanging in there with us."

"Why wouldn't I? We're family. I only wish Vesta was part of it."

"Me too." He rubbed his hands together. "Hey, I'm in the mood for Scrabble. Up for it."

"Absolutely. After dinner, I'll put on a pot of tea, and we'll see who comes out on top."

The small package, no more than sixteen ounces, came wrapped in thick, brown paper bag material. An abundance of cellophane tape held it together. It offered no forwarding address. Hawksley's name and address appeared to have been stenciled.

He shook the package near his ear. "No idea what's in here." Using a kitchen knife, he sliced through the rough paper to reveal box and lid. A note, again in stencil, read, "Anyone you know?"

Katie next to him, Hawksley pried off the lid to find Vesta's red collar. Underneath, in a clear plastic bag, they stared at gray ashes.

Katie's hand flew to her face. For the briefest moment, Hawksley's mind would not comprehend what his eyes took in.

The telephone rang. Neither moved to answer it. Both remained fixated on the horror in front of them.

The ringing stopped. Katie came out of her absorption first. She pried the box away from Hawksley, and led him to the living room. She pulled on his hand. "Come, sit with me."

Neither spoke for long minutes. Hawksley shed the first tear. Katie pulled him to her. He sobbed with a violence, barely able to catch his breath. The last tear spent, his nose running, he pulled away.

Katie rose, found a box of tissues, and handed several to him. He wiped at his face and blew his nose.

Full of swelled sinuses from the crying, he mumbled, "Thanks."

Her lips set in a grim line, Katie said, "I apologize for doubting you, love. It is Kimball. What kind of monster would do such a thing? What did Vesta ever do to him? Poor, lovely, darling Vesta. Bastard. Fucking bastard."

Hawksley closed his eyes and opened them again. His level of composure surprised her. He lowered his voice.

"I've said all along he's a psycho. Now there's not a shred of doubt left."

He broke off. She waited for more. He obliged. "I'm going to kill him. I'll pick the time and place; do what he's been doing to me all along, but before this year is over, he's dead."

"Hawk, you don't mean it. Maybe we should call the police."

"And say what exactly, Kate? He had me stalked, run-over, and he's free. He had my shooter, Casper Foley, murdered, and he got away free. And I go to the cops with no evidence, and say he killed my cat?"

"There must be something they can do—maybe trace, I don't know, the crematorium?"

"Assuming they could. Kimball's smart. He'd have someone else, one of his flunkies, have Vesta taken there." He slowly shook his head. "It's a waste of time and effort to go to the cops."

"I suppose you're right."

"I am. This is it—he's not getting away with this."

He stopped, slowly shook his head and bore on. "It's more than Vesta. He's a monster, the worst kind. I intend to rid the world of him. If this is too scary for you, offends you, or both, I'll understand if you quit me. Nothing will stop me from killing him."

Katie took his hand. "Nobody's quitting anybody here, now or ever. I hate the sonovabitch too, but I don't want you to go to prison."

Hawksley shook his head. "I promise you I'll finish my days as a free man. I need to think about this, and do it in a way no suspicion will ever fall on me. But I intend to kill him."

"How?"

He couldn't answer in specifics, only told her he'd work on it, plan it out with care. "And even when I've worked out how I'll do it, I'll keep it to myself. If anything ever comes to light, you can say you knew nothing about it."

She slouched into the couch, patted his hand, and said, "I can't believe I'm about to say this, but Kimball does need killing. I'm not agreeing with what you're about to do, but I understand."

Both lost in their thoughts, a silence enveloped the couple on the couch.

Katie had no illusions Hawksley would make good on his promise; to the same degree, she had little confidence he'd get away with it. She'd watched enough crime shows. He wasn't some kind of professional assassin. He intended to take someone's life. People like him always got caught. And even if he got away with it, what about any fallout? Would it haunt him later when he considered it with a more objective appraisal? She didn't know. The only thing certain is she'd have to sabotage his plans somehow.

Easier said than done, she told herself. What could she do? For starters, she could tease out bits of information, see what kind of action plan he'd come up with. Easier said than done. Hawk wasn't stupid, and he'd get suspicious if she asked too many questions. She'd have to be real careful. More though, she needed her own plan.

She scoured her brain for something, anything.

A distant memory flashed through her mind— Hawksley telling her about one of the Italian brothers approaching the family at his father's funeral. What had he said? It came back to her; something about a promise to help if they needed it. The way Hawksley described the man, and his supposed connection to the underworld, maybe this would be the way to go.

She tried to think of his name. She recalled Hawksley telling her about the city garbage contract. The trucks, the trucks, yes, they were all over the city with their logo on the side. It came to her. Mantachie. Yes.

She had a name. Now she had to puzzle out how to start a conversation with him. She couldn't exactly say, *Hi, Mr. Mantachie, my boyfriend's about to kill a drug dealer next door. He's really got no talent for murder. Seeing as you said you could help the family, will you take care of this for us? That'd be great. Thanks.* No, this required finesse, and even then Mantachie might not do anything. Well, she had to do something. She had to try, to save Hawk from himself.

Long minutes later, a morose Hawksley rose and placed the package on the coffee table with care. "Comes the warm weather, I'll plant this under the honeysuckle vine Vesta loved."

Neither of them spoke of the ashes or Kimball afterward. Hawksley didn't quite pull into himself, but Katie sensed a difference in him. *He's focusing his energy and attention on something big.*

*   *   *

"This could blow up in your face, you know," Bailey said the next day at the coffee shop. "If he finds out."

Katie gave a half shrug. "I don't intend for him to find out, and you're never to tell him."

"Don't worry. But what about this Mantachie character? Have you thought of what you're going to say?"

"Pretty well. All I have to do now is muster up my courage to call him."

"I hope Hawksley appreciates how much you love him, and to what extent you'll go for him."

"Me too."

"Good luck with this Mantachie. Let me know how it works out."

"Thanks. I may need more than luck."

Chapter 27

It took some time before Katie mustered up a measure of nerve to phone Victor Mantachie.

Several tries and messages later, the businessman returned her call at work. She didn't want Hawksley to learn of her plan.

"Katie Maines."

"This is Victor Mantachie," a low, rough voice said. "What can I do for you?"

Katie heard wariness in the reply. A quick scan at nearby desks told her no one showed interest in her. Still, it wouldn't hurt to keep her voice low. She swallowed and introduced herself. "I'm Hawksley Pardee's girlfriend," Mr. Mantachie–Daryl Pardee's son. He's uh, he's not doing so well these days."

But for the subtle suggestion of someone breathing, nothing would have told her a man listened to her on the other end. *Oh, dear God, this is not going well. He probably thinks I'm blathering.*

He spoke again. "Go on." Encouraged, she said, "He can't know I'm calling you, Mr. Mantachie, but he needs help. You're the only one I can think of."

Another anxiety-provoking pause before Mantachie said, "Um, Katie, slow down and tell me more."

She took some comfort from the response.

"Sorry. I'm not calling about money, in case you're wondering, but the matter's sensitive, and best I tell you face-to-face. Like I said, I have to call from work, here at city planning. You can call here to confirm if you like. Switchboard will put you through."

Another long, anxiety-provoking passed before he said, "Are you familiar with Feraghelli's Bakery & Café?"

"On East Market? Yes, yes sir, I am."

"Friday morning at ten. I have to go over some things with my manager. We can meet later and talk. I'll be in a corner at one of the tables."

*   *   *

Feraghelli's Bakery & Café always did a thriving business—in the mornings, when office workers were eager for a fresh cup of wake-up coffee, along with a pastry or scone; in afternoons, when housewives shopped for fresh rolls or breads for their family's dinner.

Katie had asked for time off on this particular morning. Her heels click-clacked with a purposeful cadence down the sidewalk, and gave proof their owner had a destination in mind.

The night before her meeting, Katie gave considerable thought to what to wear. No power suit; a hint of elegance, and nothing else. Easy on the makeup. Understated, she'd go for understated.

She chose a red pencil skirt and complimented it with a black blouse. For shoes, she rejected her killer heels in favor of lower ones.

Katie allowed herself a quick glance in a nearby store window, arrived at the bakery, and opened the door. At any other time the wonderful smell of baked goods, coffee, and the array of inviting shelves filled with delicacies, would have caused her to take in the full experience. Not this time. Her stomach doing flip-flops, she navigated past the refrigerated section of pastries, and past customers at the counter waiting to be served.

Her eyes roamed across the dozen nearby tables and spotted three men sitting at a corner table, two with their backs to her. The other man watched her approach. He had to be Mantachie. She didn't remember him from the funeral, only from Hawksley's brief description. He shot her a lips over teeth smile, and a nod of acknowledgement.

His two companions turned and glanced at her.

She approached, and he rose, the other two with him. He held out his hand. "And you are the lovely lady I spoke to on Monday—Katie." He smiled again, this time revealing full upper teeth. They reminded her of an old co-host on one of those late night talk shows who liked to show off his cosmetic smile.

She forced herself not to stare, and took his hand. Hers disappeared almost at once in his. "Hello, Mr. Mantachie, and thank you for seeing me."

"Victor, please." He released her hand and invited her to sit. At once his two companions stepped away and chose a different table.

Katie hadn't known what to expect. Perhaps from watching too many movies, she imagined Mantachie might wear a top-of-the-line Italian suit, shirt and tie. Instead he donned a black, soft leather jacket over a blue button-down, untucked shirt, and khaki slacks.

"Coffee, or something else?" He pointed to his own small cup. "As you see, I already have something."

She didn't want coffee or anything, her stomach too nervous. Still, it wouldn't do to refuse. Good manners at least dictated she say yes. "Be wonderful, thank you."

He raised his hand and signaled to someone over her shoulder. A moment later a waitress appeared. Her eyes moved from Mantachie to Katie. She smiled up at the server. "Cappuccino, please."

A fast nod and the server turned and left.

"A lovely day," Mantachie said, making small talk.

Katie held up her end of it. "It is, yes. The kind of day you'd rather be outside than in a stuffy building like mine."

The cappuccino arrived. The server left. Mantachie raised his expresso to his lips. In spite of the fleshiness of his face, Katie thought it had character. His small, evenly-spaced blue eyes held hers with determination, but not provocation. Put a few more years and a white beard on him, and he could probably be a modern-day Orson Wells.

Uneasy on how to lead into the purpose of her visit, she waited for an opportune opening. He provided it. "So this sudden—what shall we call it, predicament? You hinted at over the phone, the one you cannot solve, you think I can?"

Oh boy, Katie told herself. *Don't muff this.* She swallowed some of her coffee to get more moisture into her mouth. "I guess the best thing, Victor, is not beat around the bush, but get at it." She moved into the story of Hawksley and Kimball. "There's no doubt in either my or Hawksley's mind, Brian Kimball poisoned our pets, and tried twice to kill Hawk. Now, with the death of our cat, Hawksley's become irrational, and determined to kill Kimball."

"You think this is, you know, just talk?"

She shook her head. "No, sorry, it's gone past the kind of empty statement people make when they're angry. He means it, and he'll do it, and get caught, somehow. I can't talk him out of it. Can you, could you see your way to doing something, anything, to help us?"

In reply, Mantachie looked over her shoulder and crooked a finger in the direction of the two men. The heftier of the two rose, approached Mantachie, bent and listened. Instructions? He at last rose to full height again, faced Katie and said, "Can you come with me?"

Katie's eyes flitted from the towering man and over to Mantachie. He answered the question on her face with, "Go with him."

Katie fought down panic. Her heart raced. *What's going on? Where's he taking me?* She had no time to uncover satisfactory answers before she found herself in the kitchen, frisked by a middle-aged female employee.

"Your purse," the woman said when she finished her pat down.

Katie handed it over.

The woman examined its contents and returned it. Without any explanation she said, "Mr. Mantachie is waiting for you."

Two minutes later Katie again sat opposite Mantachie again, a fresh cup of coffee in front of her.

"You'll appreciate, I hope," Mantachie said by way of explanation, "it's not always an easy world. I have competitors, and an often law enforcement intent on bringing about my ruin. I have to protect myself."

He stopped, drank from his own coffee, and set it back into the saucer. "To the matter of your presence, Katie, what is this specific 'something' you want done to this man?"

She reminded herself not to rush her speech.

"Beyond being desperate and clutching at straws, I don't know, Victor. I only want to stop Hawksley from taking the law into his own hands. Our cat's ashes were a deliberate attempt to provoke Hawk. It worked. I have to save him from himself."

She hung her head, reached for her coffee, and took a sip. She set it down and raised her eyes. *Don't say anything,* she warned herself. *Wait for him to talk.*

She didn't have long to wait. "Go on," he said.

A fast nod and Katie said, "I don't have anything more. This is it."

He again retreated into silence. She again swallowed. "I'm embarrassed, this coming from me, but maybe a good old-fashioned beating to Kimball, something to have him hobbling around for a long time. It might warn him off Hawksley, and convince Hawksley he doesn't have to do anything else."

The speech took a lot out of her. Her earlier resolve to solicit Mantachie's help, crumbled. She wished she hadn't come. *Foolish girl,* she told herself. *Why did you think this would work*? She resolved to finish her coffee, thank Mantachie for his time, and make the hastiest of retreats.

He at last spoke. "Do you suppose all Italians are mobsters, Katie, like in the movies? Do you think our specialty is beatings and cement shoes?"

She paled at the comment. "I'm sorry, Victor, if I've given offense. I didn't mean to. I am a desperate woman struggling for a desperate solution. Perhaps I should go."

He peered at her for a moment. "By chance, I know this Mr. Kimball. Beyond this, I'll leave it there, but I will give your worries my deepest consideration. I understood, too, time is of the essence."

He twirled his cup in the saucer. "It was brave of you to take the risk of finding and meeting me, a stranger. You're to be admired. Now, what do you say we put the matter aside? I've enjoyed meeting you, and please visit my store anytime. It's not often I get to enjoy conversation with a lovely young lady."

Thank you … Victor." She rose and held out her hand. He took it. "Perhaps at some future time we might meet again, you, me, Hawksley. Under better circumstances. Who can say?"

"Exactly, Mr. Mantachie. Again, thank you for your time and everything. Goodbye."

Katie left the bakery a nervous wreck, undecided whether she'd influenced Mantachie or not. She played her conversation with him over and over in here head. She entered the lobby of city hall. *All I can do now is wait and hope Hawksley doesn't act before Mantachie does. Assuming he'll do something.*

Victor Mantachie watched her leave and waggled his index and middle finger for his two men returned to join him. They sat and leaned across the table to hear what their boss had to say. Both held an abiding curiosity as to the nature of Victor's meeting with the good-looking chick; neither felt brave enough to ask. If he wanted them to know, he would.

Mantachie drained the last of his coffee and set it in the saucer. "We got a problem with Kimball. Calling a lot of attention to himself lately. Only a matter of time before it finds its way to us. And he's again behind in his payments on the crack we supplied him."

"What do you wanna do with him, boss?" the smaller of the two men asked.

"Do? I want him clipped, is what I want. He's a pain in the ass, drawing unnecessary attention. He's become a liability. Can't have that."

"So who?" the larger man asked.

"Good question."

The small man spoke again. "The bikers?"

Mantachie shook his head. "They're not a whole lot better than Kimball these days, taking up arms against each other. We need somebody more low key."

"Hopping Owl?"

Mantachie ran his tongue over his lower teeth and considered the suggestion. "Yeah. Good choice. Get a hold of him, and tell him to add a little pain. Make Kimball wish he'd paid up on time."

*　　　*　　　*

Hawksley set the table while Katie fussed over the preparation of the evening's meal. They sat and ate.

Hawksley hadn't said anything more about Kimball. Katie knew he wouldn't, yet the worry consumed her. Would Mantachie act, and if so, before Hawksley did? She cleared her throat. "Can I ask you a question?"

"Sure." He forked some greens into his mouth and chewed.

"Have you thought some more about how to handle Kimball?"

He chewed, swallowed. "Like I said, I've gotta make sure whatever I come up with works to perfection. I'll give him some time to let his guard down, the way he does it with me. When I'm ready, I'll spring my trap"

"So nothing yet?"

"No. Haven't got anything I like so far. Why do you ask?"

Katie made sure to keep her voice light, to say nothing to cause Hawksley suspicion. "It's not the kind of thing normal people have in everyday conversation. Or how to bump somebody off. Just wondering."

"Like I said, nothing's off the drawing board yet. And besides, the less you know, the better."

She let out a quiet sigh of relief. *Ironic. He's still planning to murder someone, and I'm hoping Mantachie will get there first.*

*   *   *

One hundred-and-ninety-one miles north of New Albany, at the *Miami Nation* in Peru, Indiana, a copper-colored Native, Johnny Yellowbird Whiskychin, took a call on his disposable cell phone.

"Yeah?"

He listened for a moment, and then said, "I can take it on."

He fell silent and concentrated on what he heard.

"No. High risk. Not enough."

Again he concentrated to the voice at the other end of the line.

"Better. You want it done when?"

He reached for a pen to write on a notepad. "I think I got it, but repeat the addresses again." His finger followed the written instruction on the notepad. "Yep. I got it. Leave the payment in the usual place?"

A few seconds later the six foot one Hopping Owl turned off his cell phone. He'd have to get Gilletina to look after Skah, his beloved Labrador.

He phoned her. The arrangement taken care of, he crouched and petted his dog. "Can't take you with me this time, bud, but what say when I come back we go after some wild turkey? You'd be real happy, wouldn't you, boy?"

The chocolate Lab wagged his tail with passion.

Yellowbird straightened, opened the fridge door and pulled out a large plastic bag. He selected one of two heavy bones and gave it to Skah. "This should keep you busy for a while until Gilletina comes. And there's water in your bowl if you get thirsty."

Yellowbird packed a few things in his small suitcase, smiled at Skah, busy with his treat, and grabbed his Stetson. He shut the door behind him, his heavy cowboy boots thumping on the wooden porch.

The driver's side of the pickup unlocked, Yellowbird threw a quick look at his metal truck cap, and climbed behind his wheel. He set the Stetson on the passenger seat, pushed his long braids behind his ears, and started the truck.

Chapter 28

Brian Kimball had every reason to be pleased. An outstanding month, March: sales were up everywhere, especially to white college kids and yuppies.

Kimball's two dummy businesses, a party store and a pizzeria, did a good job of washing his profits. At this rate he'd definitely look to trade up to a better house by the end of the year. Maybe in the new gated community.

He knocked on the door of apartment 3 at 84 Carlyle, one of three apartments he used to stash his products.

The 4-plex residential building had long ago seen its best days, as had the neighborhood. New Albany had its share of urban problems, yet managed to avoid the large-scale decay of many of its sister cities. Only a few pockets of the city could be considered poor and unsafe. Carlyle and its adjacent streets satisfied the dual definition. Street lights were shot out; vandalized and rusted cars commonplace. Almost all the houses had iron grates on their doors and windows. Many boasted steel fences around their front yards.

Every welfare cop, parole officer, welfare worker and social worker in the city had stories about Carlyle.

Alvin 'Snuffy' Pickens, an emaciated, twenty-five-year-old addict and current resident of apartment 3, looked through the peephole before he opened the door. Pickens' rotting teeth, shifty eyes and zombie-like stare, should have scared customers away, but he remained Kimball's best pusher. The fear of being cut off from his source made Pickens a loyal employee. Kimball, though, had no illusion would last out the year.

"Okay," Kimball said as he stepped out of Pickens' apartment, "You know where to pick it up."

"I do, yeah."

"Good. And stop sampling so much. You're cutting into my profits. I don't want to lose you, but if I find you've been cutting the product again, you're gone. I got a reputation to maintain. Can't have people complaining about what I'm selling."

Pickens squeezed his eyes shut and opened them. He wished Kimball would shut the fuck up. Man, if he was in charge, he'd put a cap in this asshole's spine. Yeah. Be great.

"Hear you, man. You don't gotta worry none 'bout me."

"I do, but don't fuck this up for yourself."

Kimball left Pickens and walked to his Kawasaki bike. A fast scan of the street told him nothing to be worried about. Even so, he liked to make sure no one tailed him. He often tore through alleys and tight spots just in case.

For some reason, Kimball's mind turned to Hawksley Pardee. He'd had his fun with him, but time to end it. The point had well been made. He'd taught the asshole not to mess with him. Still, if only he could have seen the look on Pardee's face when he opened the package …

One thought led to another, and an image of Foley came to mind. Too bad he turned out to be such a bad shot, and then a rat. Damn near caused him a long stretch in the joint.

Encouraged by the day and his prospects, Kimball allowed himself to cruise around town. He couldn't imagine life any better, the only small hiccup the Mantachie boys. Victor had managed to get his tighty whities in a bunch lately over late payments.

"Payments are to be made in a timely fashion," the older Mantachie had lectured Kimball the last time they met. "In a timely fashion, not when you feel like it. Is my meaning clear?"

Yeah, you fat greaseball. Clear enough. Well, no point riling up Mantachie any further. He'd make his payment today, ahead of schedule, and offer sufficient respect with a nice present. What could he get? Nothing came to mind. He'd think on it further.

*   *   *

Kimball's stomach growled. Lacey had offered to make breakfast, but he told her he'd stop at *Mo's* instead. He drove into the rear. Only two vehicles—a crappy old Buick, and a silver-and-black pickup. He pulled up next to the truck.

Kimball entered through the back of *Mo's*. A big-muscled man with braids, a Stetson, and cowboy boots sat at the counter drinking coffee and reading a paper. Must be the guy who owned the truck. Kimball slapped him on the shoulder while he passed and made for a booth.

"Morning, chief."

With low speed the Indian swiveled on his stool and stared after Kimball. He spoke with a rich, deep voice.

"Excuse me. Do I look like a Native chief to you? You're making a racist and derogatory comment about me and my people."

Kimball held up both hands in surrender. "Kidding, all right? Didn't mean nothing by it."

"Then think before you speak, and don't go around offending people."

"'All right. Sorry."

Kimball took his seat in a booth. *What the hell's the matter with the world? Everybody's so touchy. You can't even have fun anymore.*

The teenaged waitress arrived. Kimball flirted with her for a moment before he ordered the all-day breakfast. "Double order of toast, Ashley."

She took the order, smiled and walked away. Kimball followed her with his eyes. *Nice legs. Wouldn't mind spending time in the sack with her.*

He reached for his cell phone on his hip. Not there. He patted himself. Had he lost it? It came to him. He'd left it on the kitchen counter. Shit. Oh well, no point going back for it now. He'd make do without. He'd already set up his appointments with the rest of his pushers.

Looking for something to distract himself, Kimball spied a copy of *U.S. News*, got up and brought it back to his seat. He worked through it while he ate, and never noticed the glances tossed his way from the counter.

Kimball finished the paper by the end of his second refill. A quick wipe of his mouth, he peeled off several bills, including a nice tip for Ashley. Outside, he scanned for any signs of a tail. Only the Buick and the Ford. The Indian sat behind the wheel of his truck, busy looking at something in his lap. Kimball lost interest in him. He swung a leg over his machine, and fished in his jeans for the key.

His attention on starting the engine, Kimball failed to respond fast enough as a powerful forearm wrapped itself around his throat. The tight squeeze denied him any air. Already spots appeared in front of his eyes.

Terror coursed through Kimball. In desperation he fought to free himself from the viselike arms wrapped around his neck. His left foot tapped and re-tapped the ground. Seconds later, his eyes rolled up into his head. He slipped into unconsciousness.

*   *   *

Kimball came to, but couldn't at first determine time, place and his situation. Awareness returned. He still remained in the parking lot behind *Mo's*. Duct tape covered his mouth. He struggled to break free against the binding plastic restraints behind his back. His abductor, the Indian, held him by the scruff of his jacket and pushed his head under the thermoplastic bed cover of the truck.

Fear, raw fear, held him in its grip. His heart raced, his eyes grew wide, and his body shook in an uncontrolled manner. Instinct warned him he'd die if he allowed himself to be snatched away. He fought to break free, braced his legs and tugged at his restraints.

His abductor rewarded his efforts with a powerful kidney punch.

Kimball had never felt such pain in his life, and folded to the ground. The pain shot through his inners, brought tears to his eyes, and made him want to cry out—if he could.

Jerked to his feet, his abductor moved an agonized Kimball around, and again forced his head down. He fed him into the truck like a load of laundry. "Stiffen your legs," he ordered in a gruff and dispassionate voice.

Unable to offer further resistance, Kimball obeyed. A final shove, and he lay under the heavy bed covering of the pickup.

The back gate slammed down. Everything went dark. Kimball couldn't see a thing. A moment later, the engine started and the truck began to move. His bowels gave out.

They drove for what felt to Kimball like a small eternity. He bounced around in the darkness, aware and disgusted with his soiled pants. The ridges in the bed of the pickup bit into his shoulder. He dismissed rolling onto his stomach or back; the first would be uncomfortable and punishing; the second meant he'd have to sit on his hands. The best of poor choices—remaining on his side.

He again struggled to free himself from the restraints. They wouldn't give. The Indian knew what he was doing.

His cell phone: he cursed himself for forgetting it. He always brought it. Not this day, the one time he didn't. If only he had it now, he told himself. He argued against himself—what would he have done with it anyway? How could he have used it with hands tied behind his back?

With nothing else to do in the dark, Kimball turned to reflection. He reviewed his life and moral choices. Next, he prayed. *Help me, please, God. I'm not a bad person. There's lots worse than me. So maybe I'm no saint, but they taught me in Sunday school if I believe in You, You won't let me down. Well, here I am, and I do believe in You. Honest. Maybe I haven't gone to church, but I never stopped believing.*

Worried the sincerity of his supplication might not satisfy God, Kimball turned to negotiation.

Dear Lord, if you help me get out of this jam, I promise to go on the straight and narrow. I'll stop dealing, get a job, sell my businesses, and give most of the money to charities. Anything you like. I promise. Please, I'm begging You; help me, and don't let me die.

At a loss to add anything else, a helpless Kimball, cold, thirsty and scared, focused on how he ended up in this dangerous situation. The "chief" thing? Nah, it couldn't be, but … Could it be anything else? A hit: maybe somebody put out a hit on him.

He ran through a short list of who might have paid for the abductor. Hawksley Pardee made it to the top of the list. Made it, but didn't stay there. He didn't have the brains, money, or whatever to pull this off. Who then?

Kimball ran through a list of suspects—Sly Panko, Chris Bartley, Ed Grogan. He doubted any of them could pull this off. Losers, all of them, always nibbling on the edge of his business, happy to take anything away, but they had no real balls.

In the end, he concluded the only ones who could pull this off had to be the Mantachies. But why? So maybe he might have been a little late with some of his payments, but he always came good.

"God," he whispered to himself, "if I could only turn back the clock. I'd convince them I'd never be late again. Ever."

With every passing mile and minute, Kimball grew more convinced he'd be dead by the end of the day. Fat tears rolled to his nose and tumbled off onto the bed of the truck. Maybe somehow he could convince the Indian to let him go. Then again, maybe this long travel delivered its own message: leave, leave New Albany, and never return. Yeah. What else made sense? The Indian would take him to the middle of nowhere, and drop him off, humiliated. He'd get the message, and stay away from New Albany. If someone really wanted him dead, why go to all this trouble? They could take him to the nearest secluded area and finish him off.

Heartened by his reasoning, Kimball felt somewhat better. The feeling didn't last long, eroded by Kimball's own logic and evidence. He returned to his former state of despair.

I'm going to die, and there's nothing I can do or say to stop it. Oh Dear God. He again addressed his Creator. *I'm sorry, Dear God, sorry for every bad thing I've ever done, and people I've hurt.*

An image of Hawksley Pardee came back to him. *I'm especially sorry I caused so much pain for him, God. We both know I can't undo it. If You won't save my life, can you at least let him know I regret doing it?*

*   *   *

A physically numbed Kimball felt the truck slow, turn, and pull onto what sounded like a gravel road. Stones pounded the bottom of the truck bed, creating a cacophony of noise, making it difficult to concentrate. With each sharp turn, Kimball rolled back and forth, banging his head and knees against the sides of the truck bed, adding to his misery.

The truck slowed again, made a sharp turn and jostled its human cargo in the back.

The sound of the engine told Kimball they'd moved onto a washboard road, probably dirt. The pull of the ruts proved it and bounced him along. He winced and groaned until the truck at last stopped.

He heard the cab door open. A moment light poured into the tailgate. His abductor crouched and peered into the truck. "Roll onto your stomach. Easier to pull you out." Kimball obeyed. His abductor grabbed his legs and pulled. Seconds later he helped Kimball onto his feet. He craned his neck and sniffed. "Smell pretty bad there, guy." He shook his head in disgust. "Now we walk a bit. You follow behind me. Try running, and you won't like what comes next. Clear?"

"Clear," a subdued Kimball said, his voice dry from fear and thirst.

*   *   *

They walked into thick bush for about ten minutes. Kimball took note of the pistol in the Indian's waistband. Not a good sign. Not a good sign at all.

In a small clearing, his abductor stopped, turned Kimball, produced a folding knife from his jeans and cut the restraints. Freed, Kimball rolled his shoulders in relief, massaged his wrists, and faced the other man. He folded his knife, slid it into his pocket, and pulled out the pistol. The action caused a violent tremor in Kimball. His teeth chattered. He had difficulty getting his words out. "C'mon, please, don't do this. If this is about calling you, chief, I'm sorry. I didn't mean nothing by it. It's not worth offing me for."

His captor offered no reply. Kimball tried again.

"Listen, man, if it's not about the chief thing, what is it? Somebody sent you? I got money. Name your price, and I'll make you a way better offer than whoever hired you. Way better."

His abductor slowly shook his head. "Oh, so now it's 'man'? What happened to 'chief' He paused. "Guess I need to educate you. I come from a proud People with a proud heritage. I'm a Native-American, or American Indian, if you like. What I'm not is a chief. My People don't go around calling each other chief any more than yours go around calling your women Buffy.

"In my culture, a chief is an honorable and earned title. Anyone who throws the word around without care is a stupid racist. Now, about making me rich, not gonna happen. I'm supposed to cause you some pain before you die, but I don't much see the point, do you? A man can't get any lower than filling his pants."

The reality of the cold, harsh words hit home to Kimball. His throat closed. Small teardrops left his eyes, and made their way down his cheeks. They increased; so too did his noisy intake of air. "Please," he said between sobs, "you don't have to do this. I can make this right for you if you let me go."

"Don't beg," his abductor said. "It only steals what little dignity you've got left." He slowly shook his head. "No matter. Strip down to your underwear and bundle up your clothes."

Kimball's tremors increased. He sobbed as he shed his clothing, and silently spoke to his girlfriend. *I'm sorry, Lacey for leaving you so soon. It wasn't my doing. I hope you'll eventually find out what happened to me, and think of me from time to time. I'll miss you, and love you.*

An order came. "On your knees, facing away from me."

Resigned to his fate, a violently trembling Kimball dropped to his knees. "This is the Mantachie brothers, who ordered this hit, isn't it? You're going to kill me, but I'll put a curse on you and them."

His abductor ignored the false bravado. "If it makes you feel better, do what you gotta do. Now, hands by your side, and don't turn around." A subdued Kimball did as ordered. His abductor walked behind him. He felt the cold muzzle of the gun against the nape of his neck. "Made you peace with your God?"

"Y-y-yes."

The crack of the pistol sent a few birds fluttering into the sky. Kimball pitched forward, convulsed twice, and released his claim to mortality.

*   *   *

Yellowbird stared down at his victim for a moment. He bent and searched the dead man's clothing. "As to why I had you strip, no point in letting wild animals struggle. Your body will help them. Cycle of life."

He made his way back to the van. Inside he extracted and pocketed eight hundred and seventy dollars from his victim's wallet. The ID he slid into his shirt pocket. He'd later send it to Kimball's home address. It'd be good for them to have some keepsake.

Yellowbird guided his truck back onto the highway. An hour later he pulled into a roadside coffee shop and entered. In the rest room, he tossed the empty wallet into a bin and washed his hands three times.

He left the rest room, found a seat at the counter and ordered coffee. A friendly waitress chatted with him while he drank the hot brew and engaged her.

Back in his pickup, Yellowbird returned to the highway, and thought about Skah, and his earlier promise to the dog.

Chapter 29

Lacey Clew, domestic partner of Brian Kimball, paced by the front window curtains, and again peeked out into the darkness. Where was he? He should have been home hours ago. He'd rushed out in the morning. "Gotta check my boys, CiCi" he called over his shoulder. "Do a couple of small things, and be back before lunch."

"Want me to make you breakfast before you go?"

"Nah, I'm good." He pressed the garage opener.

She'd heard him drive out the garage, the automatic door closing behind him. On the kitchen counter she spied his cell phone. He'll remember and come back, she told herself.

He didn't return. The small worry settling in Lacey's chest, grew more with each passing hour.

By dinner, she found herself in a near-panic mode. She phoned everyone who knew Brian. A short list. He only had a sister, and few friends. She didn't know his pushers. He'd only referred to them by nickname, and used his disposable phone whenever he had to call. She had the phone, but not his password.

What about the Mantachies? Lacey knew they supplied Brian his drugs. Maybe so, but she also knew they wouldn't help, let alone talk to her. She once asked Brian about them. He stared at her for a second, and said, "Not a good idea to tell you much about them, CiCi. Ever. The less you know, the better. Let's get off the subject."

So Brian's pushers and suppliers were out. Who else then; who else could she call? The obvious: the jail and the cops. Brian had more than a working familiarity with both.

She called the County Jail first. The cheerful female voice at the other end said, "Nobody here in custody by the name of Brian Kimball. Why don't you try the police?"

Lacey did, and got a heavy male voice. "Police Department. Sergeant DeAngelis."

"Hello. My name is Lacey Clew, and my domestic partner, Brian Kimball, hasn't come home since he left early in this morning. I'm wondering if you got a report or something, like maybe he's been in an accident, or something."

"Spell the name."

She did, and heard the faint tippity-tap of fingers on a keyboard. "No, ma'am, sorry; we've got no occurrence report for a Brian Kimball. You could try the emergency rooms. And if he fails to show up in forty-eight hours, file a *Missing Person's Report* with us."

Worried, Lacey next called all the emergency rooms. Again no luck. "Where are you, Brian?" she called out. "Something's happened. I just know it."

She couldn't sit, and paced. "I'm wound up like a spring. I need a smoke." Cigarette package and lighter in hand, Lacey stepped outside and lit up. Brian didn't like her to smoke, especially in the house.

By three in the morning, weariness and a sleeping pill at last forced Lacey to bed. She twitched all night, her feet moving back and forth, as though she were running.

In the morning, Lacey woke, groggy, and studied the empty spot beside her. A wave of sadness washed over her. Shoulders slumped, feet on the floor, she let out a dramatic exhalation. "Please be safe," she whispered to a partner unable to see or hear her. "Please come home to me."

Washed and dressed, but uninterested in putting on makeup, she made her way to the kitchen. Should she eat? She decided against it; she had no interest in food. Instead, she made a coffee, moved to the couch and lit up. She'd happily face an annoyed flesh-and-blood Brian scolding her about smoking. On her third puff she let her mind drift back to when she first met him.

With little education and no real prospects, she'd left school after grade eight. The only work for someone like her would be in a factory or waitressing. The country still found itself mired in a recession, and factories weren't hiring.

She took a job working for a fat Greek with grabby hands. Disgusted, she quit. She'd have to find other work. Nothing much beyond waitressing, curb crawling (prostitution), and exotic dancing. Curb crawling, no. She ruled out being a hooker—too dangerous. Exotic dancing? She'd heard they made good money. Tax free.

Model-thin, long-legged nineteen-year-old Lacey Clew, with small, firm breasts, wheeled about in her tightest jeans and heels for the manager, Donny Kyka.

"Nice, hon," the double-chinned manager said and tapped ash into a tray, "but I gotta see what I'm getting if I take you on. Strip, but keep the heels on."

"My clothes?" she stammered. "You want me to take off my clothes?"

He leaned across his desk. "That is what I'm asking. I wanna get a look at what my customers see when you're trotting your stuff in front of them."

With reluctance Lacey pulled off her sweater.

"No, no," Kyka said. "Put some seductiveness into it. You're stripping in front of horny, drunk men. You're not taking your clothes off for your doctor. Do it right. If you get good at it, you could make a lot of dough."

Lacey did her best imitation of a stripper.

Kyka studied her the way another man might study a serious piece of art. She'd expected him to leer and even make a pass. He did neither, and made eye contact while he talked.

"Your tits are a little on the small side, but you got nice legs. Most of the attention is gonna be down there anyway." He pointed to her groin. "I'll get one of the girls to show you how to strip. All right, put your clothes back on. You start tomorrow night at six. Get yourself a stage name."

*   *   *

Kyka hadn't lied. Lacey made more on her first night stripping than waitressing for three days. A fast learner, she colored her mousey brown hair blonde. She also bought neon pink baby doll outfits, and high, open-toed heels. Customers liked to see the girls in intimate apparel, and tipped better.

Self-conscious at first, it took some practice for Lacey to strip and tantalize in front of inebriated middle-aged men— young men, old men, all men who walked through the doors of *Gentlemen's Choice.*

As "Desiree" she also discovered she could make extra money giving private lap dances. And the other girls taught her the litany of lies to weasel more money from customers, or keep them at bay.

You're my favorite customer.
I go to college during the day—so I strip to pay my bills.
My bills are adding up. I need to make more money.
A date? Sorry, sugar, but I'm lesbian.

Most girls at the club lasted between three to six months. Soft drugs, alcohol, general burnout, working for and living with wild biker pimps, were but some of the reasons.

By her tenth month, Lacey had already seen too much, and asked herself how long she'd last? A regular customer, Brian, ten years her senior, changed her life. He tipped well, never pressured her to do anything she didn't want, and showed a genuine interest in her as a person.

She asked the other girls about him. Word had it he dealt drugs. In the sordid world of "titty bars," drugs, and alcohol went hand-in-hand. Saying so-and-so dealt drugs wouldn't raise eyebrows. Lacey didn't hold it against him.

She broke her rule about not dating customers.

Brian didn't disappoint. He took her to Chicago to a Cubs game. In the evening they dined at an upscale Italian restaurant. He ordered wine for them, and impressed her with his sophistication. He even booked separate rooms. By the day's end she invited him to share hers. Two months later he asked her to stop stripping. He promised he would look after her. She said she would on condition he gave up going to *Gentlemen's Choice*. He agreed.

She moved in with him five days later.

Life with Brian didn't disappoint. She always had lots of fun. He took her to exotic places she never imagined she'd see — the Mexican Rivera, cruises on the Caribbean, standing in Times Square with thousands of others on New Year's Eve. So much fun, and now somebody or somebodies tore him from her life. She missed him, and it hurt.

Her phone rang and jarred her from her trance. At once she sprang to her feet and raced to it. Brian, or maybe news about him?

The call display on her cordless phone read, Amber Davey, Lacey's best friend. Amber still "danced" at the *Gentleman's Choice* under the stage name of Silk.

Lacey picked up the handset. "Hello."

"Hi, Lacey. Any news?"

"Silk, hi. No."

"Aw. Why don't I come over?"

"Would you? Be great. I don't want to be alone right now."

She no sooner hung up than the phone rang again. Once more her heart raced with excitement.

Her call display read, *Mo's Diner*.

"Yes, hello."

"Is Brian Kimball there?"

"No, sorry. I'm his partner. Can I help?"

"Um, yeah, his bike's in our parking lot. We don't know what to do with it. He came yesterday, left, but without it."

Lacey let out a whimper and dropped the phone.

*　　　*　　　*

The light coffee-colored Silk knocked. The door opened to a weepy Lacey, eyes rimmed red. Halfway through a box of tissues, Lacey managed to bring herself under control again. "My eyes are sore, and my throat's worse."

"You have a good reason," her friend replied and stroked her arm. "Why don't we get some tea or coffee in you?"

"Yeah, I guess."

Over coffee, Silk asked what Lacey thought might have happened.

"I don't know for sure, and it's what makes everything worse. Maybe if I knew. I called the cop shop, the jail, and all the emergencies. No Brian anywheres." She told Silk about the motorcycle. "It's sitting there in *Mo's* parking lot without Brian. He loved his bike. He'd never leave it. Never."

She drank and set down her mug. "I'm starting to think he's been kidnapped or murdered. What else explains it? On his bike yesterday morning, and poof, he vanishes. And you know what?"

"What?"

"I think it's the asshole next door who's responsible for Brian's disappearance."

"Why do you think him?"

"I don't know. I just do. He and Brian hated each other. And he beat him up once, you know."

"Who? Brian beat him up?"

"No, the other way."

"So you don't think anyone else could have done it?"

Lacey shook her head. "No. People didn't mess with Brian. Except for the guy next door. Has to be him."

"Huh. So what's the next step?"

"The next step? Well, if Brian's not home by tomorrow, I file a *Missing Person's Report*, and get the cops looking. Not sure how hard they'll look." She reached for a cigarette and lit up. "It's bad, Silk. All's I know is something's happened to him. Something bad. I feel it in my bones."

Silk didn't answer, but leaned toward Lacey, and once more stroked her arm. "You know," Lacey said, "there are people in New Albany who think Brian was, is a low life. Like the cops, this street, especially the asshole who lives next door. They're jealous. Probably half of them were buying drugs from Brian. He's not like they made him out to be. He treated me good. He took me to nice places, and we dressed up and had fun."

She stopped herself. "Why do I keep doing that?"

"Doing what, luv?"

"Keep talking about Brian like in the past, like he's not here anymore." She took a deep pull on her cigarette and exhaled. "So, what was I saying?"

"About Brian being good people."

Lacey nodded. "Yeah, yeah he was. He loved me and took care of me."

The following morning Amber stood alongside Lacey while she filed a *Missing Person's Report*. Later they had an early lunch downtown, although Lacey found it hard to eat. Amber dropped her friend off at home. Lacey entered, again reminded of the crushing emptiness of life without Brian. Nothing. "He's not here," she said to the silent house. "Not here."

Bit by bit over the following days Lacey resigned herself to the fact she'd never see Brian again. In spite of being weighed down with her grief, she forced herself to face life without him. Could she cope financially, she asked herself? "You know the answer well enough," she murmured.

A memory of a past conversation with Brian returned. He'd told her the Feds would come after his possessions if he died. "They'll use RICO."

He referred to The *Racketeer Influenced and Corrupt Organizations Act.*

"Rico. Who's this Rico guy?"

"It's not a guy's name. Its initials, and stands for *The Racketeer Influenced and Corrupt Organizations Act*—a government thing where they grab your property because they say you got it illegally."

"Oh."

"Yeah. Anyway, like I said, if anything happens to me, dollars to donuts the government will make the case my party store and pizza business, this house, came from profits from the drug trade. In other words, organized crime."

"But you're *not* organized crime."

"Not me, but the Mantachies are. The Feds will find some way to connect me to them. Now you want organized crime, *there's* organized crime."

"How do you know all this?"

"All *what*?"

"This RICO thing."

"They've told me—a number of times when they tried to squeeze me."

"Well then, why haven't they acted before now?"

He gave a slight shrug. "Hafta ask them. But I've got a rainy day backup plan—an investment. It's eight hundred grand. Use it wisely, and don't go back to dancing. Get some kind of legit job, and the funds should top themselves up. You won't be on a yacht in the Caribbean, but you won't be poor neither."

"Wow."

"Glad you think so. All right, I'm now going to tell you how you get at it … In my desk, bottom drawer, there's an envelope with a long letter and a key. Read the letter, and then take the key to First National on Union. Give them your name, ID, and the password. They'll take you to a safety deposit box.

Inside the box you'll find the money and the name of a guy who'll invest it for you offshore, without attracting attention."

*   *   *

Lacey pulled herself out of the memory. Would the cops come and take the house, she asked herself? She doubted it, but didn't know for sure. The businesses—if they wanted those, fine, but not the house. It would always connect her to Brian. Another woman might not have wanted to stay. She did.

Four days passed and Lacey hadn't heard anything about Brian.

The morning of the fifth day, a small, thin Manila envelope arrived. She didn't recognize the handwriting; the narrow cursives suggested maybe a feminine hand. Whoever sent it left no forwarding address.

Lacey moved to the kitchen counter, and used a knife to slit the opening. She tipped the envelope upside down. Brian's plasticized license, birth certificate and social security card tumbled out.

Lacey's hand flew to her mouth. She stared at it for a long moment before she peered into the envelope again. Nothing else. She scooped up Brian's ID, picked up her purse, and made for the garage. She'd take these to the cops. Further proof somebody did something bad to Brian.

The following day the police phoned. A sergeant Bill Corey identified himself from Homicide department. "Would you come down to police headquarters as soon as you can?"

Homicide? She stopped breathing for a moment. At last she gulped air and said, "Why? What's this about?"

"It's about your *Missing Person's report*, ma'am. Sorry, but it's best if we talk to you in person. Whenever you're ready, ask for anyone in the Homicide Department."

"Homicide,'" she repeated, a tremor in her voice. "Can't you tell me something?"

"Whenever you're ready, ma'am." The line went dead.

On the way, Lacey's stomach tightened. How bad would the news be?

She sat on an uncomfortable wooden chair at the reception counter and waited until someone called her name. Her eyes found a pot-bellied detective named Farrer, in a suit he should have retired a decade ago. He introduced himself.

She rose. "Can you tell me anything about Brian?"

"Why don't you come down to my office," Farrer said, and led the way. In his small office he invited her to sit. She took one of the chairs. He hemmed and hawed before he got to the point: the State Police had found and identified the body of Brian Kimball.

"You filed a *Missing Person's Report*, Miss Clew. Can I assume Brian Kimball was your boyfriend?"

"Domestic partner," she corrected.

"Huh?"

"Domestic partner." She pronounced each word with care. "He was my domestic partner husband."

"Oh, yeah, right. Sorry. Your domestic partner husband."

She blinked several times before she again spoke.

"Who found it—the body?"

The detective looked down at a sheet of paper on his desk. He studied it and then raised his head. "From what we were told, a couple of local kids out at a conservation park. Quite a piece from here. Off I-65."

"How did he get there?"

"No one knows yet. It's a State Police investigation. They pulled fingerprints off the body, and contacted us."

"How did he die?"

Farrar exhaled. "You really want to know?"

"Yes. Tell me how he was killed."

Farrar sucked on his bottom lip and glanced down at the paper. "Execution-style, a bullet to the back of his neck. Whoever killed him took all his clothes."

Lacey pressed her eyes shut and opened them. "Bastard. Can I see it, him?"

Farrer gave her a fast shake of his head. "You'll have to contact the State Police."

Lacey pulled in a lungful of air. "Well, I want the body back. I want him to have a proper burial."

"Like I said, you'll have to contact them."

Lacey felt her eyes constrict into slits. "I know who killed my husband, and I want him arrested."

"Who?"

"My neighbor, Hawksley Pardee, is who!"

Chapter 30

A featured story in the local paper's front page read, *Reputed Drug Dealer Found Slain In Conservation Park.*

Those who read the story learned how State Police recovered the remains of a body identified as Brian Kimball, 34, of Delaney Street, New Albany. The victim had been slain gangland style. The article noted the police were following several leads. No arrests had yet been made.

The piece detailed the dead man's criminal record, alleged ties to local drug suppliers, and his vindication of a recent murder charge. It finished by noting he had shared his residence with a former dancer at *Gentlemen's Choice.*

Reporters arrived at Lacey Clew's house. They found the curtains drawn and no one answering the front door.

Word of Kimball's death swept through the neighborhood, but also at Houghton. Almost everyone knew of or had followed Kimball's arrest over the conspiracy to commit murder charge.

The day the news broke Hawksley swore he couldn't go five minutes without someone commenting on or questioning him about Kimball. He had no time to process this significant, unexpected event. People slapped him on the back, congratulated him for something not his doing, joked about whether he iced Kimball, and said he wouldn't have to carry his gun anymore.

By day's end Hawksley found himself eager to get away from all the unwanted attention. More attention awaited him when he pulled into his driveway. A TV news truck and reporters crowded his car, and called through the closed window.

"Do you know anything about your neighbor's death, Mr. Pardee?"

"Can you give us a couple of minutes for a live interview?"

"How do you feel now Brian Kimball's dead?"

"Will the police be interviewing you? Do they suspect you of having something to do with the murder?"

Frustrated and on the verge of anger at this sudden intrusion into his private life, Hawksley made it through the media crowd with care, and pulled into his garage. He entered his house. He looked down at Torchy, her tail wagging in delight. "Can't let you out the front, Torch. Let's go do your business in the back."

He waited while the dog sniffed around the yard. *Poor Torch. This has been hard on her—Vesta gone. She really misses her. They were the best of friends.*

Worried Torchy no longer had a companion during the day, Hawksley asked Nancy and Logan if Torchy could stay with them while he and Katie were at work. Companionship would be good for her, he reasoned. It might speed up her recovery.

"Yeah, sure, no problem," Nancy said. "We love Torch, and she'll be good company for Logan when he goes out for his walks."

*   *   *

He re-entered the house. Katie wouldn't be home for a while; she was off to a baby shower. He let himself imagine what she might say about today's big news.

His answering machine flashed. Katie. Several messages from news outlets wanting to talk to him. He erased them. One message from Katie. He played he played her message. "Hi, Hawk. Did you hear the news? Yeah, you had to. Talk to you when I get home. Love."

A moment later the telephone rang.

"'Lo."

"Hawk," a male voice said. "See you made it through the mob outside."

"Yeah. Had to be real careful not to hit anyone in the driveway. Took me back to the picket line."

"I can dig it. So it's true?"

"Appears to be, Logan."

"Incredible. Nancy and I sat there gawking at each other when it came on the radio. Neither of us could believe our ears. That asshole's gone. I bet everyone's wondering who did him in."

"Yeah, including me," Hawksley answered. "I doubt being a drug dealer wins you a lot of friends, or makes you *Man of the Year* at Rotary. Be interesting to see if the police catch his killer."

"No kidding. Say, why don't you and Katie come over later, and we can discuss it, and whatever else."

"She'll be home later tonight. She's at a baby shower. I'll be happy to come over and have a beer with you later."

"Sounds good, and listen, don't get frazzled by the media outside. They knocked here, and asked me if I knew anything. I told them to get lost."

"Way to go, and thanks for having my back. Be glad when this whole thing is over."

"I hear you. Take care. Later."

Hawksley unbuckled his holster and stared at the weapon. With Kimball dead, he'd no longer have to walk around with it. He placed the gun on his closet shelf. How did he feel about not needing it anymore? Fine, no, better than fine. But what would he do with it? Ah, he'd deal with the subject later. Probably sell it.

In haste he opened the front door, ignored the calls from the street, and scooped up the newspaper. He fed Torchy and re-heated yesterday's casserole.He read the coverage about Kimball while the casserole turned in the microwave. It dinged. He pulled out the dish, scooped out a portion onto a plate and ate while he read the rest of the piece. So the girlfriend used to be a stripper? He snorted. It shouldn't have come as a surprise, considering who she lived with. Like goes to like.

Later, standing over his sink, washing his plate, Hawksley asked himself what he felt about Kimball's death.

Feel—easy answer. Kimball's death removed a tremendous weight from his own life. It didn't have him dancing a jig, but he'd shed no tears either. He considered his deceased neighbor wicked, cruel, and a lousy human being. Maybe Kimball wasn't in the same league as a Hitler, Ted Bundy, or bin Laden, but bad was bad. Good riddance. And if hell existed, Kimball had to be there for sure.

*   *   *

Katie came home to find Hawksley studying his textbook. He rose to greet her. Torchy pranced around her feet. She hung up her coat, turned and faced him. He pulled her closer and kissed her.

"Got past the crowd outside?"

"Yeah. So much attention."

"They'll get bored and move on."

She pulled back. "You don't think they suspect you?"

It took him a second to decipher the message.

"Me? I gotta admit it's crossed my mind today. More than a few times. Some people at work even joked about it—me offing him." He gave a slow shake of his head. "Somebody beat me too it. I've got no blood on my hands."

He stepped closer. "I didn't do this, Kate, honest."

"I know."

His forehead wrinkled. "How? How do you know?"

She flushed. He stopped and peered at her. "You all right?"

"Sure, why?"

"I don't know; you look kinda stressed-out. Do you need to sit?"

Her hand flew to her face. "No. Rough day. I guess I'm like you—I don't hide stress well."

"Wanna talk about it?"

"There's not much to say. I'll be fine now I'm home with you. Back to your question of how I know … You were angry back then. And with good reason. Maybe you would have done it, we'll never know, but this isn't on you. It's on someone else. I think the calmer part of you would have decided against doing anything rash."

She stroked his face. "Now, we have to make sure we never, ever, talk to anyone about this, about murdering Kimball. I'm pretty sure we'd face some serious charges if it came out. Agreed?"

He kissed her. "Agreed. "You're the best, Katie Maines."

Still revved up from the news of the day, Hawksley chatted away while Katie slipped into her jeans and Stanford sweat shirt. "I tried studying," he said, "but it's not working. The words all jumble together. Did you have the same thing in college—read pages and not the foggiest idea what you've read?"

"More times than I care to remember. Your mind's elsewhere. Who could blame you?"

"Funny, I kind of held it together most of the day, especially when everyone kept asking me or talking about

Kimball. Then when I got home and did the dishes, it really hit me. He's gone, the sonovabitch is gone. Now here I am, babbling on."

Katie answered with a fast nod, turned and put her dress away.

Hawksley continued. "I know I shouldn't say this, you're supposed to keep it classy when people die—ah, what the hell, I'll say it. I can't imagine Kimball will have more than two people at his funeral. I mean who else would come to his funeral?"

"His girlfriend for sure."

Hawksley heard the edge in her voice, but pressed on.

"Why are you defending her?"

"I'm not. I thought we were having a discussion. Look, he's gone. Just because we hated him, but doesn't mean his girlfriend – and maybe others – feels the same way."

"And you don't remember the dirty look she shot me at the New Year's Eve party?"

"I do. She glared at you because she was his girlfriend. The same way I might glare at someone who wants to do you harm. I'm defending her."

"Feels like it."

Katie softened her voice. "Come on, Hawk. Why do we have to fight about this? Let's judge her on her own merits. And besides, maybe she'll now move."

The conversation rolled to a sudden stop. The lovers gazed at each other for a moment. Katie broke off eye contact, gave him a soft smile, a fast shrug, and left the room. A puzzled

Hawksley stared after her. Had he said something to offend her? This wasn't like her.

He reviewed their conversation. Well, he had to admit she had a point. Kimball no longer walked amongst the living. Why carry the grudge forward?

He joined her in the kitchen while she put the kettle on. "Feel like tea?"

"I do, yeah," he said. "Do you think now is a good time to discuss about the house, and what we do next?"

"I think it's a great time." He circled her waist. "I'm sorry if I said anything to upset you."

"Forget it. Not worth worrying about. Rough day, long day, and this Kimball thing creeps me out. I mean we talked about, well, he's really dead, and I'm trying to get my head around what happened." She gave him a fast half-smile. "Can you get out some mugs?"

*   *   *

In bed, a sleepless Katie had a lot of thoughts about Kimball. She stared at the ceiling. On his side, his back to her, she heard Hawksley's barely audible snore. She put out a hand and ran her palm softly over his forearm.

Her mind returned to her earlier meeting with Victor Mantachie. Afterwards, she'd questioned why she'd met with him in the first place. Over the following days she told herself she'd been foolish to meet with him, he wouldn't help. Then...

How could she have been so naïve, she asked herself? She recalled the phrase he'd used—his "deepest consideration." If he did anything, she assumed it meant a beating, not murder.

And Hawksley. She recalled how careful she'd been in asking about his plans for Kimball. He told her he hadn't found anything foolproof yet. She took comfort from his statement; if only Mantachie would send someone to talk to Kimball. He did, and Kimball died.

A saying came to her: *be careful what you wish for: you may get it*. So true. She could offer herself as living proof. She'd used Mantachie to kibosh Hawksley's plan. It didn't work out the way she planned. Kimball's death never entered into the equation.

Kimball's dead. What did it matter if she didn't want him dead? The facts spoke for themselves. She, Katie Maines, had a hand in his demise, albeit an unwitting one. Would she be able to live with the outcome?

Sleep at last claimed her, and denied her any breakthrough in resolving her role in Brian Kimball's death.

She woke. While brushing her teeth after breakfast she made up her mind to talk to Bailey about what happened.

They met for coffee at their usual haunt.

Bailey set down her coffee. "Hate to say it, Katie, but I did warn you this could backfire."

Katie's eyes crinkled in frustration at her sister. She let out a dramatic huff. "Not helping, Bails; not helping at all. Whenever anyone starts a sentence with, 'hate to say it,' it means the opposite. And has anybody, ever, in the entire history of the world, benefitted from an I told you so?" Katie's fingernail tapped the side of her coffee mug. "I need support and any wisdom you can offer. What I don't need is a lecture."

Bailey raised a hand. "Point taken. I apologize. I shouldn't have been so quick off the mark." She looked around at the nearby tables, lowered her voice, and leaned across the small table. "So you're holding yourself responsible for this dealer's death?"

"Somewhat, a little … I don't know."

"But sounds like you are."

Katie stared into space for a moment. "What I didn't do is think this through enough. I wanted Mantachie's boys to give him a good thrashing, and hoped Hawk would see him limping around, and let things be."

Bailey leaned forward. "But now you're stuck with unintended consequence?"

"Exactly. There's good reason to believe this guy would still be alive if I hadn't approached Mantachie."

"But you don't know for sure."

"Not a hundred per cent, no," Katie said, "but unless some competitor took Kimball out, odds are excellent Mantachie made or ordered the killing. I can't shake the feeling this will be with me for the rest of my life. How do I reconcile myself to what I've done? Kimball was a bad man. He deserved prison, a beating, maybe both, but not a death sentence. I mean I did say, but didn't really mean it.

She folded her arms across her chest. "It's one thing to wish someone dead in the abstract. It's a whole different thing when it's real."

Bailey's eyes left her sister, stared out the front picture window, and returned to Katie. "Your conscience is tearing away at you, blaming you for this."

"Duh, haven't you been listening, Dr. Bailey Freud? You've stated the obvious."

Stone-faced, Baily waited her out. "Finished? Do you want my take on this or not?"

Katie heard the hint of annoyance in her sister's voice. "My turn to apologize. Yes, I do. Go on."

"What I'm trying to say is there are other variables to consider. Let's say, for example, this Mantachie *was* behind the kidnapping and killing, maybe it didn't go the way he wanted it to. There could have been some kind of screw-up, you know, like this old movie you see on late night TV, *The Gang That Couldn't Shoot Straight*? It happens."

Katie ordered herself not to fidget, not think of replies, but to listen.

Bailed pressed on with her thoughts. "You and Mantachie had this conversation about Kimball. You didn't say what exactly you wanted to happen to him."

Katie interrupted her sister. "Yeah, I did. I wanted him roughed up."

"So beat up enough so Hawk would give up his plans?"

"Right."

"And Mantachie didn't commit to anything?"

"No. I couldn't get a good read on him. One minute I thought he would, and the next minute the opposite."

Bailey leaned forward. "Think about it, Kate. Two people have a conversation about a third person. One wants this third person beaten up; the other says he'll think about doing it. He doesn't say he will. A little while later the third person is killed."

"So what are you getting at?"

"What I'm getting at is we know what you wanted. We don't know what Mantachie intended to do. In a sense, you two had a fuzzy kind of social contract. Nothing was agreed on. And no one but him can say whether Mantachie ordered the execution. If he did, maybe, like I said, it went wrong. The takeaway is you accept you ordered up a good thumping. Take responsibility and make your peace with that, and maybe the self-blaming diminishes in time."

Katie stared at Bailey for several long seconds. Her eyes welled up. She swallowed several times, afraid her response would come out as a croak. To make doubly sure, she took a long sip of her coffee.

"You, Bailey Ambrose Maines are the best sister in the world, in the universe; the best sister anyone could ever have. What would I have done without you?"

"Muddled along. But thank you anyway. You're pretty special too. It's why I put up with you."

Both laughed. Katie stretched out her arm, took her sister's hand and squeezed.

Chapter 31

In the fast-paced news cycle world, Kimball's murder soon lost traction. The media packed up and left Delaney Street. A day after, the media stopped reporting on Kimball's murder. The next day a car pulled into Hawksley driveway.

Torchy's furious barking announced its arrival. Hawksley, busy vacuuming, didn't hear, but Katie, looked out the window. Two men in conservative business suits, one in blue, the other in brown, walked to his back door and knocked. Her heart raced at the sight of them. She wheeled about, hurried over to Hawksley, and tapped him on a shoulder. "Turn off the vacuum. We've got company."

Her palms sweating, she rubbed them on her jeans.

Hawksley shut off the machine and met the arrivals at the door. Everything about them said cops. They had to be here about Kimball. He'd been expecting someone.

He opened the door and let his gaze settle on the two men, both about the same age and close in height. They'd probably played football at one time. The blue-suited cop, his suit pulled tight under his arms, already had more than a paunch. Another ten years, Hawksley guessed, and he'd be all flab.

"Help you?"

Both men reached into their suit pockets and brought out ID wallets with mini badges. The blue-suited cop spoke first, a mid-range tine with the hint of Midwest inflection. "Indiana State Police. I'm Detective Pete Melkin, and my partner is Detective Carter Payne. Are you Hawksley Pardee?"

Hawksley glanced at the badges. "Mm-hmm."

"We'd like to talk to you, if you don't mind? Can we come in?"

Hawksley hesitated for a split second, opened the door wider, and stepped aside.

The visitors entered. Hawksley closed the door, glanced past them at Katie, and gave her his best *No idea* look.

Torchy greeted the visitors with happy wags of her tail.

Payne bent to pet her.

Hawksley moved past the detectives, stood alongside Katie, and introduced her.

Social pleasantries over, Payne spoke up. Full-toned, his voice commanded attention. It took nothing for Hawksley to imagine him barking out defensive signals at a line of scrimmage. He gestured to the kitchen table. "Why don't we all sit down?"

It's our house and our table, Hawksley thought. *Isn't it up to us to extend the invitation*? He held back on the opinion.

All four sat. Malkin pulled out a pocket notebook and ballpoint pen from his brown suit.

Hawksley opened the exchange. "So, you gonna tell us why you're here?" His gaze turned from Malkin to Payne.

"It's about your neighbor," the fleshy-faced Malkin said. "Or more accurately, your late neighbor, Brian Kimball."

"Yeah. What about him?"

Melkin answered. "Well, as you probably know—it's been all over the news—Mr. Kimball was killed. You wouldn't happen to know anything about his death, would you?"

"Am I under suspicion?"

"Not so we're aware," Payne said. "Is there any reason to believe you should?"

Katie jumped in. "I can think of a few, starting with how your first question came out."

All three men stared at her. Hawksley took note of the raised pitch in her voice, her shoulders bunched.

If the detectives noticed, they didn't say.

Payne spoke again. "Mr. Kimball's body was found in a state park. We have to investigate, to piece his life together, and follow every lead, no matter where it takes us."

"Where it takes you," Hawksley said. "So, am I—what do they call it—a person of interest?'

"Your name has come up in the investigation."

Malkin nodded. "And we understand you had something of a combative relationship with Mr. Kimball."

Hawksley played with his wrist watch. "'A combative relationship.' Yeah, but so what? Kimball was a Grade-A asshole. He broke into my house, killed my cat, shot and tried to kill me. What it added up to was a lot of stress for me. What it doesn't add up to is murder." He stopped. "A wild guess here, but the woman next door, Kimball's girlfriend, did she sic you onto me?"

Melkin shook his head. "We're not at liberty to say."

"Then what exactly are you at liberty to say?" Katie asked. "Beyond casting out the widest net and stopping short of implication."

"Maybe you should calm down," Payne said. "You're getting pretty excited."

Katie's eyes narrowed. She stared at the detective. "Did I hear what I thought I heard—telling me to calm down? Do they teach this kind of thing in the Academy or wherever—to come into somebody's house and tell them to calm down?"

Hawksley reached for her hand to dampen her agitation. She ignored it, and kept her eyes on the detective. Her mouth twisted into a wry smile. "You know, maybe you're right. I am, to use your word, excited. It's a personal failing of mine. I'm a mama bear. I protect my own, especially those accused of murder."

"We're not accusing him," Melkin said, and turned to Hawksley. "Your cat—when did this happen?"

"About ten days ago. We received a package with Vesta's—our cat—ashes inside. Pretty sure it came from Kimball."

"And you reported it to the police?"

"No. What were they going to do—search for our cat's killer? And how could I prove Kimball did it? I *know* he did it."

Malkin again wrote in his notebook. Finished, he met Hawksley's gaze. "So, Mr. Kimball disappeared on—we guess—the morning of..." He consulted his notebook, "the fifteenth. Can you account for your time then?"

"Course. I was at work."

"Can anyone confirm it?"

Hawksley gave a small laugh. "Sure. Let's start with my time card, and then about a hundred-and-forty-seven other folks at the factory. Houghton. Check if you want."

"We will," Melkin said and closed his notebook.

Hawksley let his eyebrows rise and fall. "I hated the guy, yeah, but look at the strength of the evidence. Twice he tried to kill me. He poisoned our dog and killed our cat. I don't know who killed Kimball, but it wasn't me. I didn't have a thing to do with his murder."

Melkin and Payne made brief eye contact. A fast nod from Melkin, and both rose. "All right, then," Melkin said. "Thank you for your time. One more thing before we go, and then you probably won't hear from us again."

"What would you like?" Hawksley said.

"You have a firearm?"

"Yes."

"Can you show us where you keep it?"

Hawksley rose and moved to the closet door, the other three behind him. He opened his door and pointed to the weapon and holster on a shelf. He made to reach for it, but Payne's voice stopped him.

"No, wait. I'll get it. I'll just squeeze by you." The detective pulled the weapon from the shelf. He pulled it out of its holster, and took his time to examine it. He brought it close to his nose. Finished, he placed the gun and its holster back on the shelf. "We're done here. We won't take up any more of your time."

"Good luck with the investigation." Hawksley opened the door to the driveway. The couple watched the policemen leave.

"I've got a feeling they're crossing me off their list of suspects," Hawksley said. "Boy, you were a real tiger there for a while. What got into you?"

Katie made a face. "Sorry. Can't explain it. Sorry if I made a fool of myself."

He pulled her to him. "I thought you handled yourself well. You ever think of being a trial lawyer?"

*   *   *

A week later Katie shook the *Indiana Report* open to the obituary section. She read for a moment. Her eyebrows shot up. "You gotta read this, Hawk." She handed him the newspaper. "The fifth one down."

Brian Stephen Kimball.

Brian Stephen Kimball, loving brother of Stella Kimball-Darney, and partner, Lacey Clew. Death comes to all of us, but his came too fast. Brian loved life and all it had to offer. He is now in God's good care. Funeral services will be held on Saturday, the 18th, 1 P.M. at Lifted Peace Funeral Home.

Hawksley's eyes moved from the page to Katie.

"Now there's an obituary for the ages. Not even his date of birth. Surprised it didn't say something like, he loved paint chips as a child, and had opposable thumbs."

Katie chortled. "Be nice, Hawk. He's dead. You're not supposed to say anything bad about the departed."

*   *   *

The following Saturday, Hawksley, immersed with feeding his lawn, worked the perimeter of his yard with his lawn spreader. By luck he looked up to see his neighbor, Lacey Clew, kneeling in front of her flower bed. Faded jeans, an open checkered shirt over a T-shirt, and a Motley Crue cap, she spread fertilizer around.

Their eyes met. She made no attempt to disguise her death stare.

His first instinct favored returning the hostile look, but he decided against it. *Let it go.*

He offered her a fast nod, accompanied by a fake smile. Neither won her over. The withering scorn remained in place.

Careful, Hawksley silently said; *your face may lock.* He continued spreading grass seed onto his lawn. Only from the corner of his eye did he catch her rise and march toward him. He straightened and waited, for what he didn't know.

"I know you did it, you bastard," she said in a matter-of-fact voice. "I know you killed Brian. Or had him killed."

He hadn't anticipated meeting her, let alone facing this level of hostility. He gaped at her for a few seconds before he trusted himself to speak.

"First," he said and felt his jaws tighten; "your boyfriend came over here, on my lawn, by the way, and picked a fight with me. Now you. What the hell's the matter with you two?"

He pulled in a lungful of air.

"Fuck is the matter with you, coming over here with an angry face, and throwing accusations at me? I don't have to take this. Either be nice, or I'll tell you what I told your criminal boyfriend—get off my lawn."

She folded her arms across her chest. "No." her voice rose high and loud. "Not until you tell me why you killed him, what did he do to you?"

Hawksley shook his head in disbelief. "I don't have to tell you anything, but I'll say it again—get off my lawn."

She wouldn't budge. "I want an answer."

"*You* want an answer?" He shook his head in disbelief. "Who died and left you in charge of the universe?" Ready to lay into her, Hawksley checked himself. He remembered Meissner's advice—take responsibility for your personal well-being. In a more placid voice, he said, "You know, this used to be a nice street until you and your boyfriend arrived, selling drugs."

"I don't sell drugs," she shot back.

"Yeah, sure. You at least lived with someone who did, and you had to know. Pretty well amounts to the same thing."

Hawksley pointed over her shoulder. "We had a good neighbor who lived in your house. He didn't have the cops calling on him, didn't poison my dog and my cat, and didn't try to kill me. Then you two arrive."

"You started the fight."

Hawksley's eyes grew wider in disbelief. In spite of his previous resolve, his voice rose to match hers. "*I* started it? Are you some kind of stupid? Do years of pole dancing do that?"

She batted away the take down. "Oh, so you think you're so much better, Mr. Tight Ass. I'd feel hurt—if your opinion mattered. It don't."

"Tight ass," Hawksley mimicked. "Wow. What a zinger. And yeah, I *am* much better, but don't change the subject. Your boyfriend came onto my lawn, same as you, and picked the fight. Same as you. How the hell you get I started all this?"

"You're the one who stuck the flyers up about the frat party."

Ouch! She had him. He colored at the memory of the flyers. "How … ?"

"Never mind. I'm not telling you nothing. We know it was you." She crossed her arms high on her chest. He swallowed. "Fine, I'll admit to it. So you two decide to pay me back by running me over, shooting me, and killing my cat. You think it all evens out? Not a chance."

"Liar, liar. Bet you can't jump over a telephone wire."

Something about the schoolyard taunt kept him from letting loose a caustic response. He forced himself to lower his voice.

"As hard as this is for you to believe, I did not have your boyfriend killed. And I didn't get anyone else to do it." He stared at the ground for a second before he returned his gaze to her. "You're wasting time and energy blaming me. I don't murder people."

They both stared at each other, yet Hawksley sensed the earlier level of hostility had left them.

His neighbor spoke again. "You told people he was some kind of monster."

Hawksley worked to keep his emotions under control. A fast exhale and he said, "Yeah, so, what's your point? I thought we were talking about whether I killed him."

"Brian didn't deserve what you said about him."

Hawksley pressed his lips together for a moment.

"We're back to this? Your boyfriend was a bad man, even if you don't think so. He sold drugs, poison. And if you knew, you're as culpable as him."

"What's culpable mean?"

"It means you deserve the same blame. Because of him, I had to buy a gun."

She didn't answer, but uncrossed her arms. "He had his ways, Brian, but he had a hard childhood."

Hawksley allowed two seconds to pass.

"He isn't the only one who had a tough childhood." He waved his hands. "Look, blame me if you want, if it makes you happy. Nothing I say is going to convince you otherwise."

He didn't expect what came next: her tone matched his. He noted the tightness around her eyes lessen. "I wanna believe you, but … I don't know. So you swear you had nothing to do with Brian's killing?"

"Yeah. I swear. I'd be lying if I said I was sorry he's gone. I get it, he meant something to you. Blame me for all sorts of things, but not his killing."

Chapter 32

Hawksley entered his house. He leaned against the kitchen counter, his cheeks the color of cherry tomatoes, and wiped sweat from his brow. He reached for a glass to hold under the tap, and saw the tremble in his hand.

Katie approached when he entered the house. "Are you all right? You don't look too good."

Hawksley leaned against the kitchen counter and waved her off.

"I'm fine. Had a little run-in with Ms. Ball-buster next door." He jerked his thumb toward Kimball's house. "It took a lot out of me."

"I can tell. Do you want to sit down?"

"In a minute. I want to catch my breath first." He inhaled deeply and then said, "Good now."

"I saw you," Katie said. I wondered if I should come out. Let me guess what you two were arguing about."

"Bingo. She accused me of killing Kimball, but you know what?"

"What?"

"I surprised myself. I thought I'd lose it, but I didn't. I told her I had nothing to do with his murder." He frowned at her. "What?"

"Nothing, nothing; just thinking."

"About?"

"It doesn't matter."

"What was I saying? Oh, yeah … " Hawksley detailed his exchange with Kimball's girlfriend. "I'm no fan of hers, Kate, but you know, at the end I felt kind of sorry for her. It dawned on me she really misses the low life. Hard to believe."

"Why? She lived with him, so they had to have had some kind of relationship. We thought of him as a louse, but she obviously has a different take. Maybe it didn't matter what he did outside the home."

"Couldn't have thought much of herself," Hawksley added.

Katie offered a dismissive wave of her hand. "Who's to say? Love is love. Maybe she offered the unconditional kind. Do only the pure of heart and noble of spirit get to pine away for someone they lost?"

"Now you're getting all philosophical on me."

"Am I? Oh. Something about all this feels unsettling for me."

*   *   *

Thanks to her talk with Bailey, she no longer felt so responsible for Kimball's death. Mostly but not entirely. Something about Kimball's girlfriend re-awakened another stab of guilt. Her inner voiced scolded her. S*top it. This is useless, unnecessary guilt. Remember what Bailey told you. Don't pick up* *this guilt again. You were not an accessory to murder. Not, do you hear me?*

The self-talk helped, yet she still went online and searched for anything about Kimball's death. She discovered his girlfriend's name—Lacey, Lacey Clew.

Name in hand, Katie made up her mind to visit Lacey.

The chance arrived when Hawksley and Logan went off to see a *Reds* game. Nancy, never a sports fan, begged off. Katie said she'd stay behind and keep her company.

"You don't mind us two going?" Logan asked.

"Nope," Nancy said. "As long as you behave yourselves, and drive safely."

"Will do. It'll give me more experience driving with my new leg. Not like I needed any; the Audi's an automatic."

"Just be careful."

"You got it. If it's too much, ol' bro' here can take over."

The brothers left at the crack of dawn for their weekend in Cincinnati. Hawksley, sensitive to Logan's amputation, offered no objections when Logan insisted on driving. He wouldn't let a simple thing like the loss of a limb affect his life.

Months after being fitted with his prosthesis, Logan contacted the DMV about his condition. They ordered him to submit to an extensive assessment as well as re-take his driver's test. He passed, and they didn't insist his Audi required any modification.

On I-65 Hawksley pointed to Logan's prosthesis. "Did it take a lot of getting used to, driving with your new, um, foot?"

Logan nodded. "I'm still getting used to it, not only behind the wheel, but with everything. I have to be extra alert about hitting brake and gas pedals when I'm driving. My physio says there'll come a day when I won't be thinking about it anymore."

"I know you're probably tired of hearing this," Hawksley said, "but I really admire how you handled all this. Right from the get-go you stayed positive."

Logan turned his head and took in Hawksley's profile. His eyes moved back to the road.

"I didn't feel I had another choice. I guess I have to thank Mom. Certainly not the old man. He passed on a few good things, but Mom … ." He fell silent for a moment. "You haven't done too badly with this Lyme thing either."

Hawksley quickly shook his head. "Uh-uh. Nothing like you. Big, big struggle for me."

They drove on. "I'm still sorry I had something to do with the leg."

Logan again looked at his brother. "You going to start that shit again?"

"No, sorry. Nancy's already gave me the lecture."

"Then you're not listening, dumbass." Logan lightly punched his brother's arm. "Besides, you've gone through enough crap—especially with your psycho neighbor."

Hawksley tossed off a fast nod. "Well, whatever. Life's good again, and funny, for both of us. I never thought I'd be living next to you."

"Me neither. It's like I'm discovering you, but different, as an adult. Maybe it's how things are supposed to be."

"But good, right?"

"Good, yeah. No, better. And we're going to have some fun this weekend."

*   *   *

At ten Nancy arrived for coffee. Katie told her about Hawksley's encounter with Lacey Clew. "Her boyfriend was a real shit, Nance," she said and poured coffee for both, "but from what Hawk said, she's really mourning his loss."

Neither woman spoke while they stirred their coffee. Katie resumed. "You probably think this is silly, and I hope you keep this between us, but I want to go see her, give her whatever support I can."

"I'm not sure I quite understand your reasoning. Maybe you should leave well enough alone."

"I hear you, but I've got to go over there."

Nancy gave her a long inspection. "Want me to come with you?" Katie set down her mug and smiled. "Really? I thought...."

"I changed my mind. Let's see what comes of this."

An hour later, Nancy beside her, Katie rang Lacey Clew's doorbell. Her butterflies wouldn't stop flitting about.

No one answered. Katie rang again. Silence from inside.

The women glanced at each other. "One more, for luck," Nancy whispered. Katie pressed the button. Nothing.

They turned and stepped away when the door opened. A shapely, long-legged blonde with visible roots stared at them.

"Yeah?" She folded her arms over her floral print top. Fierce, suspicious, chestnut eyes stared out at the intruders.

Katie had never been in such close proximity to her neighbor. Now she took in the hardness around the corners of Lacey Clew's mouth. She offered her best disarming smile. "Hi, I'm Katie Maines, and I live next door with my boyfriend, Hawksley." She turned and gestured to Nancy. "This is my friend, Nancy Picton. She lives on the other side of me."

Nancy put on her happiest expression.

"Hi. Pleased to meet you."

Neither Katie nor Nancy managed to melt the icy stare on Lacey Clew's face. The tone of her voice matched her facial expression. "I know who you are. Whatcha want?"

"Want, want, yes, um, well, nothing really. We thought we'd come over and see if there was any support we can lend you. Because of your loss." She followed the statement with a combined shoulder shrug and raised eyebrows.

"I'm not looking for pity," Lacey Clew said.

Katie questioned her decision to visit. It's only her wounded pride and anger speaking, she told herself. Look past it.

"I'm sorry if I might have said something to upset you."

"Hawksley Pardee send you?"

"No … no. He and his brother are in Cincinnati this weekend. I'm pretty sure he wouldn't be too happy if he knew I was here."

"So you come here to snoop, to tell the rest on the street about the druggie's girlfriend?"

Katie heard the bitterness in the accusation.

"You don't know me, I get it, but I'm not … a gossiper, and neither is Nancy." She turned to Nancy for confirmation.

A fast shake of Nancy's head supported the claim.

"In this last year," Nancy said, "I had to witness the humiliation of my ex cheating on me and leaving." She tossed her head in Katie's direction. "I watched her boyfriend deal with a sudden disease. Now his brother, my boyfriend—he's lost his leg. We've gone through enough stuff on our own, so we don't need to go looking for dirt on anyone else."

The answer softened Lacey's face. Her gaze moved between the two friends. After a moment's hesitation, she opened her door wider and stepped aside. "Do you want to come in?"

The guests entered a living room darkened by thick curtains. The stale odor of cigarette smoke hung in the air. Two leather sofas, one long, the other small, took up much of the room's space—both angled to face a large flat screen TV on a wall. A five-sided glass coffee table sat between the sofas. Pride of place however went to a long, mahogany trunk with brass fittings, the kind found in imported home furnishing stores. Sports, celebrity news, and fashion magazines graced the top.

The smaller coffee table caught Katie's eye. Their host had converted the surface into a small shrine to her boyfriend. Pictures of various sizes showed Kimball on his motorcycle, on a tropical beach, at a party, and riding a snow mobile. Two round, smooth, flameless candles kept vigil in front of the homage.

Lacey stretched her arm and gestured to the sofas. "Hava seat."

Her guests complied.

Katie chose the larger of the two sofas, Nancy the other. Both offered up their best warm smiles to their host.

Lacey crossed and uncrossed her arms. "I can't believe you're sitting here, in my house."

Katie agreed. "Yeah, I guess it's going to take some getting used to for all of us." She broke off. "Sorry, but I don't even know your name." She mentally flinched at the lie, but realized it wouldn't do to say she read it in the newspaper.

"Lacey," their host said, "and pointed her finger at them. "And you're Katie and Nancy?"

Nancy answered with a fast nod. "The very same."

"Can I get you something—tea, coffee?"

"Terrific. Either one's fine."

Lacey rose and disappeared into her kitchen. They listened to their host move around the kitchen.

Nancy pointed a finger at the shrine. *I know*, Katie mouthed silently.

Lacey returned with a tray laden with mugs of coffee as well as milk, sugar, and sugar cookies. "Don't know what you like." She placed the tray on the table. "I brought everything." Satisfied with her effort, she sat back on the larger sofa.

Katie sipped her hot beverage and again searched for a conversation starter. Lacey beat her to it. Her mug still in her hand, she directed her ruby red forefinger at the pictures of Kimball.

"Guess you think I'm strange, having pictures of Brian here like this."

Nancy spoke. "Not really. Your way of grieving, is all; hanging onto and keeping his memory alive. My cousin lost her husband. For weeks after the funeral she kept smelling his old pipe, his clothes, anything to capture the scent of him. It took a year before she could make herself take his clothes to a charity drop-off box."

"So I'm not crazy?"

She wasn't, her guests assured her.

Lacey sank further into her couch. Her gaze settled on Katie. "A lot of bad stuff went on between your boyfriend and Brian."

Katie nodded. "True, but it's them, not us. I can't change what happened, and don't want to point a finger. What's done can't be undone, except to say how sorry I am, we are, and to give you whatever support we can."

"I could do without all the stress. I gotta be careful. I know we—wait, it's only me now—have a bad reputation in this neighborhood. Me and Brian been talking about moving somewheres new. It's not gonna happen now; not gonna happen ever." Her eyes filled. She reached into her jeans and pulled out a tissue. A moment later she said, "Wish this wouldn't have happened."

Katie saw an opportunity, and with it risk. She drew in a breath and said, "It's none of our business, do you think you'll stay?"

No one spoke. For a moment Katie questioned her impulsiveness.

Lacey wiped at her nose. "This is where Brian died; I mean the last place I ever seen him. The Justice Department grabbed his pizza and party store under RICO. Do you know about RICO?"

Both women shook their heads.

Lacey gave them a general outline and finished with. "It took me a bit to understand it all. Anyway, Brian's lawyer sent me to one of those lawyers specializes in, um, racketeering. He swore they wouldn't get their greedy claws into this place." She broke off. "I'm sorry. I didn't mean to blab about all this."

"Don't worry," Nancy said. "You probably needed to get things off your chest."

"You won't spread it around the neighborhood, will you?" Lacey asked.

To Katie, the question had a child-like innocence to it. It made her feel protective toward Lacey.

"No. Nobody's business. We won't, and thanks for trusting us."

"Thanks."

"So, you think you'll stay here?" Nancy said.

Lacey exhaled. "Yeah, get on with my life." Her eyes moved to the tray. "Can I get you more coffee or cookies?"

"I'm good, thanks," Nancy said.

"Me too." Katie set down her mug. "And what will you do now?"

"I'm not sure. Right now I gotta get through all this crap with the lawyer."

"Good luck," Katie said. "We want you to know we're not your enemies, and you're not ours."

"What about Hawksley?"

"He'll come around. He's a good guy, and he's got no beef with you. Soon this'll be ancient history for him. But can I ask you a question?"

"I guess."

"Before I do, I guarantee Hawksley had nothing to do with Brian's death. If he had, I would have known. Trust me."

"All right. I believe you. So what's the question?"

"Do the police think they'll ever find who killed Brian?"

"Easy answer. No, and I don't see them trying too hard. The cops think anyone who deals in drugs is a sleazebag." She placed her mug on the tray.

"We better get going, Lacey," Katie said, "before you feel obligated to make lunch for us. Thanks for opening your door to us. Things take time, for you to heal, even for you and Hawksley to trust each other. We'll go slow and not rush anything."

Lacey nodded. "Makes sense."

"Before we go," Katie said and rose, "will it be all right to tell Hawksley we were here? I won't say anything about the other stuff you shared, only about having a good visit."

Lacey stared up at the ceiling for a moment. "Yeah, I guess. It'll be fine, and thanks for asking me."

The guests embraced their host at the door. "It'll be nice to wave to you when I see you," Nancy said.

"Yeah."

"See you soon," Katie said, and stepped out the front door. "Thanks for coming along," Katie said to Nancy on the way back to her house. "You were great."

"Welcome. Life's strange, isn't it?"

"You bet. Wait 'til Hawk hears who we had coffee with today."

Chapter 33

While Katie calmly poured tea into Hawksley' cup, he stared at her.

"You're kidding, right?" He jerked his thumb in the direction of Kimball's house. "This Lacey—you and Nancy had coffee with her?"

"The very same."

"And it went well?"

"Better."

Hawksley shook his head in amazement.

"So I go away and come home to find you've smoked the peace pipe with our neighbor." He leaned over, pulled Katie to him, squeezed and let go. "You are one amazing woman." He rubbed his hands in anticipation. "So, tell me how everything." He pulled his chair closer to the kitchen table and listened while Katie recalled her visit.

She finished with, "It's all water under the bridge now, Hawk. She is nice, and Kimball's dead. We hated him, but she misses him. We have no quarrel with her, and have to give her a chance."

"Hard to imagine anyone missing that asshole."

Katie gave him a wearied look. "Let's not go through this again. She, obviously, has a different take on Kimball. And we can't call him that anymore. He's dead, be nice, be understanding, and give her a chance."

Hawksley held up his hands in surrender. "Fine. I'll get it together, I promise."

"I know you will."

They sipped their tea, absorbed in their own thoughts. Katie spoke again. "What will you do about your gun?"

"Oh, yeah I've been thinking about it. Sell it."

*   *   *

A few days later while watering the flower bed Hawksley saw Lacey walking across her lawn in his direction. He studied her. Something different; he couldn't pinpoint it at first. It came to him—she'd changed, at least outwardly. She'd cut her hair short; dark roots now pushed out her familiar peroxide blonde. The tightness around her mouth had all but vanished. As did her noticeable slouch.

He searched for a word to describe what he saw. Together? Yeah, maybe. Even in those clothes she gave off a more together look than he remembered.

Her eyes found his. For a moment her face gave nothing away, followed by something akin to a smile.

It's a start, he told himself, and raised a hand in greeting. Katie was right—new beginnings. He'd better make the effort and extend himself. It wouldn't cost him anything.

He dropped the garden hose and moved across his lawn to hers. She glanced up from her kneeling position by her flowers.

"Hi. It's Lacey, right?" He forced himself to hold her gaze. Had his tone conveyed the right amount of warmth needed to make the grade? Butterflies gathered in his stomach.

She rose. "Lacey, yeah."

"Lacey, I haven't formally introduced myself. I'm Hawk. Listen, I don't even know where to start." He paused and licked his lips. "I'm sorry about my behavior. My emotions got the better of me."

She waved it off and slowly shook her head. "I'm trying to get past everything too." She kept her eyes on him. *Say something, anything,* Hawksley silently willed her.

She did. "It don't matter anymore. Well, it does, but there's nothing I can do about it."

He gave her a fast nod. "You're right. I also wanted to say I admire you for talking to Katie. And Nancy. Took guts."

"It took more guts for them to come over. People around here look past me like I don't exist."

Hawksley drew a step closer. "Maybe things will change."

"Yeah, maybe. It'd be nice."

Don't drag this out, Hawksley's inner voice said. *You succeeded in what you set out to do. No point hanging around any longer.* Still, some deeper instinct told him to stay. "Is there anything we can we do for you?"

She answered with a fast wave of her hand. "Not unless you can bring Brian back. Or find out who killed him, and why?"

"Nothing from the cops, huh?"

"Nah. O.J.'ll find Nicole's killer before the cops find Brian's. And everybody knows how hard he's lookin.'"

Hawksley couldn't find a suitable response beyond a fast nod of acknowledgement. "Hope you're wrong. Well, best get back to watering my plants. I'm glad we're good now." He offered her a fast smile.

He later shared his meeting with Katie. "I'm proud of you," she said.

"Thanks. I wonder if they'll ever catch his killer."

Katie didn't reply. Her eyes grew distant, and her shoulders twitched in a shrug.

*   *   *

Months passed.

In mid-August Hawksley and Katie visited Dr. Helen Calley, ND, at her practice in the old *Penobscot Medical Arts Building* in Louisville.

The lovers stepped into the small elevator. Hawksley pushed the button for the sixteenth floor.

The door closed. They felt a small jarring. Katie spoke.

"This is stepping into a piece of the past. Surprised this thing doesn't have one of those grill gates, and an operator with one of those organ grinder monkey caps, like you see in the movies."

"Right. I bet they did at one time. Pretty impressive, you gotta admit, this building. They don't build like this anymore."

Inside the reception area of Calley's practice, they approached the reception wicket. Hawksley said to the woman at her desk.

"My name is Hawksley Pardee. I have an appointment with Dr. Calley to get the results of my tests."

The woman consulted a datebook. "All right, then. Have a seat. Dr. Calley will see you shortly."

The two turned, spied vacant chairs and claimed them. Six other patients waited along with them. Few spoke, and when they did, whispered.

Katie leaned in to Hawksley. "Nervous?"

Hawksley recalled the day Katie told him about the naturopath. "Oh, before I forget," she said over dinner, "I want to tell you something Bailey told me. She read about this naturopath doctor in Louisville who specializes in patients like you. Supposed to be very good, according to the magazine article. Why don't you make an appointment to go see her? It can't hurt."

He resisted at first, but Katie wore him down. Now he matched his tone to hers.

"Not as nervous as the first time I met her. I always imagined this Lyme thing to be a life sentence. Now, fingers crossed, maybe not."

Katie squeezed his hand.

"Hawksley," the receptionist called out.

He raised his eyes.

"The doctor's ready to see you," the woman said.

Hawksley and Katie rose and followed her into the doctor's office. Once in, they sat and waited next to her desk. A minute later the specialist arrived. She wore her age well. Blonde streaks highlighted her shoulder length hair. High arched eyebrows over gray eyes considered the couple while she took her seat.

She smiled and introduced herself to Katie, turned away and opened her computer. She typed in a few characters on the keyboard and waited. Less than a minute later she turned to Hawksley.

"So, Hawksley, as you know, we re-did all your tests. You have some Lyme pathogens for sure, but there is good news." She paused as if to let her words sink in with him.

"In spite of what you've struggled with, yours isn't a worst case scenario. Far from it, and you show no signs of heading in that direction."

"Well, I'm glad to hear this. So I'm getting better?"

The hint of a smile appeared on Calley.

"Better is a subjective word, but yes, there's a good probability you are. Medically-speaking, you have a good quality-of-life in front of you. We'll look at and adjust any medications with pain and inflammation, and recommend things to boost your immune system. I'll also give you some literature about nutrition, and meet with you on a regular basis. Sound good?"

"Sounds great. To think I'll get my life back … "

*　　　*　　　*

If asked, Victor Mantachie would always say he "slept good."

Not last night or many nights before. He dreamt, always the same dream, and always involving Brian Kimball.

No matter how he tried, Victor couldn't rid himself of the image of Kimball. The dreams bothered him enough to cause him to be nervous about going to bed. As a result, he grew testy and difficult to be near during the day.

Victor knew he needed to talk to someone about these dreams, and what they meant. But who? Grazia? Nah. Quiet, great in bed, good with his kids, but otherwise dumb as a doorknob.

So not Grazia. Their priest, Father Stefano—should he make a confession? Maybe it would help. They kept saying confession was good for the soul. And he well knew anything he laid bare in the confessional couldn't be betrayed. But how would he start—*Bless me, Father, for I have sinned. It's been eleven, maybe twelve years since my last confession. I put a hit on one of my dealers. Deserved it. He was a punk, and started bringing me unwanted attention from the cops. Oh, yeah, and I'm still schupting Anthony's wife, Maria. I can't keep my hands off her.*

What about his foot soldiers, Victor asked himself? Could he talk to them? Uh-uh. Worse than talking to Grazia or

Father Stefano. They'd think he'd gone soft, and rat him out to his brother.

Reason it out, he ordered himself. There had to be some logical explanation for these dreams. They might have made sense if Kimball had been some kind of saint. He wasn't. He, Victor, had ordered better men than Kimball wacked. None of those came back to haunt him. So why Kimball?

Try as he might, Victor could not rid himself of the dream.

Grazia, worried about his health and talked him into seeing a psychiatrist.

Nervous, Victor sat across from a plump East Indian with a white goatee. *Over three hundred million people in this country,* he told himself as the psychiatrist waited for him to begin, *and Grazia couldn't send me to a white shrink?*

The two men studied each other for a moment. Dr. Dhanial spoke, a rich timbre to his voice. "So, what is it you would like to work on, Mr. Mantachie?"

Victor shifted in his chair. "What goes on here, it's, uh, what do—they call it, privileged? You can't tell anyone outside of this room?"

"Yes, you are correct."

"And I don't want our conversation recorded or any notes."

"You can be assured nothing is recorded," Dhanial said with a pronounced syllable-timed accent. "As for notes, you have concerns?"

"Damn right I do."

Dhanial studied Victor for a moment. "You are guaranteed confidentiality, Mr. Mantachie, under doctor-patient law, nothing you tell me can be used in court. If this is your worry."

The answer satisfied Mantachie. He relaxed his shoulders and pulled his chin in.

"Okay, it's about this dream I keep having. I dream about the death of someone I knew. I guess you'd describe him as a scuzz bag, so it makes this whole thing harder to understand ... And he comes to me in my dreams, like, like, in that movie, *Scrooge*."

About the Author

Both an avid reader of history and politics and a prolific writer, Robert T. Hunting writes stories that illuminate people against their time. He holds a B.A. in history and an M.A. in social science.

Made in the USA
Columbia, SC
10 May 2024

35111314R00231